A WARRIOR'S FURY

❖ S. M. SAVOY ❖

بساله

Published by
Ace Lyon Books
June
2017

Ace
Lyon

Published by
Ace Lyon Books
Acelyonbooks.com
First Edition
Cover Design by S. M. Savoy
S. M. Savoy *A Warrior's Fury*
ISBN 978-1-947122-06-2

Dedication

To Jim, the magic in my life.

TABLE OF CONTENTS

A WARRIOR'S FURY

- 1 -

THE TEAM

John Hayes placed his radio headset on the table. For three hours now he and his wife, Mary, had been waiting in this room.

Captain Sanders had called him at three a.m. and told him their son Rick might be in a group of soldiers trying to reach the border of Turkey on foot and a rescue attempt was in progress.

Mary had insisted they come to Incirlik Air Base at once. They'd been shown to this room and ignored. Though, to be honest, he hadn't made much of an effort to contact the people in charge. Before he spoke with anyone he needed to know if the kids had been seen using magic.

While he paced the room, his wife sat unmoving in the chair as if willing the safe return of their children. His anxiety was too much for him to contain, so he paced as he waited.

The window overlooked the runways and air base, which bustled with activity. Numerous helicopters and planes, departing and landing, provided the only distraction from his thoughts. He suspected the activity had to do with his children but no one had told them anything.

Mary hadn't looked out the window once. Her eyes stayed glued to the walkie-talkie, obviously hoping the kids would be in range soon. Every few minutes she tried to speak with them.

Moments ago he'd pried the radio from his wife's excited grasp and spoken briefly to his son Charlie.

Tears ran down Mary's face when she'd heard Charlie's voice. She jumped to her feet and threw herself into John's arms.

Tears filled his own eyes as he hugged his wife.

Before he could do more than greet Charlie, the door to the conference room burst open and armed men escorted a general inside.

John hesitated, unsure how to proceed, unsure of what was known.

The general motioned the men holding

the rifles to wait outside. "My men have picked up your sons along with the other missing soldiers. I was informed your youngest son and his cohorts jumped from the helicopter and ran away." The general stabbed the table with a fingertip, tapping in a rapid rhythm as a red flush covered his cheeks. "So many impossible rumors are flying it will take weeks to sort them all out. Get them here to clear this up!"

John nodded. General Flores seemed angry, but he guessed that was understandable. The situation was sure to be confused while the facts got straightened out.

He needed to clear his throat before he could speak to his son Charlie on the radio again. "I'm so glad you're back safe. Your mother and I were so worried. They just informed me you jumped from the helicopter. It's okay for you to come here to report."

"You and Mom are at the base?"

General Flores snatched the radio from John. "Yes, and we have your brother in custody as well."

"Please, whoever this is, stop talking right now," Charlie said, sounding strained. "We'll come in. We don't want to be enemies; we want to become friends, but you're making it impossible. Let me talk to my father again, please."

John held out his hand.

The general glared and slapped the radio into his palm.

"Don't worry about us. Your mom and I are fine. Rick is on base, but we haven't seen him. When can you be here?"

"Dad, someone better explain reputation gains to them before we come. Otherwise, they'll make it impossible for us to work with them. Right now, they're at neutral with us but rapidly getting lower. Rep is a passive trait, so we can't control it."

"Okay, they don't understand. I'll do my best to explain it, but you have to understand how anxious everyone here is."

"Sara called her lawyer and plans on calling Liz Harris and Mr. Lewis. The people we picked can help us, and we trust them. When our representatives get here, we'll turn ourselves in. Please, tell them not to do anything, um, unfortunate to any of you."

Mary tugged at his sleeve. "Tell them it's Project Blackout," she whispered.

"Okay, son, we can work this out. Your mom sends her love and wants me to tell you this is Project Blackout."

"I love you guys. See you soon."

Dead air crackled and hummed.

The general scowled at him and held out his hand for the radio.

A giddy mix of elation and terror made John dizzy. His children were safe, but only for the moment. Now that the magic had been seen, he needed to convince this man of the truth. Before speaking, he took a deep calming breath, kissed his wife's pale cheek, sat beside her and took her hand.

The general remained standing, his expression stiff and disbelieving as John told him his story.

John leaned back in his chair. General Flores hadn't believed him when told about the magic, and he didn't believe him now about the passive abilities. The children's return was only the first hurdle. Now that their secret was out, he needed to keep them safe.

Somehow, he needed to protect the kids from those who'd want to control them, while simultaneously keeping them under control; he was way over his head.

The impossibility of trying to convince the general made John wince. He didn't blame the general for his disbelief. Magic was almost impossible to believe even when you'd seen it with your own eyes, but he kept trying to explain.

"Look," John made a real effort to keep his voice level and imbue it with sincerity. "If you threaten them, in *any* way, your reputation with them will lower."

General Flores placed both hands on the table and leaned forward until his face hovered inches from John. "Don't mistake my presence here. My time is valuable. My coming to speak to you personally is a courtesy because of the unusual circumstances. Your children are disrupting the smooth operation of this base. I have no interest in being friends with them; they'll be lucky if I don't arrest them. They had no business being there, never mind the supplies they stole. If they don't turn themselves in, my men will apprehend them. Your lies aren't helping them."

"I don't think you understand what my husband means," Mary said in a soft, conciliatory tone. "It's a gaming term. If we might speak to someone with gaming experience?"

General Flores straightened and brushed imaginary lint from his immaculate uniform. "I assure you, Mrs. Hayes, that this isn't a game. Those—" he paused for a moment. "Delinquents," he finally spat, "are in serious trouble. They've stolen government property and attacked enemy insurgents, escalating hostilities and disrupting negotiations. We need them here to clear this up!"

"Yes, we realize that." Mary laid a hand on her husband's arm when he started to speak. "We'll make sure they come in but you need to understand—"

General Flores angrily interrupted, "No, you need to understand! This is now a matter of national security. This isn't trouble *you* can buy your way out of, and there's no time to coddle a child's hurt feelings!"

Mary stared at him helplessly a moment before turning to John.

With another heavier sigh John tried once more to explain. "General Flores, we all want the children to turn themselves in and resolve this peacefully. But they aren't normal children anymore. The magic changed them and we need to be sensitive to those changes. They can't help how hostile actions will make them react—"

General Flores interrupted again. "This magic bullshit isn't helping you. Once we find out what weapons they used, charges will be brought. I'm aware of Miss Mitchel's influence, but I doubt even Tomas Mitchel has enough money to quiet this." He paused a moment then snapped, "Don't count on your so-called witnesses staying bought." The general stepped back from the table. "I have reports to read and file. They have one hour to turn themselves in before my men arrest them." After gathering the radio and headset, he stalked from the room.

John gave his wife a comforting hug. The general's mind was made up. Nothing either of them said would get through to him. The kids couldn't meet with this man. He'd destroy any hope they had of working with the government.

Then, a new idea occurred to him.

Did he want the children to work with the government? Maybe they'd be better off if they couldn't.

John turned to Mary. "Dear Lord, he thinks Sara's father is paying for those people to lie. What would be the point?"

Mary shrugged, her face pale and her eyes wide. "Who knows what her father is into? Maybe he has a weapons deal on the table or something. And who cares? Once the children are here, they can prove what we're saying is true."

John leaned back in his seat and rubbed his temples. "Mary, they'll never be able to catch them, but they could cause a lot of harm trying, and what about Richard? We have to get through to them. We need to talk to someone who understands how MMO's work."

"Let's get the kids and just go home." Mary shrugged and cracked a small smile. "No one will believe they did any of that. What can General Flores prove? No weapons were used, and he doesn't believe in the magic."

John rubbed his temples hard, then pinched the bridge of his nose with two fingers. "As much as I wish we could just go home, we can't. The general doesn't understand what we're trying to say. This hostile attitude will make it impossible for the kids to work with the government. It got me thinking that might not be such a bad thing. The magic is so powerful it might be better if the military can't work with them."

John paused to gather his thoughts and didn't like his conclusions at all.

"Sweetheart…. Think about the big picture here. We have two choices. Help the government connect with our kids— or run. And, honey… If we run, we're a serious liability for them. With their magic, the kids could escape, hide, and remain unseen and untraceable. We can't. When we're caught, and we *will* be caught, they'll hold us, and the kids will come for us. You know they will, and they'll fight to get us. Fight the entire United States military."

Tears trailed down Mary's cheeks each drop a hurt in John's soul.

"Maybe we wouldn't be caught, John. We could all just disappear."

John squatted in front of her and took both her hands. "No. Once word of what they can do gets out, every government will hunt them down. What they can do is too valuable, too unique… too dangerous. And not only governments, unscrupulous men everywhere will want them. Whoever has them can potentially control the world."

"The world… isn't that a little extreme?"

John leaned forward and kissed his wife's cheek, resting his face on hers for a moment. "Imagine if you had a thousand warriors and ten thousand mages and sun-priests," John whispered through a constricted throat. He squeezed his eyes closed but couldn't block his imaginings. Visions of fireballs and destroyed cities overrun with rampaging warriors and rogues filled his mind. "Imagine if you had thousands of rangers and rogues," he continued, feeling sick. "Who could stop you?"

"But they don't. There's only five." Mary

pulled back and framed John's face with her hands. "Try not to panic here, John."

"Mary…honey… there's only those five now, but what's stopping them from making more?"

Mary looked confused. "How?"

"I have no idea, but do you think that would stop people from taking the kids and experimenting on them to find out?"

Mary paled and swayed.

John grabbed her in a tight hug and said, "Now you see why we need to get through to the general. By ourselves, we can't protect them. We need help. But it might be better if the kids can't help them either and can only be studied."

Mary trembled in his grasp. "Maybe Sara's lawyer can help when he gets here. She said she called him. God knows we can't do anything locked in this room. We really need to talk with someone with gaming experience before reputation is ruined."

- 2 -

SEEING IS BELIEVING

Captain Sanders was listening to the last seconds of their conversation from an intercom in the room he'd just entered.

He'd met Mr. and Mrs. Hayes three days before when they'd come to Incirlik Air Base looking for information about their son Richard who was missing in action. A gamer himself, he knew what they meant by reputation. How it applied he didn't know, but he understood it.

Something big was happening, but he wasn't quite sure what. The hostages had been rescued from ISIS and a major engagement had taken place in Iraq, but the snippets and tidbits he'd heard were fantastical. He wasn't in the need-to-know loop.

A thoughtful expression crossed his face as he stared after General Flores. The general was a good man to work for, but he was strictly by the book.

Deciding to put himself in the loop, he went to speak with Mr. and Mrs. Hayes.

"Oh, Captain Sanders," Mary said, sounding glad to see him. "Please, tell me you've played Ultimate Battle Magic."

Captain Sanders nodded. "Yes, I have. Why is that important?"

"So, you understand reputation gains and losses then?"

"I do. If a faction is hostile, you can't interact with it. You can only interact with factions friendly with you. You gain rep with different factions by doing quests and getting rewards and lose rep when you interact in a hostile manner."

"Exactly."

Mary sounded so relieved it surprised him.

"What's that have to do with them coming in?"

"They'll gain and lose rep the same way; they can't help it. If General Flores persists in being hostile, they won't be able to use their magic to benefit the United States services at all. That isn't necessarily a bad thing, but he won't even try to understand it." Mary twined her fingers in her lap and stared at him intently.

"I don't think I'm following this conversation," Captain Sanders admitted.

"The magic is from the video game. It follows all the same rules, the cooldowns, the cast speeds, everything. They can't change that, it's the way it is, but they also received all the passive buffs, including reputation gains."

Captain Sanders gaped at her, first in amazement, and then concern. "Do I understand you correctly; you believe the children can use magic from a video game?"

John laid his hand on his wife's shoulder. "Mary, he doesn't know what's happening. I don't think he can help us."

Captain Sanders tapped his fingers on the table. "Okay, I see you believe that, and you won't let the children come in unless you think our actions won't influence rep gains." He cleared his throat. "I'll speak with the MP's sent to get them and tell them to be as gentle as possible. Nothing will stop the general from sending them... unless you can get them to voluntarily turn themselves in?"

John stared at him thoughtfully. "Captain, you've been extremely kind to us, and we appreciate it. And yes, we could get the children to come here, but trust me when I say you don't want that to happen if they aren't coming as friends. If you could— I don't know— somehow convince the general that all the characteristics got transferred over, not just the magic, that would be an enormous help."

Captain Sanders eyed them doubtfully. Both Mary and John looked hopeful as if they thought what they were saying was entirely believable. The small hairs on the back of his neck rose. *They must be insane or pathological liars.* His frown deepened when John bit back a laugh, turning it into a cough.

John said, "I see you think I'm nuts, and believe me, I thought my wife was nuts too when she told me, but there are witnesses of the kids using magic. Could you talk to them?"

The captain rose. "I don't know what's going on, but I'll speak with General Flores and explain rep and tell him you believe it. I can't say that'll help, but I'll try."

Mary and John thanked him, and he left the room.

Captain Sanders headed to the barracks the rescued hostages occupied. The private guarding the door saluted and stepped aside, not attempting to stop him from entering a small anteroom where a Marine major sat viewing a video on a small screen.

The major wore heavy armor and held his face a foot from the screen, staring, his expression intent. His nametag identified him as Major Nelson.

Major Nelson stopped the video, looking up in annoyance. "Can I help you, Captain?"

"Excuse me, sir. I'm Captain Sanders, from General Flores staff."

The major shrugged and restarted the video.

On the television screen five bald teenagers, two girls, and three boys, dressed alike with black caps and headsets, were standing close together on a rocky hillside. They wore black shirts with long-sleeved, desert-camouflage shirts over them, and black cargo pants with knives strapped to their legs. Four wore dirty bulletproof vests already pockmarked with bullet holes and stained with dried blood.

One girl wore a ragged, black cloak and carried what looked like a wooden staff. One boy held a rifle. Another carried a garbage can lid and a fire ax painted black. Another ax was strapped to his back. The other two children had nothing noticeable about them.

The picture panned over destroyed

helicopters that still smoldered, giving off thick plumes of black smoke. The camera left the helicopters and scanned three tanks and a large group of armed men in jeeps and trucks approaching in the distance before panning back to the grouped children. Suddenly, one girl disappeared from the image.

Major Nelson stopped the video. "The girl wearing the cloak yelled something the recording didn't quite pick up, but I think she shouted the other girl's name and one of the boys. She said something like, 'Stacy and Leroy' and they ran forward." A sharp jab of his finger started the video again.

The camera jerked and bobbed as the man holding it argued with someone. The argument escalated to a fight, and Captain Sanders realized the men were arguing over the kids. Major Nelson was yelling for them to come back and threatening someone Captain Sanders couldn't see.

"The rescued hostages grabbed my men and wouldn't let us go until the fight started," Major Nelson said dryly as the image in the video steadied and panned back over the approaching enemy.

The kids stopped about six-hundred-yards from the approaching tanks and took what appeared to be very deliberate places, forming a triangle with the biggest boy who held the garbage can lid, in front.

Captain Sanders stared in wonder as a ball of fire formed in front of one of the boys and he threw it at an oncoming tank. His amazement grew as a silvery curve of something formed around the boy who'd thrown the fireball and the girl holding the staff.

A tank shooting high-explosive warheads at them exploded when the missiles circled the silver sphere and headed back to the tank, impacting so hard the tank rolled over, crushing the men behind it. Bits of tank spun off in all directions and fire and smoke covered the upside-down wreck.

The boy formed more fireballs in his hands, which slammed into the tanks with such force they jerked. Twelve fireballs flew from the boy's fingertips in under a minute. All glowed orange, shimmered with heat, and grew in size as they traveled from him to the tanks.

The tanks rocked with the impacts and men ran screaming as fire engulfed them. The boy didn't stop casting until the tanks smoked and burned, half sunk into the ground from the force of the explosions, clearly out of commission. It had happened so fast he couldn't catch the details.

"Could you replay that?" he asked.

Major Nelson restarted the video, and this time Captain Sanders looked for the other four kids. It took effort to spot them as they appeared to flicker all over the screen.

He finally spotted a boy kneeling about twenty feet from the girl with the staff, taking shots with a gun because the boy making the fireballs stopped beside him and spoke for a moment.

Captain Sanders asked Major Nelson to rewind and replay the recording, finding it almost impossible to see the boy even though he knew he was kneeling in plain sight. He finally gave up and looked for the others. The boy making fire had returned to the girl with the staff, and in the distance, the boy carrying the garbage can lid and ax jumped forward in impossibly huge bounds and fought hand-to-hand. The fireballs and vivid lightning strikes kept distracting his eyes.

The fight progressed.

Magic, he thought in awe, *it really was magic.* Then, *no, it's movie special effects, incredible ones, but not real.*

With another jab of his finger, Major Nelson stopped the video where the kids walked back toward the camera. "It took them eighteen minutes to destroy three tanks, four helicopters, assorted jeeps and trucks, and about one thousand men. Not a hair on their heads was harmed, I mean, if they had hair."

"You saw that happen?" Captain Sanders rose an eyebrow.

"Yes, thirty of us did. I hardly believe it myself, even though I was there. There's no doubt what they did was impossible, but we watched them do it."

Major Nelson pointed at the teenager wearing the cape. "That one makes balls of light that heal them like— um— magic, instantly. Not a lot of shots got through, but some did, and she'd throw a light ball at them, and they glowed a second and were completely healed. Their vests and clothing showed bullet holes and bloodstains, but they themselves were unharmed when they returned.

"She can fly or something too. I've watched this video over twenty times now and see something new each time. The boy carrying the garbage can lid held back ten men rushing him with it. Then he yells and they dropped their weapons, and the other girl appears out of nowhere and uses a knife to kill them all."

He rewound the video until he found the

part he'd described. "See, here, and look, the girl with the staff flies there. It happens so fast, it's like she teleports, which is what I'm pretty sure the other boy is doing." Stunned amazement laced Major Nelson's words.

Captain Sanders was more than amazed. For a moment he wondered if this was an elaborate joke, but the dead bodies looked all too real.

"Holy Christ!" Captain Sanders said, his voice soft and full of awe as he watched the video again, trying to keep his eye on the boy throwing the fireballs, and now that he observed him closer he noticed the boy caused the lightning as well.

His eyes widened and the hair rose on the back of his neck again. He recognized the motions the boy made to cast. His glance flitted to the boy with the garbage can lid and his eyes narrowed. He recognized those moves too. Just three days ago he'd dueled a warrior who'd cast the same exact spells.

"Oh, man, we have a big problem. Has General Flores seen these?"

"Yes, he has copies."

"Then the problem is bigger than I thought. I've just spoken to one of their parents and they tried to tell me... well, anyway, that doesn't matter, I didn't believe them, but now I do. It's imperative the general makes no moves that will affect reputation gains."

"What are you talking about?" Major Nelson sat back in his chair, stretching and rubbing his eyes.

"You agree those kids were using magic, correct?"

"Well, I suppose it's as good a word as any for what they did."

"The parents said they got it from a video game and received all of their character's characteristics, including the passive ones, like reputation gains."

"I'm sorry, you've lost me."

"Okay, there are different abilities a character in the game can do. Some they cast, like a fireball or healing, and some are what they call passive— they just are— like strength or agility. They don't do anything to get them; they have it automatically and can't control it."

"Okay, I'm with you so far."

"Well, they also received the reputation gains. They can't do a thing about that, it's a passive ability. They can't control it or turn it off."

"What exactly does that mean?"

"They can obviously control when they

cast a fireball or heal or whatever, but they can't control how strong or fast they are, that just is. It's the same with how people are perceived in the game. It's called reputation. When you meet a group of people, you start at neutral, do quests and get rewards, and it increases your reputation, your rep with them. The opposite is also true. If the group interacts with you in a hostile manner, you go from neutral, to unfriendly, to hated, to at war. That means you can't interact with that group in any way except hostilely."

"Still not understanding the problem here."

"If we act in a hostile or threatening way, our rep with them will lower. It will be automatic; they can't stop it. They'll be unable to interact with us except in a hostile manner." He pointed at the screen where fireballs blew up tanks. "Hostile, like that."

"Well, that doesn't sound good. You're saying if we make them mad, they become our enemy?"

"I'm saying, until we assure we're friendly with them, we need to tread lightly. While they could choose to be our enemy at any time, they'll be forced to if we aren't careful in our approach."

"And you know this how?"

"I play the occasional online video game and understand how they work and I recognize the casts. The parents said they got the, err, magic from UBM. There's no reason to doubt that at the moment. Until we know better, it would be in our best interest to be friendly."

Major Nelson rose. "Let's go see the general before this is fubar."

"How did we lose sight of them?" Captain Sanders asked as they left the room together.

"They jumped from the helicopter when one of my men waved a gun at them." Major Nelson continued telling his story as they entered the main building and went to speak with General Flores.

General Flores narrowed his eyes and flared his nostrils when confronted. "So, you've investigated without authorization from me and believe the fairytale magic explanation. We don't have time for this nonsense. We need to find them and make them tell us how they did those things. You're obviously unaware of their earlier run-ins with the law. They're suspected of dealing in nuclear weapons and causing a plane to crash. This wasn't magic!"

He spat the word magic derisively.

"This was spoiled, teenage brats with too much money thinking they could do whatever they wanted. Sara Mitchel is Tomas Mitchel's daughter. Tomas Mitchel who owns Coren Tech – the makers of the warheads we use in our F-16's – and who the hell knows what else. Those kids stole something and used it."

Captain Sanders exchanged a dismayed glance with Major Nelson.

"These are dangerous criminals and will be treated as such until such time as adequate answers are provided. Those of you who have accepted bribes to stay silent will be dealt with as well. Dismissed." General Flores returned to his paperwork, not acknowledging their parting salutes.

"Okay, that could've gone better." Major Nelson grimaced at Captain Sanders as they stood outside the general's closed door.

Captain Sanders wore a matching scowl. "This could rapidly become a serious disaster. If they do have magic, which, I can't believe I'm saying this, but I believe they do after seeing that video, it won't be an easy job to get them somewhere they don't want to be."

"Oh, they for sure have something, and if the parents are right and we pursue them, we'll be burning our bridges. I for one want to know how he did that fire thing. I wouldn't mind being able to do that myself."

"So— now what?" Captain Sanders asked.

Major Nelson's grimace deepened. "Now we do what God frowns upon, we go over his head.

- 3 -

SPECS OF MAGIC

Major Nelson took out his cell phone and made a call. "Terry, I need a favor. It's huge and more important than I have time to explain. I'm sending you a file. Bring it immediately to Major General Campbell's attention. It's for his eyes only. Tell him I'm breaking every rule in the book to get him this file, and I need to talk with him faster than ASAP.

"Everything in the report is true. Multiple witnesses can confirm it. If I don't hear from him in fifteen minutes I'm calling someone else. I have critical information that needs to be acted on pronto if we want to control these assets." Major Nelson listened for a moment. "Yes, I'll owe you one for sure. Do it right now. Interrupt whatever he has going on, this is more important." He hung up and

27

turned to Captain Sanders. "Now, we wait."

His phone rang twelve minutes later.

"This better be for real," a gruff voice said.

"It is, sir, and those kids are running around doing god knows what, god knows where. One of the kids parents are here and explained some stuff, and I really think you should speak with them before anything, um, unfortunate happens."

"Is Brigadier General Flores unaware of this video?" Major General Campbell asked in disbelief.

"No, sir, he's seen it and has copies, but prefers to believe they're using secret weapons, or it's a fake, which I assure you, sir, it isn't. The kid's parents say it's magic, and well...." He explained the reputation system as best he could.

General Campbell listened politely before saying decisively, "I'll be there in four hours. I'm calling General Flores now and assuming command. Stay with the parents until I arrive. Find out what you can. Assure them I'm taking over, no arrests will be issued, and the children will be free to go after an interview. And, Major, you by god better be correct!"

Captain Sanders escorted Major Nelson to the conference room where Mary and John

Hayes waited. He sent the private at the door for food and water.

Major Nelson shook their hands, saying, "Mr. and Mrs. Hayes, I've seen compelling evidence that the children can, in fact, do magic. Can you tell us how they can?"

"Well, no. I have a theory, but no— we don't know— they don't know either." Mary shrugged.

"What's your theory then?" the major asked as he sat.

Mary explained about the lightning and plane crash and how they went to the tournament and played brilliantly even though they were so ill. Then she told them how Charlie realized what he could do.

That was the first time John heard the story and he gripped her hand hard. "Oh my god, Mary, we came so close to losing both our boys! Thank God for Sara."

Tears filled his eyes and he hugged her tight, burying his face in her hair for a moment before clearing his throat and sitting back in his chair.

"So, you think what? The radiation transformed them?" Major Nelson's voice exuded doubt.

"Yes, I think because they were being their characters so hard in their minds that, somehow, they became them," Mary said. "I know that sounds nuts, but you've seen what they can do."

"Speaking of which, can you tell us exactly what that is?" Major Nelson leaned forward, his eyes intent on hers.

"You can see their exact specs on the website," John said.

"The what?" Major Nelson sat back in confusion.

"I know what he means. I'll be right back," Captain Sanders said and hurried from the room.

Major Nelson said, "I understand you can get them to come in and talk with us?"

"Yes, but it was in your best interest to wait until we straightened things out," Mary said.

"Yeah, Captain Sanders told me about reputation. We understand it now, or at least he does anyway. Major General Campbell is coming here and taking over. He assures me no arrests will be made and the kids will be free to go after they're debriefed."

Mary sagged in relief.

John said, "Richard was threatened in their hearing. To boost rep, I think it would be smart to have him here unharmed, where they can see for themselves he's in no danger or trouble." He put an arm around his wife and they exchanged relieved smiles.

"I agree, but I'm afraid I don't have the authority to get him here myself. Don't worry about it though; General Campbell will appreciate the wisdom in that. The kids went to Iraq and fought a small war to get your son Richard once; we don't want them doing it again."

"A war?" Mary cried in dismay. "I knew they'd used their magic, but I thought just defensive spells to escape."

"No one told you?" Major Nelson said in amazement. "They fought in three encounters. One of which was a major engagement. I was there and can honestly say we would've suffered casualties without them, possibly even total casualties. We were severely out-gunned."

He took out his phone, queued up the video, and handed it to John. Dismay, fear, horror, a myriad of emotion crossed their faces as they watched.

"The plan was to sneak in and out," John explained as he handed the phone back. "They didn't intend to fight."

"Which one is your child?"

"The boy with the ax and garbage can lid, but we love them all. That was horrible!"

Mary turned to her husband, weeping into his shoulder. "Oh, John, what have we done?"

"Honey, we couldn't stop them. We'll get them help." He patted her back.

"Yeah, they could probably use counseling after that," Major Nelson agreed. "Not that they have anything to regret, but battle, fighting for your life, is a hard thing."

Captain Sanders returned with a laptop and a small printer. He handed the laptop to John, who pushed it to Mary.

She looked up the children's characters, printed them out, wrote their names at the top of the corresponding sheets and passed the sheets to Captain Sanders. "This is the most current spec. I'm not sure how often it's updated, but I'm sure this spec is close."

Major Nelson examined the pages. "I see Sara has two points in staff expertise but not what that means."

"Oh, that's easy. Just go to the game website and look it up." Mary returned to the keyboard and typed a minute. "Two points gives a fifty percent chance to proc blade flurry, which incapacitates opponents for three seconds. It also has a passive boost to all spells cast with a staff by twenty-five percent."

"You understood that?" Major Nelson asked Captain Sanders doubtfully.

The captain nodded and said, "Yes. I'm looking these spells over. She's extremely powerful; almost all of her spells are upgraded. You say she can do all of this in real life?"

"Well, honestly, I don't know." Mary tapped her pursed lips with one finger. "I've seen her cast Ascension, what they call levitate, and she understands languages I'm pretty sure she couldn't before. Protective Companion, what they call pull, she's used in front of me. Soothe and heal she's cast on me, but I haven't seen her cast every spell Seraphim has."

"If you'll excuse me a minute, I'll set my men to finding out what all these different spells do. General Campbell will want a complete report." Captain Sanders stood to leave.

"If you wouldn't mind, I'd love a copy of that report." John smiled and shrugged one shoulder. "I could look it up myself, but if you're going through all the trouble anyway...."

Captain Sanders laughed. "I don't see why not; it's all public knowledge."

Major Nelson turned back to them eagerly after Captain Sanders left. "You say you can get them to come in to talk?"

"I won't have to. Charles won't leave his family here. I'm sure they'll come no matter what I say. But I can leave messages for him, and hopefully, he sees them and comes in peacefully." John leaned forward and spoke very seriously, "I can't stress this enough, they're children with extremely powerful abilities. Please, please, do nothing to make them react badly."

"I've seen them in action, and believe me, I don't want them as enemies. We'll be as friendly as possible. What do you need to get in touch with them?"

John leaned back and drummed his fingers on the tabletop.

Mary placed a hand on his arm. "Trust has to start somewhere, John."

John nodded. "I'll need my phone, and if you could get our radio back that would be awesome. And my wife can leave an email for Charles."

The major retrieved those items and listened while John left a message on Sara's phone canceling Project Blackout and told them they could come in.

"Project Blackout?" Major Nelson lifted a quizzical brow.

"It's a scenario name. They'll tell you about it if they want to," Mary said. "Maybe you're unaware they're champions of their game. They don't just possess magic now, they have serious skill in using it as a team."

"I've never been into video games. I've played a few, but they seem pretty much alike to me, players as well."

"That's true to a certain extent, but you can see them play if you want to. The latest tournament is on the UBM website. You'll notice they play much, much, better than most of the others."

"The girl with the staff said something about looking up Stasis online."

"That's Sara, the girl with the staff, and Stasis is Stasia, the rogue." Mary used the laptop again and slid it to the major.

A clip of video game characters behaving almost exactly as the kids had played. The fight took place in a rock-walled castle with werewolves, but the techniques and abilities remained the same. The title of the clip was 'Stasis Leroy's Underhill.' Multiple links with her name and Team Valor filled the page. Pages of video links followed the clip.

Randomly picking another titled, 'This is How It's Done' Major Nelson watched the same characters battle a giant blue dragon. He clicked a link from the dragon and watched another group fight it. After watching two more groups fight the dragon, he re-played Team Valor's video. The difference amazed him.

Team Valor was organized, their movements precise, almost choreographed. In the other videos, people ran trying to avoid the tail and gaping maw, bumping into each other and running through the fire covering the floor while the dragon ate people and threw the bodies. In Team Valor's video, the dragon turned in small, precise circles. The characters moved quickly and in sync with each other, sometimes pausing or stopping completely before rapidly changing positions.

"Yeah, I see what you mean. They clearly play very well. You can tell from the other videos that others are trying to copy them with moderate success. Team Valor makes it look easy, but I guess it isn't."

They were still talking about the game when an older, tall thin man with skin the color of rich coffee, entered the room. The uniform he wore identified him as being in the Army, his stars told his rank. Cropped short and close to his head, his graying black hair framed a distinguished face. He offered his hand to Mary and John, introducing himself as Major General Campbell. Captain Sanders followed behind him.

- 4 -

REPUTATION GAINS

Earlier that same day

Team Valor jumped from the helicopter and landed on a rocky hillside sparsely covered with pine trees and small prickly shrubs. They hiked for an hour before reaching a road.

Charlie had no idea where they were other than Turkey, somewhere near Adana. Dawn had just given way to daylight and not a single car had passed, which was good, they needed a plan.

"So, now what?" Stasia frowned at her ripped sleeve.

Bullet holes and dried blood covered their clothing. Three battles and four days since their last shower while sleeping rough, and filthy didn't begin to describe them.

"We wait." Sara handed Charlie back his cell phone. "Agent Lewis said he'll call when he arrives. Once we talk with him and Mr. Martin we'll have a better idea of what to do. Major Harris said she'd come. You know they'll want to do a million tests; we insist she's involved. We need someone we trust looking out for us."

"These clothes are just rank. We need new ones," Stasia insisted after giving her arm a quick sniff.

The dried blood and sweat from their escape from Iraq had combined to form a powerful stench that made her grimace and wrinkle her nose.

"Let's head to the hotel. I bet they won't think we'll go there. Stasia can check it out and make sure it's safe," Oz said as he took off his bulletproof vest and camo shirt and stuffed them into his backpack.

The others did the same.

"Okay, but, Stasia, if anyone is there, or things seem off, just leave. We can't afford to do anything that would inadvertently lower our rep." Charlie met their eyes, his own serious.

Hawk kicked a rock on the road and sighed. "Yeah, we avoid them until someone has time to explain what's going on before their reputation with us is so far down we can't get it back."

"Fine, let's go to the hotel." Stasia turned to Oz. "Where is it?"

Oz pointed. "That way."

"Darn, I wish one of us had a chariot key bound or something. I'm sick of walking," Hawk complained as they trudged along the deserted dirt road.

"Yeah, that would be subtle, a Phoenix pulling a giant chariot; no one would notice that." Oz snickered.

"I could always borrow a car," Stasia offered.

"No!" Both Sara and Charlie said.

"We can't go around stealing things just because we can get away with it. We stole the gear, but that was an emergency, life, or death. This isn't. We walk!" Charlie took Sara's hand.

Stasia heaved a sigh and nodded, then brightened. "We have money, let's call a cab."

Sara laughed. "Oh, my god, we're too used to magical means now and forgot real life. Yeah, call one, Stasia. But first, let's look up the address of the hotel. We just want to go near it; not directly to it."

Stasia stayed in the shower for twenty minutes

humming and singing snatches of songs. When she finished showering, Sara was already dressed in a pair of jeans with her Team Valor sweatshirt zipped over a white t-shirt, making a face at her reflection in the mirror.

"Being bald sucks!"

Stasia wrapped herself in a towel and peered in the mirror with Sara. "I agree. This isn't a good look!"

She scowled at her reflection and grabbed her small makeup bag. Turning Sara to face her, she applied the makeup. After stepping back to critique her work, she rubbed the line she'd drawn for eyebrows and redid it. Then she handed Sara a lipstick and added face powder before stepping back and checking again.

"Better, but I hope our hair grows back quick." Stasia went to dress while Sara frowned at the mirror.

Still scowling at her reflection, Sara jammed a white knit cap on her head.

Stasia dressed similarly, putting on clean jeans and her Valor sweatshirt over a light-pink t-shirt. She was applying her makeup when a soft knock came at the door.

Sara let Charlie in and returned to the chair where she sat with a thump.

The door closed behind him with a dull click, and he faced them smiling.

He was dressed like them in jeans and a black t-shirt. A sweatshirt dangled from his hand and he wore a black knit hat on his bald head.

Charlie grinned. "You two clean up nice. What do ya say we find somewhere to eat?"

"Sure, I could eat." Stasia glanced at Sara hunched in the chair, then the oblivious Charlie. "I'm going to see if Hawk's okay. We'll be next door when you're ready to go."

Sara rose to follow her out.

Charlie stepped into her path as the door closed behind Stasia. "Are we okay?" he asked as he reached to touch her arm.

Avoiding eye contact, her hand went self-consciously to her head. She dropped it quickly and understanding lit his eyes.

"Sara, this doesn't matter to me." He removed the white hat and ran a gentle hand over the curve of her skull. "When I said I loved you, I meant it."

Soft skin shivered under his hand and he wanted to touch more. Cradling her head in one hand, he leaned down and kissed her.

The warmth of her neck where his hand rested filled his entire body. Without meaning to, he found his other hand on the bare skin of her back, under her t-shirt. Her low moan caused his breath to catch, and she moved closer.

The two inches she stood from him wasn't close enough. She felt so good he wanted to get even closer. The kiss deepened, and she slid her hands under his shirt, making him groan. Both of his hands were now under her shirt, caressing the bare skin of her back, and her breath came faster.

The pulse in his neck increased as he deepened the kiss, and she moaned again.

He was moving too fast and knew it. It took all his willpower to break from the kiss and release her.

When he spoke, his voice was husky with emotion. "I love you, not your hair, you!"

The brilliant blue of her eyes met his, and he couldn't resist stealing another kiss. The heat from her body excited him. Her firm softness pressing against him made him shiver and press even closer. If they were alone and had time… he wanted to feel her warm skin against his everywhere. But they weren't alone; their friends waited right next door. And they didn't have time; they needed to leave before someone came here looking for them.

She stepped back and smiled at him. "I

love you too, Charlie Hayes. I could kiss you forever."

As she leaned in for another kiss his stomach gurgled. She giggled and took his hand.

"Let's go eat."

Hand-in-hand, they went next door.

Five bald kids would be remembered. After conferring a moment, they decided they didn't care and entered the first restaurant they passed.

"How long until Agent Lewis gets here?" Oz asked when they'd finished eating.

"He didn't say, he just said he'd come. Major Harris won't be here for five or six days at least; she has to get leave. Mr. Martin will arrive in a day or two as well," Sara answered.

"I don't know; can we wait that long? Who knows what they're doing to my family." Charlie frowned.

Hawk slapped his shoulder reassuringly. "The most they'll do is lock them up. It's not like they'll waterboard them or anything."

"Let's not worry about it; I'll check," Stasia said. "I won't do anything except look. Imagination will do more harm than knowing."

"Let me call Agent Lewis and find out where he is, and we'll all go. We'll wait outside for you." Sara placed her hand on Stasia's. "If you need us, we'll be ready."

She called Agent Lewis again. "Hi, it's me again, Sara Mitchel. We wondered how long before you got here? Well, sort of in a rush. I don't think I should say over the phone. No, not exactly life or death. Yes, I do know what caused it, I did, but I shouldn't say more on the phone. That would be amazing. I'll call you in three hours. Thank you. See you then." Sara handed the phone back to Charlie.

"A jet will have him here in three hours. Let's go see where your parents are." Sara handed out the radios and headsets while Stasia called another cab.

A copse of windblown pine trees across from the fence made a good spot to wait while Stasia spied.

"Keep up Project Blackout, Stasia," Charlie said. "Sara will turn on her radio every twelve minutes for fifteen seconds. If she hears the word port, I'll summon you using her summon. Don't take any action, call us first, just get information. Come back here, and we'll decide what to do depending on what you discover. If you miss two check-ins, we'll summon you."

Charlie watched her sprint across the base a moment before turning away. He'd debated stealing her invisible spell but didn't trust he'd be able to resist breaking his parents out if he saw them in person. *It was better to wait and plan their moves,* he told himself and forced his hands away from the knife sheathed on his waist.

Mary and John were easy to find. Both sat in the same small conference room with a private guarding the door. She slipped away to find Rick without trying to enter.

At the twelve-minute mark she reported locating Charlie's parents and Rick. He was in a lightly guarded barracks with the rest of the hostages they'd rescued, and she planned on sneaking in and talking to him.

A quick reconnaissance located an open window eight-feet from the ground. An effortless, graceful leap and she swung inside, landing silently. Rick hadn't canceled the raid; sidelong glances followed her across the room.

She held a finger to her lips, asking for quiet, and everyone went about their business, pretending she wasn't there.

An MP patrolling the room took no notice of her. Guthric wandered over to where Rick lay reading a book.

"They're holding us for questioning; it's nothing to be alarmed at," Rick whispered. "Are you all okay?"

She nodded.

"That was a lawyer Sara called on the helicopter?"

Another nod.

"Couldn't hurt."

"Your parents are here," Stasia whispered.

Rick jerked upright, then lay back down, flicking the guard a guilty glance. "Like on the base here?"

"Yes, they're holding them for questioning. They appear fine. They're alone in a conference room right now."

Guthrie turned, acting as if he spoke to Rick. "You have reinforcements coming?"

"Yes, we called an FBI agent and a few others. We didn't want only one agency to know about us and make us disappear or something."

"Yeah, this is something of a pickle," Guthrie agreed. "Rick explained how reputation affects who you can deal with, but I'm afraid the guy in charge here doesn't believe a word we're saying. I'm sure they'll work it out," he added hurriedly. "Try not to let this snafu affect you."

"We can try all we want, but they pulled a

gun on Sara for making a phone call. Hostile actions lower rep, it's a fact," Stasia whispered.

"Well, not always." Rick frowned. "If both parties agree, you can duel and stuff, but yeah, I see your point. You can choose not to attack them, but they'll make it impossible for you to help them. But honestly, will that matter? It's not as if you wanted to be in the service anyway. Well Charlie did, but it's not like it would really matter if you couldn't work with them, is it?"

"I don't know," Stasia admitted. "But if they remain hostile, we won't come in; we'll just disappear."

"And do what?" Rick asked. "Run away? Never see your families and friends again?"

"If we have too. We don't want too, but we don't want to be dissected in a lab somewhere or go to jail either."

"Stasia, that won't happen. This'll get straightened out, you'll see," Guthrie said soothingly. "We'll explain, and eventually someone with imagination will believe us."

"Maybe." Stasia climbed off Rick's bed. "I'll be around keeping an eye on things to see where this is headed. Rick, they know we came for you, which makes you a valuable hostage. If we run, we'll have no way to contact you or assure your safety. You need to decide if you're staying here or coming with us."

Rick stared at her sadly. "I'm a soldier; my duty is here."

Stasia nodded but didn't look happy. "I understand that, but I hope you don't regret it."

She took his hand a moment and released it with a heavy sigh. At the window, she paused and gazed back, her expression worried, before leaping gracefully through the window.

"Me too," Rick whispered, watching her leave.

MEETING GENERAL CAMPBELL

Major General Campbell arrived on the base two hours and forty minutes later. Captain Sanders escorted him to his office while debriefing him.

Charlie had spell-stolen Stasia's invisible and had checked on his brother and parents himself. He followed the general into the office and peered over his shoulder with interest. General Campbell sat at his desk where a tall stack of files waited. The reports contained printouts of their character specifications with descriptions of what each skill point did.

"This is a full list of their abilities?" The general asked as he glanced at each page of the thick report. "Why are some highlighted?"

"Yes, this is a complete list. The highlighted ones are confirmed abilities," Captain Sanders explained.

"You're telling me, they can do everything

on this list?" General Campbell waved the paper disbelievingly at the captain.

"I don't know, sir. We're assuming so. We only have eyewitness confirmation on the highlighted ones though."

"Jesus Christ!" General Campbell exclaimed after taking a moment to read the document more thoroughly. "This says the warrior, um...."

"Charles Hayes, aka, Chief," Captain Sanders supplied.

"Right, this Chief can yell and cause his enemies to drop their weapons just like that?"

"Yes, we even have that one on video," Captain Sanders agreed. "I know its hard to believe but the evidence supports there claim it's magic."

Charlie stifled a laugh. Stasia's eyes danced with mirth and she'd clapped a hand over her mouth to stifle her giggles. He had to look away before he burst into laughter.

"I'll keep an open mind although I find it incredible. But even if Miss Mitchel has stolen something from her father's lab, I want to know what it is. I've never seen anything like that recording. "The general turned back to the reports. "And you say they received the passive abilities as well?" General Campbell asked as he ran his finger down the long list of passive talents.

"They claim so, but it's hard to tell for most of them. Most of the passives aren't visible, we'll need to test."

General Campbell continued to read Charlie's spec. "Chief has quite a few passive abilities, commanding presence, damage conversion, damage reflection, look at this one —fearful presence— enemies won't attack until he gets very close. And this one— protective presence— it forces enemies in range of him to focus on him, not his party. I wonder how that translates to real life?"

Captain Sanders shrugged. "We'll need testing that's for sure."

"Okay, so assuming what the parents say is true, that they've received all the character traits, we'd best proceed with the utmost care concerning our reputation with them. They'd be an unbelievable asset to our armed forces it this isn't all an elebroate hoax of some sort."

Captian Sanders held out his hands and shook his head and General Campbell tapped the paper in front of him.

"Don't forget they're minor's, just children. We can't recruit them," Captain Sanders said.

General Campbell sat back in his chair. "Exceptions on age can be made. The real point is will they want to help us?"

"I guess we could ask them and find out, but I guarantee they won't if they think Richard Hayes is being held against his will, or if we threaten them, or their parents in any way."

"Well, that isn't a problem." General Campbell slapped the folder closed. "We have no intention of doing any of those things." The chair creaked as he leaned even farther back and rubbed the bridge of his nose. "Well, Lance Corporal Hayes could be problematic. He's a Marine, subject to their rules and could be stationed anywhere. But I suppose, exceptions could be made for him as well."

"Normal discipline or orders for Richard Hayes shouldn't be a problem, but we can ask. If they don't want him assigned far away, I'm sure we can work something out," Captain Sanders agreed. "I'd suggest he be present, at least at first, to assure them of our good will. Then if he has duty elsewhere, we see what they say."

"And you say they'd already called a lawyer and we're trying to call someone else when the incident with the gun occurred?"

"Yes, Sergeant Rinto reports he took the phone from Sara Mitchel and told her to remain seated. He says he pointed the gun at her seat, not her, but the threat was implied. They jumped from the helicopter immediately. We can assume they finished making whatever calls they'd intended. We know they returned to their hotel rooms and changed clothes before visiting a local restaurant. The waiter there said they appeared calm and weren't different from any other group of teenagers, except for the baldheads, which he clearly remembers. After that, we don't know where they went."

"Okay, let's talk with the parents and see if we can set up a meeting." General Campbell pushed back from his desk and strode out, followed by the captain, and unbeknownst to them, Charlie. He signaled Stasia to follow and ran back to Sara.

General Campbell entered the conference room where Major Nelson still spoke with Mr. and Mrs. Hayes. Someone had brought food, drinks, and another laptop. Three copies of the report General Campbell had received lay on the table. Mary's eyes lit and she stood when the general entered. A flush stained her cheeks as she looked away and returned to her seat.

Her husband also stood and stepped

forward, offering his hand.

The captain made introductions.

General Campbell surveyed them and sighed. "So, Anastasia is here?"

Both John and Mary couldn't help glancing at her and away. Neither answered him.

General Campbell cleared his throat and turned to where they'd glanced. "It's perfectly safe to show yourself, young lady. No one will be held here against their will. Your friend Richard is safe and will be brought in soon."

A slight frown creased his face as he waited, and John wondered if he felt foolish for talking to thin air.

The general startled as Stasia appeared with her hand placed protectively on the back of Mary's chair.

Mary pulled her into a tight embrace. "Oh, Stasia, sweetheart, thank you for saving Rick, but I'm so sorry I let you go. I shouldn't have." Mary's voice shook with emotion.

"You're welcome, and you know you couldn't have stopped us." Stasia returned Mary's hug but kept her gaze on the general.

General Campbell took a seat at the table. "Your friends are here too?"

"No, just me."

The general thumbed through the pages

in front of him and brought out the one containing her information. "They're waiting for you to report?"

"Yes."

"And will you ask them to come in?"

"Yes." She glanced at her watch. "In three minutes, when I can contact them."

"Okay, why don't you have a seat and, Major, maybe more food, and drinks would be in order," General Campbell said.

Major Nelson left to round up refreshments.

"Would you mind telling us who else you've called?" the general asked Stasia.

Stasia tapped her fingers on the table in front of her and paused a moment before leaning forward. "An FBI agent and a nurse we want put in charge of our medical care. We understand you'll need to test us, and we're willing to cooperate, but we also want safeguards in place."

General Campbell frowned slightly but nodded. "Yes, I can see that, but we want to keep this classified. Civilian personnel will be hard to manage."

"We understand that as well. The nurse is a major in the Navy and had access to our medical records. She was there the entire time we were so sick. The agent we called has also seen our records. Agent Lewis is nonnegotiable. We don't want only one branch of the service to know about us, so picked a civil branch to broaden our protection."

"Okay, I'm sure we can work with that too. When will they arrive?"

"Major Harris will arrive in a day or so. She wasn't sure about getting leave but said she'd come as soon as she could, and Agent Lewis should be here already." Stasia glanced at her watch and turned on the radio.

Agent Lewis exited the F-16F and stretched. Riding in the back of a jet, traveling faster than sound, wasn't something he wanted to do again. His boss had set up this ride. The mysterious explosion on flight Two-Twelve and the disappearance of flight Four-Fourteen were a top priority for the FBI. If the kids knew anything about the radiation, they needed to know it too.

The fact that Sara Mitchel had connections to Coren Tech excited him. Coren Tech was already being investigated for violating safety procedures and illegal arms dealings. Maybe Tomas Mitchel was using his daughter and her friends to smuggle a new weapon from the country. Finding out what was used to cause the explosion could make his career.

Mystery surrounded Sara. First, the explosion, then the miraculous survival. Not to mention her father abandoning her in the hospital. The only reason he could imagine a parent doing so was guilt. *Maybe Tomas had been afraid to be found out?* He wished now he'd thought to track down Mr. Mitchel's whereabouts and gotten actual eyewitness collaboration. If Tomas had skipped to a non-extradition country it would explain his leaving.

Agent Lewis had read all the reports and spoken to multiple witnesses. The illness hadn't been faked, he was sure of that. That the kids had survived was indeed a miracle. And now, here they were in Turkey of all places.

His boss had practically had a stroke when he'd called and told him Sara wanted a meeting and where she was. The speed with which his ride had been arranged told Agent Lewis just how badly the FBI wanted this meeting. He'd been ordered to make Sara an asset. She was in a unique position to give intelligence on Coren Tech, assuming she knew anything at all and this wasn't just a wild goose chase.

He hated to get his hopes up for nothing, what could a fourteen-year-old girl know, but the facts seemed too big to be a coincidence.

He called Sara, informing her of his arrival.

"Can you meet us alone?" Sara asked.

"Yes, where?"

"Leave the base and walk west. We'll find you."

With a grumble under his breath of too many spy movies, he agreed and hung up.

More armed men than usual guarded the base gates, but he exited with no problems.

Vehicles passed him on the busy street, but he remained the sole pedestrian. A dirt berm separated the street from the open space in front of the fence that encircled the base.

He walked on the berm through the dead grass, staying off the street, keeping a watchful eye out for the kids. Dead grasses lined both sides of the road with an occasional prickly looking patch of bushes. Meager looking pine trees grew in clumps on the side of the street opposite the base. The sudden appearance of Charlie and Oz in front of him made him jump.

Without giving him time to talk, they led him to a group of straggly trees and sat cross-legged in the brush, so he did too.

"How did you do that?" A gasp escaped him as Sara and Sebastian became visible. "How are you doing that?" He knew his face was a study of amazement and snapped his gaping mouth closed.

Charlie explained what had happened. Sara interrupted right after Charlie told the astounded Agent Lewis about the battle in Iraq.

"Stasia says the general had food brought in and seems nice." Sara glanced anxiously at Charlie.

"Tell her we'll come in with Agent Lewis, but we need more time with him first. Is she okay there, or should we get her out?"

Sara held a quick, hushed conversation with Stasia. "She's fine with your parents, and Rick is there and unharmed. He says they're being treated well and in no trouble."

Charlie turned back to the stunned agent. "We want you to represent us when we turn ourselves in. If they try to hold us there, we need you to get us out. I don't mean physically get us away, we can do that ourselves. I mean legally."

"This is a bit much to believe, even with the evidence of my own eyes." Agent Lewis took a moment to think. "This will obviously be classified. There's no way we'll want word of this to get out, but with that being said, the word is already out in some places. I'll need to contact my superiors, and I'll have to leapfrog quite a few to keep this secret." He straightened and reached for his phone.

His earlier thoughts made him smile and then grimace.

No one was going to believe this. Hell, he had a hard time believing it and the proof sat before him. His boss was sure to think he'd been bought off or was hiding the truth for other reasons. He'd have to think of something to convince him Sara knew nothing about Coren Tech.

His frown deepened. A lot of effort had gone into getting him here. He'd need a believable story on why she'd asked for this meeting.

"Okay, let me make a few calls first to get things in motion. Then we'll retrieve Anastasia."

"You'll do your best to make sure we don't get confiscated by the military?" Sara asked.

"I'll do my best to make sure you don't get confiscated by anyone," he said in a voice thick with repressed excitement as he turned away to make the calls.

- 6 -

SHOW AND TELL

General Campbell met them at the gate and escorted them to the conference room where everyone took seats after the kids had hugged Mary and John.

"I've seen the videos, but for verification purposes, and my own curiosity, could you show me some of the things you can do?" General Campbell leaned forward, his eyes eager.

"Uh, sure," Charlie said, "but most of what we can do is destructive, so our show-and-tell will be limited."

Charlie cast Waylay on Stasia, appearing instantly by her side. Then Sara pulled him back to her side, using her Protective Companion spell.

"Wait, what was that?" General Campbell asked in confusion as he read his notes.

"I cast Waylay on Stasia. It's an instant cast spell we call intercept with a one-minute cooldown. I can use it on friend or foe. Then Sara used Protective Companion, which we call pull, and pulled me to her side. That's also an instant cast but has a three-minute cooldown. She can use it to pull herself to her target too," Charlie explained.

General Campbell read his notes and ran a highlighter over the corresponding spells. "Okay, could you cast one at a time and name them, please?"

"Sure," Charlie said. "I'll go first. I can only show one more," and he jumped across the table. "That was Valorous Leap. I can jump forward up to thirty feet at a time, its instant cast with a ten-second cooldown. Leap can be used to jump upwards or backward too." Charlie sat by his brother.

Hawk said, "I'll go next," and faded from sight. When he stood, he became visible. "That was Imperceptible what we call invis. I can only do it while staying still and it works faster if I sit down. It's a two-second sitting, five-second standing, channeled spell and can't be used while I have aggro unless I break L O S."

"Okay." General Campbell rifled through the papers before him. "I see from my notes that L O S is short for line-of-sight. So, if someone can't see you, you can disappear, but if you move, they can see you."

"Yes and no," Hawk agreed. "I can disappear and then, if I'm outside, my passive ability works and I'm very hard to spot. You'd have to be actively looking for me and look right at me. Even if I'm moving, I'd be hard to spot." Hawk jumped across the room, clearing the table and landing gracefully. "I have Valorous Leap as well. That's pretty much all I can show you here too."

Hawk sat, and Stasia said, "Me next, I guess. You've already seen me go invisible, but I can also intercept like Charlie can, while invisible or visible, and mine can be cast ten times in a minute." Suddenly, she appeared behind Mary. A second later, she stood behind General Campbell. With a smile and wink, she placed his wallet and keys on the table." I can also pickpocket in both stances." Stasia jumped across the room, landing right next to Mary. "I have a leap too." She sat beside Mary.

Mary took her hand.

Oz shrugged. "Me next, I guess. I can make food and water." Oz conjured a loaf of bread and a flask of water and handed them to General Campbell. "I can conjure bandages too that work like healing potions, but they'll disappear in three hours. I can make glass bottles and large packs, but I have no idea how long they last. In the game, they last until I log out."

Oz conjured samples to show the general. Thick-walled glass decanters with decorative silver stoppers and ornate etching sparkled in the sunlight coming through the window as if they were made of crystal. Decorative silver trim laced the brown leather pack Oz placed beside the decanter.

"In the game, packs could hold differing amounts depending on the characters base strength. A warrior like Charlie could carry much more than a priest like Sara in the same space. Mage packs were used while raiding because they could hold hundreds of bottles of conjured water as well as your normal packs and anything placed inside them entered stasis. Items with countdowns stop counting down," he clarified when the general frowned.

"I have no idea if that translates to real life or not. We didn't want to use conjured packs because the guild symbol gives off a low glow," Oz said and turned the pack to show the back where an ornate V seemed to give off a subtle yellow light.

Oz waved his hands and before you could really see it the pack and decanter turned to blue mist and disappeared. "I can dispel magic and low-level enchantments."

"Could you make another set? I want to take them with me and see how long they last."

"Sure," Oz said as blue mist solidified before his outstretched hands. "Conjured items are only usable by the recipient though.

The general nodded he understood and took the items, turning them in his hands as Oz continued, "I can make a duplicate of myself; a decoy."

An identical Oz stood beside him when he cast Chicanery, the decoy spell. "My decoy casts the same spell I do but does much less damage. It doesn't move, remaining wherever I cast it, but I can choose where that is within thirty yards of me. I can cast a blinding flash, but it really will blind you for six seconds, so be prepared." A brilliant white light lit the room.

The general blinked rapidly, shaking his head, and rubbing his eyes. "That works even with closed eyes."

"I can also silence you for one minute. Mage silence makes you unable to make any noise, including firing weapons that make sound. You could still use a knife, but you can't call for help or cast spells when silenced."

Charlie laughed as the general pounded soundlessly on the table, then rose and smashed his chair against the door. It was clear he was yelling by the movement of his mouth but not a peep emerged until a minute had passed.

"That's amazing. Everything you can do is amazing," the general said wonderingly as he resumed his seat.

"I can shield myself in flame or ice, but I don't think I should use the flame in here."

The ice shield glistened as it formed around Oz, solidifying into a wall of clear ice. The general tapped it with his fingertips then scraped frost off with a fingernail.

"I can disguise myself or a party member." The surrounding air shimmered, and his appearance changed to that of General Campbell. "Invisible Duo works on me and the target of my choice but only lasts three minutes and has a five-minute cooldown."

General Campbell watched in amazement as Oz and Sara disappeared.

"Wink lets me teleport up to twenty yards at a time, through walls too, but I have to be careful doing that because I could kill myself if I get stuck in a wall or furniture. In the game, you wait for a rez. In real life, I don't know what would happen."

He showed General Campbell a simple teleport across the room. "That's my Wink; I can do it twice a minute and choose where to land within twenty yards. I can open portals, but we won't use them. Portals in the game were notoriously buggy. You could use one and fall through the air from any height. Sometimes it killed you, sometimes hurt you, but the worst was when you fell endlessly through the earth or space and a game master needed to reset your character. If it were life or death, it might be worth trying but it would be a serious risk."

"So that portal there comes out where?" General Campbell stared in fascination through the square doorway hanging in space.

"That's my room at home. There's one more spell I can try. I'll try to summon a dagger. It's a channeled spell with a thirty-second cast and no cooldown, but I can only have one active at a time."

A barely discernible twitch of his fingers followed, and he held his hands out. A blue glow solidified into a metal dagger with a curved blade and a very sharp tip. The hilt formed an ornamental relief of lightning that glowed so brightly it appeared as if it would be hot to the touch.

"Guess that one works, Chief," Oz said with a small laugh. He hefted the blade in his hand thoughtfully. "In the game, if I have my conjured dagger out it increases my cast speed and every cast has a chance to proc a lightning bolt on my target. I have no idea if that's still true." He held up the dagger, the bright silver blade glittered in the sunlight. "Try to take it."

Chief, Hawk and Stasia stood. The dagger appeared in Charlie's hand, it flitted from Hawk to Stasia, and back to Charlie, appearing instantly in their hands as they cast their Grapple Weapon spells.

"How often can you grapple a weapon?" Captain Sanders asked.

"Allies and my own weapon, any time I want to, but enemies can only be grappled once every three minutes," Charlie said as he handed the dagger back to Oz.

"That's all I can show you, I guess." Oz sat.

"That leaves me," Sara said. "Most of my spells can be cast on my friends." She showed the general her heal spells, followed by Ascension, which they called levitate, Soothe Spirits, and her Hands-of-Sun, which caused her hands to give off light.

Then she cast her minor shields. "I have defensive spells as well, and I can use my staff if I have one to make my spells more powerful and to store magic that can be unleashed as bigger attacks or heals. We know that works because I used it in the fight. I can show you the difference with a shield."

Sara opened her staff and tapped it on the ground, casting a mirrored shield. The silver glow took a few seconds to form above them. "Notice how it's bigger? It takes me three seconds to cast it instead of instant, but it's much stronger. This reflective shield will cover an entire raid, which is thirty people in a thirty-foot radius. It has a five-minute cooldown and lasts three minutes or until damage destroys it. If I dispel it, the magic left returns to my staff, and I can use that instantly by banging it on the ground, which lets me cast two spells at once. The staff will store any magic I want, but I have to remember what kind is in there and plan ahead to use it."

She banged her staff on the ground, and another silver shield instantly formed above them. "If I'd casted more shields and dispelled them, my shield would be stronger and larger, but that's almost never done because I'd have to only use my staff for that. The time spent casting shields and dispelling them is wasted, but sometimes it's the only way to live through a giant damage spike you know is coming."

"I see," General Campbell said. "Anastasia can tell the future, do you use that to see those spikes?"

"Rarely." Stasia gave a small shrug. "Most of the game battles are scripted with timers available so it's not needed. Occasionally, I use precog if I can work it into my DPS rotation without too much loss of DPS or losing my dots."

"You lost me, I'm afraid," General Campbell admitted.

"We cast our spells or damaging moves in a certain order to be sure of using all of our bigger hits when they're off their cooldowns. That's a DPS rotation. Some abilities leave damage-over-time effects on our targets, we call them dots. The idea is to never miss a big damage ability and to always keep these dots up on your target. Casting See-the-Future takes me fifteen seconds to do. It's a channeled spell, so I have to do it remaining stationary, and it has a five-minute cooldown. So, has limited combat use. It's not incredibly often you want to see what the next big attack is within five minutes."

"Can you use it to see anything else?"

Stasia grinned. "I could see the next card in the deck; I'm betting I'd own a roulette table."

"So pretty much everything you guys tried worked?" Captain Sanders asked.

"Yes, but we haven't tried everything either. We assume it will work, but we don't know for sure," Oz said.

"What haven't you tried?"

Oz frowned thoughtfully. "Well, Stasia hasn't tried her silent kill or disarm trap, and Hawk hasn't tried to breathe underwater or half his traps. Sara hasn't tried to summon us or purify food. Neither has tried to cure poison. Charlie hasn't given anyone in our raid one of his abilities. Let's see, what am I forgetting?"

"I haven't cured blindness or deafness yet, and Hawk hasn't had an animal pick up and deliver something, and he hasn't tracked anything or tamed anything, and he hasn't called for help either," Sara added.

"We'll need to set up a testing facility." General Campbell leaned back in his chair and rubbed his temples.

"Um, excuse me, General," Mary interrupted, putting an arm around Stasia's shoulder and pulling her closer. "I understand you want to find out what they can do and how they can do it, but they're minors, still in school, they're not soldiers."

"Yes, that needs to be considered as well." The sound of his drumming fingers on the tabletop filled the room. "Okay, how about this. We keep you for a few weeks and do our tests. We'll need a cover story of some sort— say your illness returns or something. That should give us time to figure out if anybody else is aware of what you can do before you're back home and potentially at risk from anyone else who might want to get control of you. I'm thinking ISIS here, but if word of these abilities leaks it might be anyone. After a few weeks, if it seems safe, you can return home to school, but there'll need to be surveillance on you for your own safety."

John nodded and glanced at his son Richard. "And my other son?"

General Campbell pursed his lips. "Will return to his unit, or we might assign him to this project as it will be need-to-know, and he already knows."

John Hayes nodded. "That's fine. Are you thinking you'll be using the children in more battles?"

"No," General Campbell said. "They're too young now. I'm hoping to recruit them when they're older, but right now, all I'm thinking is we need to understand this, especially how it happened."

"While I can let Charlie stay here or in your care for a few weeks, I can't agree for the other parents," John said.

"Yes, I can see that. You say they're unaware of any of this?" General Campbell asked.

"As far as I know." John glanced at Stasia sitting by Mary.

"There hasn't been a chance to tell them. This isn't something you say over the phone, and we didn't want to tell them while we were in the hospital before we found out what we could do. Then there was Rick to find. It all sort of happened very fast," Stasia explained.

After a moment's consideration General Campbell said, "I'd prefer to keep this completely confidential for now. I'm thinking we send the children back to the states and announce they picked up a virus that would keep them in quarantine."

"Uh, you say a few weeks, and while we're willing to cooperate, we don't want to stay back a year in school either." Charlie's gaze shifted to Sara sitting beside his father. "And we want an absolute guarantee we won't be separated and can contact anyone we wish at any time. We'll promise to never mention anything on the phone, but we want to stay in contact with our families."

"Okay, let's do this," General Campbell said. "Everyone returns to your hotel for the night. I'll arrange transport back to the states. We'll put you somewhere secure for a maximum of six months under the pretense of being infectious. Major Harris will be assigned as your nurse and oversee any medical testing. Mr. Lewis will attend all meetings and keep you and his superiors informed. Access to telephones will be granted on request, but you won't be allowed cell phones. Charlie's parents will be allowed entrance, but I'm afraid the rest of you must keep up the charade of an infectious disease, at least for the time being. No testing that isn't agreed upon in advance will be done."

"And school?" Oz asked.

"We'll make certain you don't fall behind," General Campbell agreed. "Tutors will be arranged for you."

"What about internet access and our game?" Stasia peered hopefully at the general.

"Well, I guess we'll have to see. I'm not sure what we'll do about that. Assume no access for the first month though."

The kids looked disappointed.

"Uh, guys." Rick cleared his throat. "I think your gaming days might be done. How can you play when what you cast online happens in real life?"

"Oh, my god, I never considered that! What if we can never play again?" Stasia stared wide-eyed at Oz.

"No point in worrying about it now," Hawk said to his sister. "I'm more worried about Mom. She'll freak if she thinks we're sick again. She can't afford to fly to us and miss work like that."

"Yeah, you have to tell her we're in quarantine, but in no danger. My mom has enough worries." Stasia took her brother's hand.

"I'm sure we can think of something," General Campbell agreed. "If we're all in agreement, I propose we break for the evening. Major Nelson will escort you to your hotel. Lance Corporal Hayes may go with you tonight, but I expect him to report for duty in the morning."

"One more thing to cover." Mary cleared her throat. "General Flores told us the kids could be arrested for stealing the vests and radio and for sneaking on the truck and helicopter."

"We can return the vests and radio," Stasia smiled hopefully at the general and clasped her hands on the table. "They're in our hotel room and a bit worse for wear, but we could pay for them or something," she finished anxiously.

"Believe me; we have no interest in pursuing that. Documents will be drawn up saying so if it will put your mind at ease," General Campbell assured her. "Now, Sara, you called your family lawyer, and I'm okay with that too, but please make sure he's your lawyer only, not your fathers, before asking him to represent you in this."

"I can do that," she agreed. "But Mr. Martin is on his way here already."

"Let's worry about him when he gets here then." General Campbell made a note.

"Can I call him and tell him to wait in the states? No sense in his flying here, then back."

"Call him now. Ask him if what you tell him remains confidential. Find a new lawyer if he has to report to your father. Tell him the Air Force is voluntarily detaining you because they think you're infectious and have him wait in the states. You can give him my number to call. But don't say a word about any of this on the phone."

Sara agreed and made the call.

Mr. Martin agreed to the changes and told her he'd meet with her when she reached home.

General Campbell stood and shook their hands. "Thank you for coming in. I'm sure we can all work together despite our rough start." He ushered them out the door with orders to Major Nelson to take his squad and stay with them at the hotel.

Charlie's mother hugged him when the general left. "That wasn't too bad," she said brightly.

"No, it wasn't," Charlie agreed, smiling at his mother.

Everyone gathered in the parent's room when they returned to the hotel. Stasia leaned on Oz whispering, and he nodded.

"I'm beat, let's hit the hay." Oz glanced meaningfully at the door. Charlie rose and headed to their room, followed by Hawk. He wanted to kiss Sara good night but wasn't comfortable doing so in front of his parents since they were unaware of their new relationship. Before he could work up the courage, both girls had hugged his parents goodnight and went to their room.

Stasia closed the door of their room, held her finger to her lips, and whispered to Sara,

"I'm going back to see what they do when they think we're gone."

Sara hugged her and whispered back, "I'll cover for you, but be safe. I'm sure they're monitoring our channel by now, but if you call me, I'll summon you here."

Stasia and Sara put on the headsets and made Stasia's bed look like someone used it with the clothes from their suitcase in case Major Nelson checked on them. Sara opened the window and Stasia jumped gracefully to the ground and ran off.

She jumped onto a car headed her way and rode it until it turned off and then hopped on another one while remaining invisible.

Ignoring the dog, which ignored her as well, she walked through the main gate directly to General Campbell's office. After a few minutes wait, she followed behind a private as he entered the general's office to leave a stack of reports, and soon spied over the general's shoulder. He made numerous phone calls putting his plan into action.

Occasionally, he looked around the room and once even said, "Stasia, if you're in here, you can go home and get some rest. I promise to do only what we discussed."

She didn't answer him, but she took a

quick step back in case he swung wildly hoping to catch her. He set up a bunch of meetings and sent a lot of orders, but nothing looked the slightest bit hinky to her.

When he finally left, she followed him to a nearby house and into the kitchen where he prepared a sandwich. After using the bathroom, he went to bed. The room was dark and quiet. She settled on the floor in the corner. General Campbell did nothing except sleep. An hour later, she snuck out and snooped around the base again. Everything appeared normal to her, so she car hopped back.

- 7 -

QUARANTINE

Major Nelson and his team escorted them to the plane the next morning where they found everyone they'd rescued in Iraq already aboard.

"General Campbell sent everybody," Captain Sanders explained. "He wasn't sure how the raid system worked and wanted everyone handy. Sara, can you still cast on them?"

She could.

"Can you cast on me?"

She couldn't.

"Could you tell by looking at them they're in your raid?" She couldn't, but Hawk and Oz could. "There's a lot to learn," Captain Sanders said, sounding excited.

An ambulance picked them up from the plane and took them to a small building on

Langley Air Force Base in Virginia.

General Campbell met them in their new quarters. The rest of their raid was quartered in a nearby barracks. When they entered the building, they passed through a complicated array of devices designed to contain and stop any infectious disease. A small, but complete hospital setup filled the first floor. A floor of empty rooms followed, leading to the third floor where they were each given their own rooms. Plain white walls and standard hospital beds were the sole furnishings. The entire building remained sealed off and empty except for them. A discreet security detail patrolled the outside of the building.

"Everyone who saw you in Iraq is assigned to this project and we'll use them to fill the ranks of this detail. They're back on active duty and are free to come and go as their duty permits. I'm asking you to stay inside at all times unless escorted by an officer," General Campbell requested.

"Is there any access to the outdoors?" Sara asked.

"No, do you need access?" General Campbell glanced at Sara and rose an eyebrow.

"Need, no. Want, yes," Sara said. "I'm a sun priest, we like being in sunlight. And

Hawk is a ranger. Being in the woods is good for him. It's not like it will hurt us, but we're happier outdoors."

"We'll work something out, but it might take a day or two," General Campbell warned. "Do you need anything else?"

"Well, we could use target dummies and weapons if you want to see what we can do," Charlie said.

"Yes, we're arranging all that already. I meant anything in particular, like Sara needing the sun, or Sebastian trees."

"Call me Hawk, everyone does." Hawk grinned at the general. "And we don't need them, we just like them."

"Let Major Harris know if you'll need anything. We want you to be comfortable here. She's been reassigned to this project and should arrive today." General Campbell returned Hawk's smile. "As soon as she arrives and meets with our doctors, she'll inform you on what tests they want to perform."

"Is she mad about getting reassigned? We didn't mean to mess up her life," Stasia asked.

"Well, I wouldn't know." General Campbell winked at Stasia. "A major wouldn't complain to a general about their assignment."

"Can we get books and internet access to

look stuff up?" Charlie glanced around the empty white hospital room. "We don't know a lot about the military and we should if we're thinking of joining."

"Yes, we can do that, but I want a promise from all of you not to mention any of this."

Sara rose her hand. "I have a question. What do we tell people about why we aren't playing? For the sports, we can say doctor's orders, but our guild will expect to hear from us and soon."

"Can you tell them you're too sick to play for now? At least until we find out if you can even play. Captain Sanders is researching your game right now. He's putting a copy on a laptop, and you can take turns trying to play."

"Okay, but if we can't play anymore, we'll need a good reason why. We have a lot of fans and our guild of course." Stasia sat beside Sara on Charlie's bed.

"Why do people normally quit playing?" General Campbell asked.

Stasia laughed. "They don't, most people slowly fade out of the game. Sometimes, a new job or whatever will stop them awhile, but they usually come back. No one at our level of play disappears except if they die."

"Yeah, and we can't pretend to die,"

Charlie said. "Too many people know who we are in real life and Sara is sort of famous. So, rumors that Seraphim died wouldn't hold up. Someone would see her and everyone knows she's Seraphim."

"Yes, that could be a problem, but let's find out if you can play or not before worrying about it," General Campbell said. "I won't necessarily be around for all these tests, but I can always be reached on the red phone in the hallway. It's for emergencies only. This shouldn't be hard for you; you all understand the chain of command. If you have a problem, tell Major Nelson or Major Harris, okay? The majors oversee you. That doesn't mean you can't talk to anyone else here or ask questions, it's just those two will be in charge of getting you where you need to be and making sure you have anything you need."

"Sure, no problem. We get it; they're our babysitters." Stasia shrugged.

"What about my parents?" Charlie sat beside Sara and took her hand.

"You're free to come and go as you wish, Mr. Hayes," General Campbell said as he turned and spoke directly to Mr. and Mrs. Hayes who stood together by the door. "But because of our quarantine charade, you'll have to use the same system as the other parents.

We've set up a room where you can speak using phones and still see each other. To lend validity to our story, we want Mrs. Hayes to stay in the building under quarantine with the children."

"Like jail," Hawk said laughingly.

"Sort of," General Campbell agreed. "Call your parents today. Tell them you've been readmitted, but show no symptoms, only that you appear contagious and the Air Force flew you to Virginia to see specialists here. Tell them you can video chat and aren't allowed visitors." General Campbell sighed and rubbed his eyes. "I really hate to do this. I'm a parent myself. We can discuss options for informing them after we have a better idea of what's going on. We'll make sure the doctors are very reassuring so they don't worry too much."

"I better call their parents and update them on where their children are," Mary said. "I'll tell them we were readmitted last night and flew here this morning from Japan. They don't know they were in Turkey."

"Fine," General Campbell agreed. "Have them contact Doctor Elliot here for details. Tell them the kids are fine but with a low white-cell count and need to be in a clean room and some people they encountered have developed mild, flu-like symptoms. We'll say we're not sure if it's related and that we're just taking precautions."

Mary agreed and made the calls, starting with Camila, Stasia and Hawk's mother. As expected, Camila was alarmed.

Mary told her the kids were fine and would call soon, gave her the number for Doctor Elliot, and promised to keep her informed. Oz's father reacted much the same way. Sara's father, however, wasn't happy leaving Sara there and told Mary he'd get his own specialists.

The kids called their parents and told the same story. Mrs. Morales seemed reassured by the sound of her children's voices. Stasia convinced her to stay home and they would video chat. Oz's father was also reassured speaking to Oz and told his son that he'd tell his mother. Sara's father informed her he was looking into specialists for her. Everyone told their parents to call and speak to Doctor Elliot himself.

"Well, that went well," General Campbell said when they'd hung-up. "Mr. Mitchel might be something of a problem, but nothing we can't handle. Take some time to get settled in. Tomorrow, we'll start testing."

- 8 -

INFORMING THE PRESIDENT

A slightly overweight woman with dyed, brown hair pulled into a fancy French knot held open the door to the oval office.

The president stood and gestured General Campbell to enter, flashing his famous smile. Clean shaven, with sparkling blue eyes, he appeared ten years younger than his fifty-two years. President Carmichael had been president less than a year. General Campbell eyed his commander and chief, hoping the boyish charm hid an iron will. He'd never had personal dealings with the president before although he approved his policies in general.

What he'd tell him would change America and the world forever. If handled badly, it could precipitate World War Three.

"Ah, General Campbell, my secretary informed me you asked for this emergency conference, and this is Agent Lewis, I presume?" President Carmichael offered his hand.

"Yes, Mr. President, and thank you for meeting us on such short notice." General Campbell shook the president's hand, happy with the firm grip.

"I'll admit I was intrigued. I don't get many requests of this nature."

"What I'm going to tell you will be hard to believe, and we thought the fewer people who know, the better. So we came straight to the top to let you decide who'll be informed." General Campbell set his briefcase on the coffee table.

The president gestured him to a nearby chair. "Please, take a seat."

The three men sat. General Campbell opened his briefcase and removed several thick folders.

"Everything I'm going to tell you has been verified by me personally," General Campbell said as he handed out files. "I've seen this with my own eyes and brought videos for you to watch."

General Campbell explained the situation.

The president flipped through the report and watched a video, stepped into the hallway, and spoke with his secretary. "Joyce, cancel all meetings for today." Returning to his chair, he picked up the folders again. "You've seen them in person?" The president's eyes widened in amazement as he watched the video footage.

"Yes, they're in custody right now at Langley Air Force base. They came voluntarily and agreed to let us run tests. We have no idea how this happened other than the radiation exposure on the airplane."

The president picked up that report and extracted a photo of the airplane. "The wing of the plane is still radioactive?"

"As of the last report, yes, but here's where it gets weird. It's not a known type," Agent Lewis said as he turned his copy of the report to the relevant page. "It's not alpha, beta, gamma or X. It has similar properties, but it's not an exact match to any."

"The wing is in our custody as well, I assume?"

"Yes, our top men are examining it, but they're unaware of the children or of the radiation's apparent effects." General Campbell pointed to the related report.

"So, how many people know right now?" The president shuffled the papers in front of him, searching for the list.

General Campbell handed him another

thick file. "All the hostages and the boy's parents, the five Marine CSO, including Major Nelson have seen them cast in person. Captain Sanders and Doctor Elliot are fully informed. And General Flores knows but didn't believe it. The children requested a Navy Major, Elizabeth Harris, as their nurse, I'll be informing her when she arrives. I'm using the rescued hostages to staff this project as much as possible, but I'll need doctors and scientists in the loop."

"Oh, and don't forget Sara's lawyer. He hasn't been informed yet, but she plans to tell him," Agent Lewis reminded him.

"Yes, and some personnel saw some hard to explain things, but have no official knowledge, like the helicopter pilot."

The president's blue eyes sharpened, and he leaned forward, folding his hands on the reports. "And ISIS, what do they know?"

"Well, we aren't sure. No survivors remained on their side, but we aren't certain what, if anything, they had time to report." General Campbell handed him a long list of names of the men killed. "My men rounded up all electronic devices on the bodies and are checking now to see if anyone sent footage out, but so far we've found nothing."

Straightening in his chair, General

Campbell rubbed his chin a moment before speaking. "I've issued a public report on the incident in Iraq. You'll find a copy in the red folder. Time was of the essence, so I fabricated a cover that I believe will hold as no live witnesses exist to disprove it. The only witnesses are our own men, and we have them gathered here and Agent Lewis is watching them. In the red file, you'll see I've made recommendations on how to stop the spread of rumors, but very few people actually know Team Valor was there at all. I really don't foresee a huge problem with this cover-up."

The president snorted back a small laugh. "A new area fifty-one in another country. I'm sure the rumors will be flying, but I must say, I believed your fake report when I received it."

"Even if the Iraqis reported it would be almost impossible to believe," Agent Lewis added.

"Yes," the president agreed. "Despite pictures, I find it difficult to accept. I can almost believe this" – he waved the folder in his hand containing the list of magical abilities— "is a complete fake and the false report is real. I'd like to see them for myself."

"We are, of course, at your disposal, Mr.

President."

"Thank you for coming straight to me. I know that can be a career stopper. Give me a few days to think about this. Meanwhile, keep this quiet."

"Yes, sir, Mr. President, I'll need the authorization to retain the hostages and Major Harris, they aren't under my command."

"I'll see to that right away. We'll need to form a special unit and assign Major Harris and the Marines to you directly. Will you be able to return to Baghdad Base soon?"

"Yes, and with no one there the wiser." Major General Campbell smiled in satisfaction.

"And you, Agent Lewis?"

"The director of the FBI is fully informed. I had to call in a lot of favors to skip over my superiors, and believe me, they aren't happy with me. They realize something big is up, but not what."

"I can handle that," the president assured him.

"The children requested me specifically. My boss demanded I return. I've taken personal time, but it will run out soon." Agent Lewis frowned thoughtfully.

"I can handle that as well," the president said. "Remain with the children. I'll speak to

Pierce Taylor, the head of the FBI, directly and get you assigned there. For now, stay on leave. We might make it look like you're somewhere else completely, we'll have to see.

"So, we have them in custody, but what exactly do we have?" The president leaned back in the chair.

The general handed over another thick file. "You'll want to pay special attention to the part there on reputation gains. All the highlighted abilities are verified."

The president read the report from cover-to-cover, then leafed through it again. Finally, he set it on the coffee table. "So, they're friendly at the moment?"

"Yes, they've been very cooperative."

"And you think they're no threat to us?"

"At the moment, no, and honestly, sir, they went out of their way to make sure they could work with us."

"This file makes for scary reading. They're extremely powerful."

"True—"

"Excuse me," Agent Lewis interrupted. "I see where this conversation is headed, and while I understand sometimes threats need to be eliminated; keep three things in mind. One, they're cooperating, two, they're children, and three, how do we know hostile nations don't have their own?"

General Campbell and the president stared at him thoughtfully. "We don't," the president admitted after a moment.

"Proceed with the testing, General. Find out how this happened. Keep a close eye on them; we can't afford to lose them."

"We'll do our best, sir. Do I have the authorization to reassign what specialists I'll need?"

"Yes, but use as few as possible." The president rubbed his chin in a thoughtful manner. "Funding for this will be tricky…"

"I have a small group picked out with top level clearance. A list is in the green file. I'll get them flown in tonight."

"Send me daily reports using secure communications." The president stood, offered his hand again and escorted them to the door. "And, General, if at any time you think they pose a threat to the United States, I want to know immediately."

"Yes, sir, thank you, sir. We'll be in touch."

Four days later, the president stood with General Campbell, looking through a one-way mirror into a small room.

"They've continued to be cooperative?" the president asked.

"Yes, extremely cooperative, even with the painful tests we've run."

"Which were?"

"To test all stages of healing we've injured them purposefully. The scientists conducted every test they could think of, measuring light, air, water, electricity, magnetism— you name it. So far, we've found out very little."

"What's the boy doing now?"

"That's Sebastian; he's controlling the animals in there. Those electrodes are monitoring both his and the animal's brainwaves."

"And have we learned anything?"

"When they use their magic, it causes activity in the left-side temporal lobe, and they possess an extra set of cranial nerves and more neurons and axons than we do. The doctors are excited about Sara; she can absorb sunlight directly into energy. Sebastian does as well to a lesser degree."

"What does that mean exactly?"

"Talk with the scientists if you want exact, but what it means for Sara is she's stronger in sunlight just like her character. She can run farther, cast more and stronger spells, and generally do more in the sunlight. The scientists say they're learning a lot about energy.

"On a more useful note," General Campbell continued. "Hawk can send those animals up to a mile away with complex directions and anywhere in what they refer to as the zone with simple instructions."

The president rested a hip against the thin lip of the window as he said thoughtfully, "Yes, I read the report on zones and found it interesting. Public perception is a limiting factor for them. Any area the general populace accepts as an individual zone becomes one for them."

General Campbell said, "Eventually, we want to take them somewhere they don't know and see if that rule still applies, but that must wait for another time. We really need to get them back home. This charade can't be kept up indefinitely."

"And we're sure they pose no threat to the United States?" the president asked softly.

"No, if anything, they could be a huge help if they still possess these abilities when they're older."

The president's eye's widened. "Do the scientists think it will wear off?"

"No one is willing to say, but there's been no lessening of their abilities so far. It doesn't appear to be an effect from the radiation, but an actual physical change. I believe it's a permanent condition."

"I want to meet them," the president said.

General Campbell glanced at his watch. "They should be gathered for lunch in twenty minutes, but you can meet them whenever you like."

"Can we interrupt this test?" President Carmichael indicated Hawk in the next room.

"Yes." The general rapped on the glass.

Hawk jumped up and spoke to the man in the white coat. The man rose and ran to the door.

"Excuse me, Mr. President, I wasn't aware you were waiting. Come right in."

"Sebastian told you we were here?" the president shook the man's hand.

"Yes, come in and meet him." The man held the door open, stepping back to give them room.

"Hello, um, Sebastian, I'm —"

Hawk interrupted. "President Carmichael. I know who you are. Nice to meet you." He grinned and held out his hand.

The president shook his hand. "How did you know we were here? Isn't that one-way glass?"

Hawk shrugged. "I don't know how I

know things like that, I just do. If I want to, I can tell how many people are around me, but I can't identify them unless I know them or have seen their picture enough to recognize them, like you. Usually, I can tell if they're enemies or neutral too."

"General Campbell tells me they're trying to figure out how you communicate with the animals. How do you think it's done?"

"I don't think I am, really," Hawk absently petted the ferret in his hand, then placed it on the floor. "I think it's me in the animal."

The man in the white coat looked intrigued and made a note in his notebook.

"So, you're using mind control then, not true communication?" the president asked.

"I think so, well, maybe a mix of both. See these ferrets? I can direct them where I want them to go or ask them. It's different when I make them."

The president watched the ferret as it tried to climb into Sebastian's arms. "It seems to like you well enough."

"All animals like me, it's a passive trait."

The president glanced at his watch. "How about you show me around a little before lunch and then introduce me to your friends?"

"Sure." Hawk showed him the lab, explaining what happened in each area as he understood it.

He brought the president to the room where they did school work and to another room where they cast their spells while being monitored every way known to man. Finally, he took them to the cafeteria and introduced him to the rest of his team.

The president stayed and ate lunch with them. "Sebastian showed me where you cast your spells. Have you notice any change in them?"

Charlie laid his fork down before speaking. "No. It isn't a good practice spot, but I guess it's not supposed to be."

Sara nodded, placing her own fork beside her plate before leaning forward to speak. "No, it's for them to observe, not for us to get better at it."

"You think you can get better at it?" The president gazed at her with interest.

"Well, sure. We practice when we can, but we don't get much time together."

Charlie exchanged an unhappy glance with Sara.

The second night of their stay here Charlie had snuck into Sara's room. That hadn't been a great idea. Not only was his mother sleeping right next door, but Sara, wearing just a t-shirt covered with a light blanket, was too much for his self-control. He hadn't snuck over again.

Twice, they'd literally hid in a closet to exchange quick kisses, but he didn't want that for her either. He wanted time to explore their new relationship without sneaking or rushing. Right now, they barely had time to speak. The doctors and scientists kept them separated all day doing tests. They spent four hours every evening doing schoolwork and then went to bed. Their only personal contact was a hurried touch as they passed in the hallways.

"I don't think I understand," the president admitted.

"To work as a team takes practice," Stasia explained. "We can cast a spell all day long, but it won't help us develop the teamwork we'll need to use it."

"And are you going to use it?"

"Well, I guess so, someday. I thought that was the point of all this?"

"The point right now is to find out how it happened and what it is exactly." The president smiled at them.

"Yeah, we understood that, but I guess we expected you'd want us to be able to use it too." Charlie shrugged, picking up his fork again.

"How do you see yourselves doing that?"

the president asked.

"We haven't really talked about it, but I assumed if more soldiers went MIA we could help. It would be a lot easier than last time if we didn't need to sneak on board transports and had a satellite phone for when we found them." Charlie tapped his fork absently on his plate as he spoke.

The others nodded.

"So, you see yourselves as a rescue force, not a fighting force?" The president leaned forward in interest.

"I would rather do rescue," Sara admitted. "But I don't want to do either if we can't train for both. I don't want to be caught unprepared."

"What would you need to get prepared?" General Campbell asked.

"Target dummy's," Stasia and Hawk said simultaneously and grinned at each other.

"Yeah, we would need those and a way to check our timing. Especially Sara, her spells rely on timing a lot. If she can't see the timer, she has to guess." Charlie gave Sara a small smile.

"Yeah, I guess I need more watches or something," Sara added.

"And time to practice," Oz tapped the table for emphasis. "It takes time to get it right."

The talk turned to other things. The president left after lunch, letting the kids return to the testing. Later that afternoon he held a meeting in his office.

"Well, General"— the president gestured his guests to seats and took one himself on the couch beside General Campbell— "I agree with your assessment. I don't believe they pose a threat to the United States. In fact, I agree with them. Let's give them some training."

"My staff and I discussed this." The general handed the president a new folder. "Major Harris thinks we should let them return to school as soon as possible to give them a normal environment while they adjust to the magic. Staff Sergeant Guthrie had an idea I think has merit. To keep them under observation, and interested in working with us, we could instruct them after school in unarmed combat, map reading, and any number of other skills they might need if and when we do use them.

"This summer they can attend a boot camp, tailored specifically to them, where we can train them to work with us. The more we interact with them in a positive way, the higher our reputation will raise. Captain Sanders recommends we give them new gear and money occasionally to boost rep. He has a team working on that already."

"So, you're saying we should send them home soon?"

"Yes, I think we should. The scientists collected reams of data to go through. There's no reason the children couldn't return to school while the scientists investigate. We'll keep them under surveillance, of course, and arrange somewhere they can train unobserved. And we could set up a small lab nearby if other tests are wanted," General Campbell said.

"And you think the children will agree to this?"

"Yes, they can't play sports or their game. This gives them something to do, and they honestly want to help, they just don't want to fight, which is very healthy at their age. Truthfully, I found the report they made of their reaction to killing those men chilling. That cold eagerness wasn't a normal response. Until we understand this more, we should limit the violence they do. I think there's a big risk of turning them into homicidal killers.

"Doctor Elliot says it's a form of split

personality; the character persona did the killing, not the children. He agrees we don't want to tip them into those personas permanently. Frankly, I'm not all that comfortable with the idea of using children in battles, no matter how eagerly they fight."

"Yes, I agree. I too would rather wait until they're older, but you're right, there's no need to delay training."

"Speaking of training, you saw the report about Sara being unable to heal anyone who wasn't in their raid?"

"Yes, have we discovered a way around that?"

"No, not yet, but I was thinking. Ten Marines know what's going on, and twelve Army personnel, and Major Nelson's CSO. I suggest we put them through training as well."

"Hmm, yes, I see." The president leaned back in the chair, rubbing his temple. "The training you're talking about costs money. Get a commitment first. Sign them up for six more years if they want this training. Make it clear they'll be working with the kids, and it will be classified. I understand one raid spot remains open. Have they tried to remove anyone yet?"

"No, we asked them not to make any changes."

"Let's do this, anyone who's already in the raid, and signs up for six years, will receive advanced training when the kids return to school. Then they'll attend the custom boot camp with them. That gives us a choice of operatives to work with them who are fully informed on their special abilities. Is there a plan for the parents yet?"

"No, sir, not yet, and I must say, I don't like lying to them."

Pierce Taylor joined the conversation, "Yes, I agree, but I don't see an alternative. Oz's father, Mr. Simmons, could safely be told, but not his mother. Mr. Mitchel couldn't be informed. We're sure he'd take Sara immediately and offer her services to the highest bidder if not sell her outright. No, we can't tell him. Two of my best profilers looked into this, Mr. President, and they both agree on Mr. Mitchel.

"As far as Anastasia and Sebastian's case, our psychologists concur it could be extremely harmful for the children to have a secret of this magnitude from the mother. I suggest you get her to sign confidentiality agreements. The threat of lawsuits would probably be enough to keep her from speaking about this casually, but it wouldn't stop her if she believed going public was in the best interest of her children."

The president eyed the head of the FBI thoughtfully. "What do you recommend, Pierce?"

"Inform Mrs. Morales and Mr. Simmons after they sign the confidentiality papers. Never tell Mr. Mitchel or Mrs. Simmons. If Mr. Mitchel causes too many problems, we can ask Sara to apply for emancipation. In one year, she inherits her mother's estate, and she meets the requirements in all other respects."

"I hate to do that to a family." The president frowned.

"Honestly, it isn't much of a family. For all practical purposes, she's already emancipated from him. Last year she saw him twelve times."

The president nodded. "And the stepmother?"

"She sees her more often, but there's no affection there. My analysts assure me being separated from her would cause no trauma."

"So, we proceed. General, you return to Iraq in three days to resume your duties there. Will you have time to get this in motion?" The president tapped the folder containing the plan they'd just discussed.

"Yes, I have plenty of officers to help organize the after-school activities and the summer camp. I'll make sure the doctors receive the access they need. Normalizing their lives is our best choice. When we return the children, we'll inform the parents."

General Campbell rose to leave, and the president stopped him. "I want to be informed immediately of any changes, any changes at all."

"Yes, sir, Mr. President." General Campbell saluted and went to put the plan into motion.

BACK TO SCHOOL

Liz Harris took a seat at the dining table beside Mary. "Okay, guys, I have good news. They're letting you return home."

Charlie turned to Sara and squeezed her hand. "You'll be home for your birthday, where do you want to go?"

Sara smiled. "Somewhere sunny. We could hang out at my house, just the two of us."

A matching smile crossed his face as he leaned closer, running a thumb over her hand.

Mary looked confused and then enlightened.

Liz cleared her throat. "The president asked me to pass along his thanks for consenting to the tests. The scientists are learning a lot. I'm also to tell you, we'll inform your father Oz, and Hawk and Stasia's mother, but not your father, Sara, or Oz's mother."

"We can tell Mom?" Hawk asked in surprise.

"No, we will. We'll sit down together, and they can ask what they like, and you're not to speak of it again, okay?"

"Um, sure, okay." Oz looked thoughtful.

Liz met their eyes briefly before returning her gaze to the printouts in her hand and passing them out as she spoke. "You'll return to school after Christmas break. The sports ban is still in effect. There's too much chance of others noticing enhanced skills, and besides, it wouldn't be fair. What we want to do, if your parents permit, is teach you things you'd need to know to go on another rescue mission."

"Like what?" Mary's eyes narrowed in doubt as she examined the long list.

Charlie almost laughed, recognizing the look from asking to do things that took convincing.

"Map reading, how to use the com equipment, how to navigate by the stars— all sorts of things. They'll have a self-defense instructor too. You'll be kept under observation, and we want you to wear these panic buttons with a GPS locator. The surveillance will be so discreet you won't notice them." Liz handed the small devices around.

"I'll be stationed in town. We plan on renting a facility convenient to you, and I'll check your health routinely. Also, they intend to build a custom training ground for you, a summer camp where you can practice your magic."

"When do we leave?" Stasia grinned.

Oz and Hawk wore matching smiles. Everyone wanted to leave the hospital.

"The day after tomorrow. You'll be home on the twenty-first."

"What will you tell my father?" Sara asked nervously.

"That you're recovered and not contagious," Liz said.

"What about these classes? Where am I supposed to tell him I am?"

"Maybe we can say you need therapy for hand muscles or you're taking a self-defense course or some other lessons. Let's get everyone home first and set up a place to train you before we worry about that."

Captain Sanders followed behind Stasia and Hawk as they entered their house. Their mother greeted them with hugs and thanked him for escorting them home.

"Actually, Mrs. Morales, if Mr. Martin and I could have a few minutes of your time, we have some things to discuss," Captain Sanders said, giving her a polite smile.

"My kids, they're okay?" Camila asked in sudden fear, gripping Stasia's arm tightly.

"Yes, they're fine. Could we have a seat and talk a moment, please?"

"Yes, of course." She gestured to the small kitchen table. "Can I get you coffee or anything?"

"I'll get it, Mom. Sit and talk with them," Stasia said as she rose to put on a coffee pot.

Mrs. Morales grabbed her son's hand and sat. "I'll help Stasia, Mom. We're fine. Captain Sanders just wants to talk." Hawk pulled his hand from her nervous grasp and went to assist his sister.

"Mrs. Morales—" Captain Sanders said when she interrupted.

"I'm Camila."

Captain Sanders smiled. "Camila, as you can see, your children are fine but there are things they want you to know. These things affect national security and require special clearance, so, before I can tell you, you must sign the documents Mr. Martin has prepared."

Mr. Martin handed her a small stack of papers. "These papers say you agree to keep everything we tell you secret. If you tell anyone, a twenty-year jail term and a three-hundred-thousand-dollar fine will be enforced," Mr. Martin explained as he pointed out the relevant paragraphs.

Mrs. Morales looked shocked and a little afraid.

"You don't have to sign, Camila. I can leave without telling you anything at all," Captain Sanders said.

"Mom, we want you to sign." Stasia laid a hand on her mother's shoulder.

"You know this big secret?" Camila took Stasia's hand and pulled her to the side to peer in her eyes.

"Yes," Stasia agreed. "Because we're minors, we didn't sign anything, but we realize how important it is that no one finds out what we know."

A frown flitted across her mother's worried face as she glanced from one of her children to the other. "Okay, I'll sign," she finally said.

Mr. Martin handed her a pen. "This is a binding agreement with no statute of limitations. You may never talk about this again to anyone. Not even to your children or anyone else who already knows without Captain Sanders present, or his express permission, is that clear?" Mr. Martin asked.

"It is. But I can ask questions now?" Camila's voice trembled.

"Yes, we'll try to answer all your questions now," Captain Sanders agreed. "If you think of more questions after this, don't ask your children, ask for a meeting instead. I'll give you a phone number to contact me, but never say anything over the phone, except you want a meeting, okay?"

Camila nodded agreement and signed the papers.

Mr. Martin placed them in his briefcase and left the house after telling the kids goodbye.

Stasia and Hawk handed out coffee no one drank as Captain Sanders explained what had happened. The trip to Iraq wasn't mentioned.

Tears fell unheeded down Camila's cheeks, and Stasia hugged her, patting her back. "Nothing is changed. We're fine, Mom, same as ever."

Her mother nodded and ran a trembling hand over the baby-fine hair that shadowed Stasia's head. "Mary knew?"

Stasia rubbed her mother's back. "Don't

be mad at Mrs. H; she just found out, and they had her isolated. She wasn't and isn't allowed to talk about this either."

"So now what? I'm supposed to pretend everything is normal? I don't know if I can do that."

"It is normal, Mom. It's just us. Nothing has changed." Hawk patted his mother's arm.

"Can I see?" Camila's eyes were wide and fearful.

Captain Sanders nodded, and Hawk and Stasia cast spells. When they disappeared, she crossed herself and began to pray.

"And you want my permission to train them for the military?" she asked through her tears.

"Yes, but not only that. We want to study them too. As far as we know, they're the only people with this ability," Captain Sanders said.

Hawk's brow furrowed as she continued to mumble prayers. "Mom, you can't tell your priest either. If word gets out about what we can do, we won't be safe anywhere."

The praying stopped, and she clutched Hawk's arm again as she cried.

"Camila, I assure you, they're safe now. Security will watch them at all times. The agents should be so discreet you never notice them. Don't let that worry you. We don't foresee any problems. We're just being cautious. This is a list of the things we want to teach them." The thick file he handed her made her eyes widen.

"What about school?" Her eyes narrowed as she read the list.

"They'll attend like always, but after school, they'll go to our facility and train until six o'clock. They'll return home after training and do homework or whatever they wish. For their time they'll receive the same pay as a private E-1 with their housing allotment going to you. This situation could change. If it does, we'll notify you. We want you to be aware of what's happening."

"But how…" She stopped speaking, then started again in a more determined voice. "How will we talk if I can't speak about this?"

Stasia gave her mother a quick hug. "When we come home, you can ask how our day was and we can answer just not in detail, same as always. When you asked how a game went, we never told you the details then either."

"Honey, they're going to train you in firearms, and I'm supposed to say, how was your day, and you say fine?"

Stasia shrugged helplessly.

Her mother straightened her shoulders.

"Fine, I give my permission provisionally. First, my children must want to participate. Second, I always know where they are. Third, if I think this is harming them in any way, I can take them out of your school, and fourth, they receive an allowance, not their full pay; the rest goes into a college fund."

Captain Sanders nodded. "That's no problem. Part of the training will include classwork. If they wish to attend university later, I'm sure we can work out a way to use the G.I. training program."

Captain Sanders straightened the file in front of him. "There's one more thing to cover. We don't foresee them getting ill, but if they ever need medical care, call this number." He handed her a card with a list of phone numbers. "The top one is for Major Elizabeth Harris. You met her in Japan. Major Harris is now their personal nurse. Don't take them to a doctor or hospital without notifying us."

"Can I call Sara? You said she can heal them."

"Yes, but you need to be discreet. You couldn't say Sara come heal them. You'd have to say something like— Anastasia fell down the stairs and hurt her leg and wants to see you."

"Fine, I'll be careful. Can Sara heal anyone

she likes?"

"No, only her teammates." Captain Sanders gathered the paperwork. "Is there anything else you want to ask before I go?"

"No. I'll probably think of more things later. I'm glad you told me, but I'm confused. I want to ask about their time away."

"You can. We'll tell you about it, Mom; we just can't discuss the magic. Everything else we can talk about." Hawk gave his mother a quick hug.

Camila stood. "I won't mention this to anyone, and you keep my children safe." She escorted Captain Sanders to the door, which shut with a soft click behind him as she hugged her children. Camila cried but didn't say a word.

Liz stopped at a gate blocking the driveway in front of Sara's house. The gate swung open with well-oiled silence when Sara entered her code.

"Now remember, Sara, if you need us, push the button, and we'll be there in minutes."

"I remember, thanks." Sara lips compressed together, and she hesitated before opening the door. With a deep sigh, she entered.

Mrs. Shaw, the housekeeper, waited. "Your father called and said he and your stepmother will arrive on the twenty-seventh."

The two women shook hands.

Liz handed over a small file. "Sara is fully recovered. As you can see, she needs therapy to regain full muscle tone, but she's completely noninfectious. The doctor's numbers are in the file if her father has questions. She has no special restrictions except for the exercise one. Do you have any questions?"

Mrs. Shaw shook her head. "No, I'm sure we'll be fine. Thank you for bringing her home."

"It's no problem." Liz turned to Sara. "If you have any problems, call me."

Liz watched the door close behind Sara and frowned.

The meeting with Oz's father went much the same way.

After Captain Sanders had left, his father sat staring at him in amazement, finally, saying softly, "No one would believe me anyway," and got himself a beer.

Oz sighed in relief and headed to his

bedroom.

He logged onto his computer, turned on voice-chat, and jumped into the officer's channel. This would be hard for everyone. They'd agreed to meet and talk to their guild before tonight's raid.

Sara hopped in the channel. Oz mumbled hello but he was busy answering the flood of texts he'd received the moment he logged in. He put up an away message just as Sara's guild message broadcasted that the officers would speak to everyone soon.

Stasia, Hawk, and Charlie, arrived moments later.

"This sucks," Charlie said. "I'll miss these guys."

"Yeah, me too," Hawk agreed. "Maybe we can play again in a year."

"Man, in a year this game will have changed so much it'll be like learning a new one," Oz said.

"I'll miss the competitions and the money." Stasia sighed.

Hawk snickered. "Poo, you'll miss being on the cover of gamer magazine."

"True," she agreed with a laugh.

"I'll miss hanging out with you guys and having fun." Sara sounded wistful and sad.

"Silly, you'll see us more," Stasia said.

"Yeah, but not hanging out like this. Playing with you guys were the best moments of my life."

"We'll make more moments, Sara, better ones," Charlie promised. "I'll see you tomorrow for your birthday."

"I miss you already," Sara said, sounding happier now.

"Oh, god, this happened just in time." Hawk made a gagging sound. "I don't think I could take the sappy talk in officer's chat."

Stasia giggled. "Yeah, let's get this over with. Voice-chat is almost full."

Their guildmates greeted them enthusiastically when they joined the channel, and the questions and comments came in a confused clamor.

"You guys rocked the tournament!"

"We've been turning down applications by the hundreds."

"Are you guys recovered now?"

"Are you going on tonight's raid?"

"Can you post the strats you used on our website?"

"The picture of you guys winning has over four million hits now."

Charlie waited until the flood of questions and greetings stopped. Finally, he cleared his throat and asked for silence.

"Most of you have been in Valor a long time and raided with my brother Rick before he joined the Marines. Some of you had a tough time accepting his younger brother as the GM, but the guild did well because we were a team. Changing officers is hard, but you've proved that even with change you can succeed. This will be a hard hit for the guild."

Silence filled the channel when he paused.

"None of us can play any longer."

The babble as everyone exclaimed took a minute to clear before he could speak again.

"Quitting, leaving the guild with no officers, is hard on us. We're really sorry about this, but you know how sick we were. While we're getting better, we can't play anymore. We play much slower now."

This was true but made him feel like a heel. The doctors thought they might train themselves out of using the magic if they persisted in trying not to cast.

"Because we can't play very well anymore, we decided not to play at all. Piper, I'm making you the GM. I'll give you complete access to the website and the guild bank. We hope you guys continue raiding and stay strong. There's no reason to let Valor fall apart. You're all amazing players, and we'll miss you all."

"Chief, can you come hang out sometime and watch us raid?" Piper asked, sounding shocked. "Maybe you'll recover more; it's only been a few weeks."

"No, I don't think so, Piper. The doctors have given strict orders, and his expectations on our playing aren't great either. As for hanging out, well, we want to, but at the same time, it's hard because we want to so much. Cold turkey might be best for our game addiction."

Charlie laughed ruefully. "We'll be on for an hour or so as we mothball our characters. Piper, I'm pulling you into a private room to give you the passwords you'll need."

"Man, this sucks, Chief. I always wanted to be a guild master, but not like this," Piper said when they were alone together.

"It sucks for us too," Charlie said as he gave Piper the passwords he needed.

"We all watched the tournament live and the news footage. Everyone here was freaking out. I'm glad you're better now. We thought you were going to die. Are you sure about quitting though? You could play casually; you wouldn't have to raid."

"We really can't play."

"Yeah, the pictures of you guys, or anyway the magazine said the photos were of you, were really horrible. We thought it might be a fake. You looked pretty bad."

"We did look bad and don't look a hell of a lot better now, but at least our hair is growing in and the patchiness is fading."

"Poor Stasia," Piper said.

"Yeah, it was rough on the girls. But believe me when I say, none of us enjoyed it."

"The doctors think your condition is permanent, then?"

"They think so but aren't sure. You know how doctors are."

Charlie received a lot of private messages, most containing the same questions, so he put up an away message.

When he logged off, he flopped on his bed completely stressed out.

His mother came to check on him before heading to bed and found him lying with an arm thrown over his eyes.

"Quit the guild, huh?" she asked, her voice full of sympathy.

"Well, technically no, our characters are still in there. But yes, we told them we won't be playing anymore."

Mary nodded and changed the subject. "I made Sara a birthday cake. Will she be coming for dinner tomorrow?"

"Yeah." Charlie sat up, smiling now. "I'm

taking a bus to her house in the morning. Her father and stepmother won't be home until after Christmas, so she's spending a few days with Stasia. Would it be okay if she spent part of Christmas Day here?"

"Sure, they're all welcome." His mother hesitated a moment. "Charles, you and Sara, you're not just friends anymore?"

"No." He met his mother's eyes squarely. "I love her, and she says she loves me."

Mary smiled. "She's a nice girl, son, and I love her too. Because I love her, I'm asking you to be careful of her feelings. You think this is love, and I'm not saying it isn't, but young people change their minds all the time. Be as kind as you can to her."

Charlie nodded. "I will. Even if she changes her mind I'd never do anything to hurt her. I really do love her, Mom."

His mother leaned over and kissed his forehead. "You're both young, take your time."

A smile crossed her face as she leaned against his closed bedroom door a moment before going to find her husband.

John lay in bed reading.

"Charles is in love," she said and giggled.

John took one look at her face and laughed. "I'll go talk to him."

He laid his book down and kissed his wife in passing. "Maybe he really is. I loved you at nineteen."

- 10 -

BUFFS

Major Harris traveled to Camp Pendleton in California, on an Air Force jet, while Guthrie organized the kids after school activities.

"Major Harris, your people are doing very well. We can go see them now if you like?" Lieutenant Colonel Garcia greeted Liz with a smile.

Liz saluted. "Yes, sir, I've brought new orders for them and have additional medical tests to run." Liz handed him a sealed file and a copy of her orders. "My orders are to observe. I'm sorry I don't know how long this will take."

After glancing at it, he placed it on a corner of his desk and gestured her to the door. "You can leave your bags here. My corporal will see to them. We're ready for you. I've received my orders. Observe as long as you like. I realize your work is classified."

"How disruptive to your normal training will this be?" Liz asked as they approached a large obstacle course.

"Some, I suppose, but the training here is flexible. The goal is the best fighting machine we can make these soldiers. Sometimes a promising candidate needs a little extra help in one area or another. We try to supply it, discreetly, you understand, before washing them out. Your group is performing very well in all physical testing, which is where we wash out most applicants."

"Overall, how would you say morale is?" Liz asked as she watched a group of men in camouflage start the obstacle course.

Lieutenant Colonel Garcia paused a moment. "Adequate," he finally said. "This is a highly unusual circumstance. Army personnel doesn't normally train with Marines in the same group."

"Is it causing problems?"

"Some," he admitted. "Nothing we can't handle."

"We're debating transferring the Army personnel into the Marine Core. In your opinion, would that cause more problems?"

"Well no, not to us it wouldn't, but to them, maybe. The Rangers are proud of being

Army Rangers and rightfully so. You're proposing taking that from them. You'd need to speak to them about it first, and they'd need to resign and reenlist."

"Well, no they wouldn't, and no I don't. My sealed orders give me permission to do as I see fit. The transfer would be totally at my discretion with or without their permission."

"I see. I've never heard of that being done."

"Which is why I hesitate to do it. If they're working together seamlessly, I'll leave it alone."

"Well, here they come now," he said unnecessarily.

Liz had already recognized them. The other soldiers wore fatigues. Dressed in solid black, with no insignia of any kind, not even nametags, her group stood out. Brenda stopped in front of Liz, and the entire unit saluted in harmony.

Liz returned the salute.

"I'm here to observe and do the usual medical testing, and I'll make time to speak with everyone. Right now, I want an all-out demonstration, please. Tony and Joy, and Andre and Brenda, I want you to work as teams and cross this course as fast as possible," Liz said as she paired Army personnel with a Marine.

Brenda eyed the officer standing there and glanced at the men in fatigues waiting to run the course.

Liz smiled and shooed her toward the course. "Proceed, I have clearance."

Liz hit her stopwatch as Tony and Joy started the course.

Tony jumped and grabbed the top of the first wall, disregarding the rope. He hauled Joy up, and they both jumped to the ground, again ignoring the rope. Tony gave Joy a boost to the top of the bars, jumped, and swung himself into a standing position in one fluid move. They ran across the bars holding hands, helping to balance each other. Again, they hopped down, this time going forward ten feet. Joy crawled under the barbwire; Tony followed.

When they reached a large rock wall, Joy ascended sure-footed as a goat. Tony went a bit slower, Joy pulled him to the top where she waited. A rope dangled to rappel down, followed by a short run and climb to the top of a pipe arrangement.

Instead of using the rope, Joy slid down the line, kicked off the wall, and dove into the pipe followed by Tony who, not quite as agile as Joy, grasped the pipe lip and pulled himself in. They emerged and ran full speed to the next obstacle, a shell of a two-story house with a ribbon to retrieve on the roof.

Tony formed a cradle with his hands, Joy sped up and put one foot on his clasped hands, and he threw her as high as he could. She gripped the edge of the roof, flipped herself onto it, grabbed the ribbon, and jumped. Tony caught her and set her on her feet, and they sprinted to the next obstacle.

"That was impressive. That's the first time I've seen anyone do that." Lieutenant Colonel Garcia shaded his eyes with one hand, watching, as they crossed a pool and a large mud puddle using the rings and narrow boards provided. They returned, crossing the same obstacles. At the pipes, Joy emerged, dragged Tony up, and jumped forward, grabbing the rope. She pulled herself up. Tony passed her and hauled her to the top where they both descended the wall, barely breaking the speed of their fall with the handholds.

Liz clicked her stopwatch as they crossed and showed Lieutenant Colonel Garcia the time.

"They aren't even breathing hard," he said in awe.

Liz waved Brenda up, yelled, "Go!" and clicked her stopwatch.

A crowd gathered as Brenda and Andre started. They crossed in an almost identical manner. Brenda boosted Andre to the top of the house where he grabbed the ribbon and jumped down, and she caught him.

"They're cooperating well, wouldn't you say?" Liz asked.

"Yes. No hesitations in either group."

Liz clicked her stopwatch as they crossed the starting line and showed it to him. A few men standing near them also checked their watches and a low mummer arose.

"Very nice," Liz said as her team gathered in front of her." I'll be doing more full-out tests, but in the meantime, return to your covert status; good enough to pass, but don't stand out.

"All physical testing will stop here and resume at the camp you'll be going to this summer. Classroom work is your priority here, and I want you working as a team before you go. If the team leaders would accompany me now, I can get started. Carry on."

Liz turned to Lieutenant Colonel Garcia. "What you saw and heard is classified. There's a report in the file regarding their enhanced speed and agility, and I'm authorized to tell you it's because of the recruitment process."

Brenda choked back a laugh, and Liz

glared at her.

"That must be one hell of a process," Colonel Garcia said dryly.

"It was," Liz agreed. "They found just the ones they wanted. Now we need to form them into a team. Is there office space available to conduct my interviews?"

"Yes, we've prepared a room for you to work and I've assigned a corporal to you. She can get you whatever you need." He turned to Brenda and Andre. "That was remarkable. Those were the best times made on that course. I'm sorry we can't put your names on the wall as times to beat."

"Thank you, sir," Brenda said.

Liz gestured to Brenda and Tony, indicating they should follow her. The office allocated to Liz wasn't far away. The lieutenant colonel escorted them to a small office complex, pointed out Liz's office, exchanged salutes, and left.

Liz conducted her inquiries and did her usual medical tests. Finally, she sat with them and asked what they thought. A notepad rested on her knee.

"We definitely gained the passive raid buffs." Brenda grinned at Liz. "Major Nelson was here with his team, and everyone can outfight them now. Our stamina is much greater too. It's hard to balance so we don't stand out too much."

"Yes, we'll do that at Camp UBM Practice," Liz agreed.

Tony laughed. "We're looking forward to Cub Scout Camp. Everyone wants to go all-out."

Liz laughed. "I like it, you're the Scouts, and they're the Cubs. From now on that'll be my official name for them." She handed Brenda a list. "Is there anything on that list you think the unit can't learn? I mean every single one of them."

"No, with training everyone can do these things, except for Sergeant Jones. He has a thing about heights, but I'll find out if he'll do it anyway," Brenda said as she examined the long list.

"The regular jumps don't bother him?" Liz looked up from her notes, gauging her reaction.

"Yes, but he does it anyway." Brenda shrugged.

Tony gave Liz a wry smile. "He closes his eyes, crosses himself, and jumps. It's braver than me. Jumping never bothered me. I don't know that I could do it if I were that afraid."

"Well, everyone will need to jump chute-less with Sara. We won't make a habit of it, but we want everyone familiar with it." Liz tapped the notebook with the pen as she spoke.

"I'm not going to lie, that makes me nervous too," Brenda said. "What if her magic fails?"

"How probable is that?" Liz said with a smile. "A chute is more likely to fail."

Brenda let out a sharp bark of laughter. "Gee, that's so reassuring. I'll be sure to tell Jones that."

"On May fifteenth, we'll be releasing you from here with orders to report to Cub Scout Camp on June third. I'm hoping everyone has passed the tests here by then and will be fully qualified."

Liz leaned forward and spoke earnestly. "If anybody is falling behind, or having problems, we need to know. Most of you weren't planning on this as a career path. If anyone changes their mind about continuing, I need to know that too. This is an unusual situation, so we're bending the rules. The mix of Army and Marines in the same unit is a concern. You'll be working and living together. When you've completed the courses here, I have presidential permission to make you Marines."

"I don't think we need to do that."

Brenda shrugged and grinned at Tony. "But I don't think any of us would mind either. I'll talk to the Army men and woman. Can they take some time to decide?"

"Yes," Liz said. "Send reports, using confidential channels as always. This is an eclectic team, our Co is Army, our Xo is Marines, Captain Sanders is Airforce, and I'm Navy. I'm leaning toward leaving them Army. Find out what everyone else thinks and get back to me. Now, let's set up a time to do my tests."

- 11 -

FIRST LOVE

Charlie arrived at Sara's house at noon the next day. The housekeeper directed him to the pool where Sara sunbathed.

"Hey," he said, suddenly shy seeing her in a bikini.

"Hey, yourself." She kissed him and led him to a chaise for two. "Sunlight feels so good now. I crave it. If you want to go though, I can get ready."

"It's your birthday; we can do whatever you want."

"Let's stay here then. We can swim if you want?" she said a while later as they snuggled together in the sun on the chaise lounge.

"I thought people would think it's be too cold to swim and didn't bring a suit." Charlie ran a finger along the top strap of her bathing suit, enjoying the way she shivered and leaned closer.

"The housekeeper might think it's odd that we're swimming in December but the pool is heated so it isn't that crazy. Extra bathing suits are in the pool house, or you could go commando." She gave him a wicked grin.

Bathing suits of all sizes and types filled a bureau in the small pool house. He picked a blue one with white Hawaiian flowers and returned to her wearing it.

They floated around for an hour, splashing and dunking each other. The play turned to kissing as they drifted by the edge.

Sara's body felt warm against his, whether from the sun or the exercise Charlie didn't know. For all he knew, all girls were this warm. He didn't care either; she felt perfect in his arms as if she belonged there.

The housekeeper's loud throat clearing brought him back to reality, and they reluctantly separated.

"Do you require lunch, Miss?"

"No, we're leaving soon." Sara glanced at him apologetically.

"Very good, Miss. I'll have the car brought around." The sharp staccato of her heels echoed off the tiles as she marched away.

Sara giggled, pulling him closer for a kiss.

"I could stay here forever." She pressed against him, running her hands over his shoulders, kissing him again.

The water sparkled like diamonds in her lashes; he could drown in the blue of her eyes. With a sigh of regret, Charlie pushed her gently away, jumped from the pool, and easily lifted her out. "Go get dressed before the housekeeper comes back; she scares me." He gave a dramatic shudder, making Sara laugh.

Fifteen minutes later, they were in the back of Sara's father's limo. The driver hadn't spoken except to ask the address.

"You have a new driver every other month," Charlie whispered as they snuggled together behind the privacy screen.

"Tara is hard on servants." Sara heaved a sigh and frowned, clearly not happy with Tara.

Charlie gave her a sympathetic grimace, reached in his pocket, and brought out a small wrapped box. "Happy birthday."

The black jewelry case held a fourteen-karat gold chain that rested right above her breasts. Sara kissed him again after he fastened it around her neck.

Charlie traced the necklace with a fingertip. "It's beautiful, just like you. I hope you like it."

"I love it." She ran her fingers over the

necklace. "And you."

Charlie leaned in to kiss her mouth and then her neck where the necklace lay. He continued trailing kisses across the necklace and didn't stop kissing her until they arrived at his house.

"Does your mother know about us?" she whispered, slightly flushed and breathless as she left the car, touching the necklace with a nervous finger.

"Yes, she likes you. There's no problem." Charlie got her bag from the trunk and thanked the driver who nodded and drove away. "Stasia, Oz, and Hawk will be here for dinner too."

Mary hugged her and wished her a happy birthday. Charlie could tell Sara was relieved.

"See, I told you she was okay with us." He gave Sara a quick kiss when his mother left them alone in the living room to check on dinner.

"I'm so glad, Charlie. Your mother means the world to me. I'd hate to disappoint her."

"She loves you, Sara, that won't change."

The rest of Team Valor arrived, and they spent a quiet evening together. Charlie walked Sara to Stasia's house afterward. "Will I see you tomorrow?"

"Nope, Stasia and I are going shopping.

But I'll see you Christmas Eve, and we're all coming over Christmas afternoon." Sara smiled and stopped walking to kiss him.

Her lips tasted sweet, like the frosting on her birthday cake. The way she sighed and touched him was sweeter yet. Knowing she liked to kiss him as much as he did her thrilled him. The brilliant smile she gave him made him feel loved to his toes. He'd never seen her smile at anyone like that except him. With all his soul, he wanted to keep that smile for himself.

The next day, Stasia and Sara spent shopping at the mall.

"Okay, we need awesome Christmas dresses and something for Christmas Eve too. Help me pick out something to send to Rick," Stasia said as she ran a finger across the mall directory.

"I want to get something for your mom and Charlie's parents."

"What are you getting Charlie?"

"Well, I want to get him cologne and a soft sweater, but I'm not sure really. Do you have any ideas?" Sara eyed Stasia hopefully.

"I have an idea, but I'm using it." Stasia's finger stopped on the Radio Shack icon.

Everyone met at Charlie's house to exchange gifts on Christmas day. His parents gave Sara a keychain with a key to their house; she cried when she opened it. The boys loved the cars from Stasia and laughed when Charlie's father received one too.

Charlie said he loved his gifts from her, but his eyes lit when he opened the picture frame she'd bought him and read the inscription, 'I picture us together forever.'

Stasia had taken a candid picture of them on Christmas Eve, sitting by the Christmas tree, smiling at each other and laughing as Charlie held mistletoe over her head.

"This is my favorite present of all time," he said.

He reached into his pocket and handed her a small box. "This is all I got you."

Sara opened it and gasped. "Charlie, this isn't real, I hope."

"As real as you are."

After removing the necklace he'd given her three days ago, he slipped the diamond pendant on the gold chain. A blush covered her cheeks as he kissed her neck and clasped it.

"I love you," he said, his voice deep with

emotion. "Someday, I plan on giving you more diamonds."

"I can't accept such an expensive gift. What if I lose it or...?"

"Sara, I can get it insured, and besides Oz can find it. When you wear this, think about how much I love you. We're too young for me to give you a diamond ring, wear this instead."

Sara hugged him tight. Her eyes filled with tears and she hid her face in the curve of his neck while he rubbed her back in small circles. Everyone continued talking and opening gifts, giving them privacy.

"Did you know that's what he got her?" John asked his wife when they went to check on dinner.

"No, I have to admit this worries me. If one of them changes their mind, hearts will break," Mary said.

Her husband kissed her quickly as he took over the job of basting the turkey. "If I lost you tomorrow, it would break my heart, but I wouldn't trade one second of our time together. Don't worry about them, sweetheart. Let them enjoy their new love. Look how close we came to losing them. Time will tell if it's true love, and no one knows how much time they have."

- 12 -

FIRST MISSION

Sara called Charlie crying two days later. "My father is taking me to New York to see different doctors."

"I'll miss you. When do you leave?"

"I've already left. He wouldn't let me contact anyone until now. I'm at the airport at a pay phone."

"How long, Sara?" Dread made his voice harsher than he'd intended.

"At least a month, maybe more." She cried harder now.

"Okay, don't cry. It sucks, but I'm not going anywhere. We can video chat and I'll call you every day. What about school?"

"Apparently, my school doesn't want me back. I'm getting a tutor. What if he decides to put me in a boarding school somewhere?"

"Then I'll come to you. Please stop crying

or I'll start," Charlie said.

Sara choked back a laugh and then sobbed again. "God, Charlie, I'll be alone in New York, and you'll be surrounded by Hannah the harpy and her horrible friends. We can't play together online anymore. You're all going to forget me, and I'll be alone and miserable."

"Sara, that won't happen, I promise. Don't panic. One month isn't too bad." Charlie tried to say cheerfully while what he really wanted to do was yell and curse.

"Can you tell Stasia and Major Harris? There wasn't time to call anyone. I love you."

Dial tone heard his answering, "I love you too."

Charlie put his head in his hands, trying to compose himself before making the calls. First, he called the major.

"Thank you for calling, but I'm sure their aware of where she is, Charlie. If I find out anything new, I'll let you know, and call me Liz, okay?" Charlie thanked her and phoned Stasia.

"Well, no," – Stasia sounded annoyed—" he can't do that. We'll go get her."

"Be real, we can't— he's her father. He can take her wherever he likes and send her to whatever school he wants too," Charlie said angrily.

Hawk got on the other line. "What about the special classes?"

"I guess she won't take them."

"He can't keep her there. New York isn't sunny enough for her in winter. She'll hate it. Sara needs the sun. She's a sun-priest! She's our sun-priest!" Stasia said with real anger in her voice.

"He can do what he likes," Charlie repeated. "When has he ever cared what she wanted? I remember when Tara fired her housekeeper right after they got married. That woman was the closest thing Sara ever had to a mother, and she begged him to change his mind."

"I remembered. She was eleven and cried for a week." Stasia sighed. "Charlie, if he sends her far away... Well, I'll give this a month, then I'm visiting like it or not."

"One month," Charlie agreed.

They returned to school the next week. Their friends were sympathetic when told they couldn't play sports or their game anymore. The Harpies were ruthless about Stasia's hair until short hair became the trend for the girls.

The special classes started, first in a small office and then at a warehouse twenty minutes away. Guthrie or Major Harris oversaw them. Different doctors or scientists showed up from time-to-time with Special Agent Lewis.

Sara had been in New York for almost three weeks, and Charlie had only spoken to her a few times. Every day, when he arrived at the warehouse, he asked Liz for news.

"Yes, there's news," Liz said with a slight smile. "The specialists her father sent her to found out the same things we did, that she's a healthy girl of fifteen. They found no trace of her special abilities and even agreed to the precautionary sports ban from the exposure.

"Private tutors visit her daily in the penthouse suite her father rents. Occasionally, they go to museums or art galleries. But generally, she's inside the building. Agent Lewis has men watching her. We have a small mission for you."

Liz grinned and handed him a new laptop. "Take this to her so we can communicate. With this laptop, she can take some of our classes remotely. Stasia could do this alone, but I figured everyone wants to visit her."

"This will be a real mission, albeit a minor one," Guthrie added. "That means complete obedience to orders. No running off and doing what you want. Our mission is to deliver this laptop to her. Leave it with her if she can guarantee to keep it hidden. No one can see you enter or leave or anything suspicious. No razzle-dazzle in public."

Charlie beamed at him. "When do we go?"

"I think you mean, when do we go, sir!" Guthrie said loudly.

"Yes, sir, I meant when do we go, sir?" Charlie grinned.

"Tomorrow is Saturday. We leave here at zero-seven-hundred hours. If you're not here, you get left behind. This mission is already cleared with your parents. Now, let's get some work done. Get into your gym clothes, we're going on a run."

The next day Guthrie took a room in the same hotel as Sara. "Okay, Stasia, go check it out. Don't be seen and don't get caught."

Stasia left the room with a happy smile and came back fifteen minutes later without one. "She's there, and alone, and says we can walk in. No one will be there until late tonight. The only tricky part is the elevator. A key is needed to get to or from the penthouse. The front desk had one I, um, borrowed."

"Sara doesn't have one of her own?"

"No, she's effectively locked in there. Basically, she's under house arrest. It's really not fair, she didn't do anything." Stasia glared and slapped the elevator key into his palm.

Sara greeted everyone with hard hugs, even Guthrie. The laptop got a smile, and she clutched it to her chest.

"I can hide it. They won't find it. Tara won't let me have a computer. She's on some weird computers are bad kick and won't have one in the house. This will be so amazing. It's so boring here all day."

"You're alone here all day?" Guthrie said, sounding appalled.

"No, just weekends. The tutors are here during the week. If you're on in the evenings, I can talk to you guys. Usually, I'm alone at night."

Charlie was worried. Other than the hug she'd given to everyone, she'd made no move to greet him. She looked thinner, almost fragile, and tired with dark circles under her eyes. The desperate way she clutched the laptop made him angry.

"Can you go outside at all?" he asked.

"Sometimes. I really miss the sun. The buildings shade everything, and it's always cloudy here." She turned away and cleared her throat. "Can I show you around or anything?"

Stasia grabbed her hand. "Show me your room, and we'll find a good spot to hide that.

We'll be back in a few minutes."

Charlie glanced uncertainly at Guthrie after the girls left the room. "Sarge, this seems like child abuse. Can he do this; lock her up like this?"

"Son, this appears unpleasant, I'll grant you that, but no, I don't think it's abuse. But I'll be talking to her lawyer about it."

Forty minutes later, Stasia returned looking angry, and Sara's eyes were puffy and red.

"I'm starving. Let's sneak out for a burger," Stasia said.

"I better not. If my father finds me gone, he might tighten the security."

"Okay, I'll bring you back one." Stasia gestured the others to head to the elevator. "Charlie can wait here with her, can't he, Sarge?"

"Yeah, we'll return in an hour or so."

Sara twisted her hands together and looked away as the others left. "If you want to go with them—"

"When you never called me back last week, I was worried. I miss you so much." Charlie held out a hand, and she clutched it, and then flung herself into his arms shaking.

"I'm sorry. I've missed you so much," she mumbled. "I wasn't sure you still—"

Furious anger tightened his jaw, and it took him a second to control it enough to interrupt. "Stop! I'll always love you! That will never change, not in five seconds, five days, or five years. Not in five thousand years!"

She nodded against his shoulder but didn't slacken her hold on him.

He tightened his grip on her.

"Tara said you had a new girlfriend by now, and I was pathetic when I begged my father to send me home. It's not like I believed her, but...."

"I love you," Charlie murmured into her hair, willing her to trust him. "We'll talk every night or at least every night you can without being caught."

She nodded but didn't release him. They still stood there when Stasia let herself back in.

"Here, I bought you a present." She handed Sara a new iPod. "Link it to my account. I'd go crazy here with no electronics."

"Tara has this thing...."

"Tara's a nut. I bet she still has a cell phone, the hypocrite." Hawk paced to the window and stared out, his back rigid.

Oz handed Sara a bag containing hamburgers and fries.

She laughed as she opened it. "God, this smells good. I miss hamburgers and pizza. I think some nights I'd kill for a pizza." She handed Charlie a wrapped burger then sniffed hers with a wide smile on her face.

He angrily bit into his burger.

"Let me guess, Tara doesn't eat meat and pizza is the devil?" Hawk turned and rolled his eyes at Sara.

Sara nodded as she ate the burger. "I can eat it occasionally if I'm out with my tutor. One of them is very nice. He always lets me take a walk, and we stop and eat at a café. The others aren't friendly."

"How many do you have?" Oz asked, sounding a bit envious.

"I'll tell you guys all about them later. Right now, I want to hear what you've been up too."

They told her what they were learning, and she asked about their school and school friends.

Guthrie checked the time. "Sorry, guys, it's time to go. We don't want to get caught here."

"Will you come again?" Sara clutched Stasia's hand.

"Yes, and we'll talk. It'll be better now." Stasia hugged her hard.

Sara handed her the bag the food came in and the packaging from the new iPod. "I don't want to explain where it came from."

"Once I get home, I'll be online," Stasia promised.

"Me too," Charlie added.

"We all will be," Oz said.

"I miss you guys." Sara's voice was sad, and her eyes had tears in them when they left.

It took all Charlie's willpower to leave her there. Only by repeatedly telling himself this wasn't a problem he could physically fight was he able to make himself leave.

Stasia returned the key, and they headed back to the airport.

"Okay, I want you guys to promise you won't return there without me," Guthrie said after they'd boarded the plane.

"I won't promise that." Charlie narrowed his eyes.

"Me either," Stasia agreed.

"Look," Oz placed a hand on Stasia's shoulder. "She's our best friend. We aren't going to leave her there alone. Anyone could tell how unhappy she is. We were willing to give it a month, not forever. Would you leave a friend like that?"

"If one of us were stuck somewhere and unhappy she'd visit if she could." Hawk glared at Sergeant Guthrie.

"That place is making her miserable; she's pale, and drawn, and needs the sun." Stasia's voice rose, and she took a deep breath before continuing. "She's having horrible nightmares."

"Now that she can talk with all of you, she'll be happier. Give it a few weeks at least. We want to call off the surveillance on everyone, but I can't do that if you might run off."

"Do what you have too. I'm not promising anything." Charlie crossed his arms and looked away.

"Is it really running off if we tell you we're doing it?" Oz asked with a laugh. "Seems more like not listening."

"Okay, promise me this then, you'll tell me before going."

"So you can raise security and stop us?" Hawk's glare ratcheted up a notch.

Stasia put a hand on his shoulder and squeezed. "Sure, that's fine, I'll tell you— I like a challenge."

Every night they talked online and during the day kept an open channel in the warehouse Sara could join if the opportunity arose. While doing her classroom work at the warehouse Stasia would video-chat with her.

Charlie's anger lessened as her smile returned. Sara appeared much happier now, almost her old self, and better yet, her father was sending her home in a few more weeks. He'd signed her up at a local school to finish her freshman year.

"How are the nightmares?" Stasia asked.

Liz turned her monitor up and put her paperwork down.

"Let's not talk about it. I hate being so clingy and annoying." Sara sounded nervous.

Stasia laughed. "Believe me, if I were alone in a strange place, I would react much worse than you. The problem is you won't make a scene. That's what Tara and your father need, a good old-fashion, foot kicking the floor, temper tantrum."

Sara laughed. "O-M-G can you imagine his expression? He'd have me committed."

Stasia frowned. "Yeah, he would, wouldn't he? Maybe you better not do that. Hey, did you see the news last night?" The talk turned to the news of the day, and Liz stopped listening.

Liz had asked Stasia to find out about Sara's nightmares. Stasia didn't know she was listening to them, but she knew the room was monitored. Liz frowned. Repetitive nightmares could be a serious problem; she needed to talk with Sara soon in person.

Resuming her paperwork, she continued comparing the graphs of fifteen-year-olds doing the same exercise's Stasia did. The report she was writing would make for interesting reading.

- 13 -

PASSIVES

Liz met with General Campbell at Baghdad base. The previous night she'd flown in, and she planned to fly back on the first transport heading her way.

A large stack of papers dangled precariously, jammed under her left arm as she dragged a projector hooked to her laptop on a small cart behind her.

She saluted as she entered and General Campbell motioned her to a seat. "Thank you for coming, Major. I'm aware of the amount of traveling you've been doing."

Liz smiled. "I find my work very interesting, and I think you will too. This is a secure room?"

"Yes, we can talk freely."

"These files will back up my presentation, but I'll sum it up for you. The magic is impressive, but I believe you'll find the passive abilities even more so."

"Hmm?" General Campbell furrowed his brow, looking doubtful. "More impressive than a fireball formed and thrown in three seconds or a girl who can become invisible?"

"Yes. I've prepared a graph to show you." Liz turned on the projector and pointed to the graph that appeared. "This line here represents Oz's academic performance. Each of these colored lines denotes a subject, for example, math. Pre-event he was extremely gifted in math, genius level really, now follow the line."

"The line goes to the top of the page."

"Yes, he's in the highest percentile in mathematics and learning at a phenomenal rate. Oz is grasping concepts that less than one percent of the population can understand. Now we look at the other subjects and see the same increase across the board. In a nutshell, he's much, much smarter than he was."

"That's impressive, I'll admit, but excuse me, not as impressive as his fireballs."

"This will be though; this graph is the raid. Individual graphs for each are in the file, but this shows overall."

General Campbell leaned forward. "The lines are shorter though."

"Yes, they aren't as smart as he is, but they're smarter than the average person, and some might potentially be as smart as him with more study. They're all busy doing more physical things, and I'll get to that in a moment. I want to make this clear; they are *all* measurably smarter than they were."

Liz lit another graph. "This is Sara. Right away you'll see she's as smart as Oz in all fields." Liz leafed through her papers and showed him another graph. "This is Chief. Not as smart as Oz, but smarter than he was, which again, was in the higher percentile for his age." The next graph was in shades of red. "This is Chief as well."

"The line goes to the top again."

"Yes, this represents his strength. He's impossibly strong, much stronger than a man should be, stronger than any of them. I'm not convinced we've managed to measure the full extent of his strength as his magic is rage based and he hasn't been angry during the testing."

She flipped to a new graph. "And this is the raid. I'll skip ahead here and tell you the green line is agility. While they're not as strong as Chief or as agile as Stasia, they're *all* - every single one of them - not only faster and stronger than they were, but much faster and stronger than a normal human.

"These videos and files will prove their decision-making skills are at least ten times faster than an unbuffed human. When crossing an obstacle course or playing a game, they plan it from the beginning including contingency. I.E. what if I fall from the bars or my opponent does X instead of Z." Liz showed him a short video clip.

"This is Joy doing a solo obstacle run. See that bar?" Liz pointed to the screen. "Joy is planning to swing from it to the tree line, but we remove the bar at the last second. In mid-leap, she changes her jump into a roll. She does it so smoothly it looks like what she intended from the start. Afterward, I asked her about it. Just like in UBM, she plans her moves in advance. Everyone plays the game by the way.

"Anyway, she explained that in the game, your character could be walking on firm ground when it turns to water, or sand, or disappears, so you need a plan all the time for that kind of thing. One minute you're fighting a man, the next he's a fire-breathing dragon. That's how they all fight."

Liz showed him another clip. "Brenda is sparring with Harrison here. See how well she reacts when Drew unexpectedly jumps in the bout? Drew and Harrison are trained Force Recon, and she's had minimal training and makes them look like the rankest amateurs. With buffs, they can all fight like that. Speed, agility, cunning, strength— they can outfight any normal human as if they were a child."

"Yes, I'm impressed now," General Campbell admitted. "With nothing except a few words they've made them superhuman."

"Yes, they have. With Sara's Sun-Rays buff, they heal twice as fast, and with Hawk's Endure Elements they can withstand cold and heat to amazing degrees.

"We had to pull them from some of the regular training sessions so it wouldn't be as apparent. They received Charlie's pain management and his and Stasia's increase to strength. Both strength buffs are minor, but together formidable. With his pain management, they don't take as much damage as a normal person, and the damage they do take doesn't hurt as much. Add in Stasia's agility buff and Oz's intelligence buff, and you get a superhuman even without the magic spells.

"Those passive buffs they give to their groups stay with them, they don't wear off. We haven't tried to remove anyone from the raid, and as far as I know, the raid leader is still Richard Hayes. For a full report I need to study someone they remove. The no-goes are the perfect choice. If Rick drops them now, before they leave the service, we can order tests for both physical and mental acuity. If we wait, I'd have to do it clandestinely."

"What are the risks here?"

Liz settled back in her chair and rolled the pointer absently in her hands. "Well, we really don't know. The raid could fall apart completely, I suppose, which would remove all the buffs from them or it might not. The buffs might remain until they die or join a new group like in the game. We simply don't know."

"Can the buffs be removed?"

"Yes, both Sara and Oz possess spells to remove them, or at least in theory they do, we haven't tried."

"So, how many raid members are there right now?"

"Twenty-nine people are in the raid now. Richard Hayes should be able to invite one more. Potentially, they could disband and form five raids of thirty each. Now, whether they'd lose buffs as they traded raids, I don't know. And while it could be done, I'm not sure the knowledge we'd gain is worth the knowledge we might lose. We know the magic is limited in some respects to their perceptions. I wouldn't recommend that we disband them until we have a better grasp on what's happening in case losing their party means losing the magic."

"Eight Marines and four Army personnel who re-upped will go to Camp UBM Practice," Liz continued. "Now they're in their respective special ops training camps. If we drop the no-goes, it leaves nine free spaces, and I believe the risk is minimal to drop them, or I should say, try to drop them."

"Okay, let's do that and see if we can remove the buffs too. We don't want people running around with them if we have no control." General Campbell leaned back in his chair and gripped the edge of his desk.

"Jesus Christ," he said, his voice soft and full of awe. "This is huge, you're right. If they can do that just by being in a group, and my god, if it stays after they leave the group…. The demand on Sara alone will be astronomical. She could spend the rest of her life healing people and giving her quick heals buff."

"Yes, the demand on Oz would also be astronomical. Who wouldn't want to be smarter? I'd like time to study the people we drop to determine if the buff is removed or not before trying to dispel it."

"Yes, all the buffs are powerful. We need to find out how long they last. I'll form your orders to give you what time you'll need, and, Major, I don't need to say keep this confidential. I'll report this to the president. Get Richard Hayes to remove those people if he can, and I want to be informed immediately of the results."

"I'll get right on this. There's one more point to cover. You're aware we're mixing service personnel here. What you may be unaware of is they've already named themselves, and you'll see in my reports I've adopted their name. They call the camp they'll go to Cub Scout Camp and refer to Team Valor as their cubs. This video clip shows this. They do it naturally as if they've been doing it for years."

Liz turned on a different video, this one showing Brenda yelling a cadence to her team as they ran. "She's saying, who are we, and they answer, we're the Scouts. Then she says, 'What do we do'? They answer, 'we protect the cubs'. Then it goes into a traditional Marine cadence, but ends with, 'and what's our mission'? And they reply. '*Arghhh, Oorah*' which translates to attack and kill both coming from Charlie; they're both his battle cries."

Liz handed General Campbell a slip of paper. "I want permission to give them their own emblem to further cement them as a group. While they can individually be an Army Ranger or a Marine Recon, together they're Scouts."

General Campbell contemplated the colored drawing of a red arrowhead with a banner along the bottom. The badge was very similar to the traditional Marine Recon emblem except it had a black bear paw with yellowed claws extended instead of a skull and the banner read 'First Scout Unit.' The same motto deadly, swift, silent, ran along the edge.

"Yes, I'll get this approved and made up for them. We're also bumping up the promotions in the lesser ranks. We'll have three new corporals and one new sergeant. I'm aware there's already some slight friction with Major Nelson's original team, and I'm sure this will add to it, but they're Marines and need to suck it up.

"The Scouts won the lottery when the cubs rescued them. Maybe, someday, we'll figure out how to pass the magic on. Until then, they need to work together and accept that the Scouts have special abilities and will receive special treatment."

"Major Nelson and I've already spoken, and we both feel the resentment is slight. Only a few have expressed unease working with the kids and have already been reassigned elsewhere. If we ever get the capability, the remainder hope to be in the first batch to receive the magic." Liz gathered her belongings.

General Campbell shook her hand as he dismissed her. "Thank you, Major, this is excellent work."

Liz saluted and left to find a ride to Camp Pendleton.

- 14 -

THE RAID

Liz arrived at Camp Pendleton two days later and went straight to Lieutenant Colonel Gracias office.

"Ah, Major, I was expecting you." With absentminded courtesy, he gestured her to a seat. "Your Scouts are doing very well. A small ceremony took place here yesterday to award the new emblems."

A startled snort of laughter escaped Liz. "Excuse me, sir. The speed surprised me. I just recommended it two days ago."

Lieutenant Colonel Gracias leaned back in his swivel chair and smiled. "Yeah, my recommendations for them happen at once or never. They skip through the chain of command as if it wasn't even there."

Liz nodded but said nothing.

"Classified, I know." The chair creaked as

he leaned forward. "I'm happy to report all the training criteria are met, including supplying personal computers and internet access."

"They've been pulled from physical testing already?"

"Yes, they still do the mandatory hikes and runs and morning PE, but now spend most of their time in classrooms. The instructors are thrilled with them. I wish I knew where you recruited them. I could use a hundred more."

"Classified, but I can tell you we're working on recruitment too. The reason I'm here is to borrow Lance Corporal Richard Hayes for a short time." Liz passed him her orders.

Without bothering to read them, he set them on the edge of his desk.

"This should take approximately five days. And I want to leave today."

"That's fine," he agreed. The chair creaked again as he turned to his computer and typed a moment. "The Scouts are observing unarmed combat training right now."

"Do they do that often?" Liz rose an eyebrow in surprise.

"Let me see here— it's scheduled for

twice a week for the next three weeks," he said after checking the computer again.

"Thank you, sir. Permission to retrieve him?" Liz asked.

"Permission granted. I'll come along. A good man is teaching a refresher course to seasoned Marines. This should prove interesting."

Warm air smelling of sweat buffeted them when they entered the busy gym. Soldiers crowded around a standard boxing ring observing as an instructor showed two men in sweatpants and gray t-shirts how to break a hold.

Liz nodded to her Scouts as they turned to see who'd entered. Joy recorded with a small handheld recorder while everyone else took notes.

Major Nelson and his team were teaching them close-combat unarmed fighting. The last report he'd sent recommended they be pulled from hand-to-hand training here. The Scout's strength and agility, coupled with their intelligence, let them win fights against normal, unbuffed humans too easily. Apparently, the Scouts felt they had more to learn from observing fights.

One of the Marines standing at the ring turned to Brenda and said loudly enough that

Liz heard.

"So, Scouts watch huh?" He smirked at the new patch on her black uniform.

Brenda nodded but didn't reply.

"So, you're not a combat group then? Well, that's good. Women have no place in battle."

Brenda frowned, staring pointedly at his patch. "Look, Recon, women have a place anywhere we want."

The man held up his hands and waved them. "Sure, sure, don't get your panties in a bunch. Whatever you say. Go back to scouting." With a last smirk at her new patch, he turned away.

Brenda's ears reddened, but she didn't say a thing, just returned to viewing the fight.

Liz approached the instructor. "Could you put one of my Scouts in?"

The instructor looked to Lieutenant Colonel Garcia saying, "This isn't a group for beginners to fight."

The lieutenant colonel tapped his bottom lip a moment and then grinned. "Put one in," he ordered, giving a hard stare to the grouped men. "Don't hold back."

With a sigh, the instructor stopped the current fight and motioned for a waiting man to enter the ring. "Pick your man."

"Joy, would you mind?" Liz grinned at Joy.

Joy laughed and handed the recorder to Todd. "Sure."

Liz leaned over and whispered, "Don't beat him too bad."

Joy nodded and hopped into the ring.

The soldier in the ring frowned. "Um, I'm supposed to..."

His frown deepened as he stared doubtfully at Joy. Over a foot taller and a good hundred pounds heavier, he dwarfed Joy's slight frame.

"Follow orders!" Lieutenant Colonel Garcia barked.

The man shrugged and threw a light punch.

Joy grabbed his arm and used it to swing over him, and then foot swept him onto the mat. Pretending to check her nails for damage, she winked at Liz as she waited for her opponent to rise.

He glared at her.

She smiled sweetly back.

The soldier took a more serious defensive stance and swung again. Joy leaned out of the way, moving impossibly fast.

Liz cleared her throat and Joy assumed a defensive position. This time she used her hands in a traditional block and kicked her opponent hard in the upper chest. He fell back but remained standing. She sparred with him a few minutes. Liz noticed she wasn't trying and wondered if it were obvious to the others she held back.

The man she fought growled and swung harder. Joy blocked every punch, lightly tapping the man on the neck or face after each attempt.

He snarled and tried grabbing her in a bear hug. Joy winked at her again as she let him bring her to the floor. A second later, she knelt on the man's back with one of his arms pulled up uncomfortably high. In one fluid move, she released him and flipped backward, landing lightly on her feet. He rose slowly.

"I can't beat her without seriously hurting her," he said to the instructor.

Joy laughed. "You can try."

The man turned to her. "I don't want to hurt you, and I will if we try for real."

Joy nodded. "Take your best shot." She backed up, taking a defensive position.

The soldier stood there uncertainly.

"Follow your orders. Take her out! Don't hold back. I want her dead on the floor!" Lieutenant Colonel Garcia barked.

The man nodded, taking an aggressive

stance.

"*Oorah*" the Scouts chorused softly, and Joy leaped forward so fast it was hard to see what she did. Pinned, unable to move, her opponent lay on his stomach, both of his hands held by one of hers. One of her arms forced his head back. A moment's effort would snap his neck. Clearly the winner, she swung herself gracefully from the ring.

"Scouts fight too," Liz said. "The Scouts are every bit as much a fighting force as you are." She beckoned Rick and strode away.

Lieutenant Colonel Garcia followed.

Liz's face flushed pink. "I shouldn't have done that, but the woman comment made me mad."

The lieutenant colonel laughed. "Overconfidence can be fatal. They needed to be taken down a notch. It'll do them good to fight people who can so easily beat them. I saw she was holding back. Can they all fight like that?"

"Classified, I'm sorry I let her." Liz turned to Rick.

"Get your gear. We're going to Elgin. You'll be back in a week, tops." She saluted Lieutenant Colonel Garcia, and he returned to his office.

Rick ran to his barracks and packed a bag.

Liz glanced at the time when he returned.

"Let's grab a bite first. I'll explain our mission on the plane. Everyone is fine," she said in reply to his worried look. "We can fit in a visit."

"Man, I need to get Stasia a present then. Her birthday was last month." Rick groaned scrunching his eyes closed and rubbing a temple with two fingers.

"Are you and she, um...?" Liz trailed off.

"Are you crazy? She's fourteen." Rick grimaced and laughed. "Well, fifteen now, but still. No, we're not! I care about her though, and she always sends me stuff."

Liz pondered informing him that Stasia had a crush on him, but decided that was none of her business.

Rick laughed again. "She thinks she's in love with me, but she's just a kid. I try to be nice to her without leading her on. That's harder to do than it sounds."

"I bet," Liz agreed, "especially as she doesn't consider herself a child."

"Should I ignore her then?" Rick asked anxiously.

Liz snickered. "Yeah, good luck with that." The laugh died as she leaned over and patted his shoulder. "Seriously though, you're handling it fine. No matter what she thinks, she's too young. Be clear, no mixed messages. Maybe, mention your girlfriend or something."

"What girlfriend? I have no time to meet anyone, never mind date. Every minute of my day is scheduled."

"This pace will slow after Cub Scout Camp, I promise. It's hectic now because we want everyone trained as soon as possible."

Once they were on the way, Liz opened her briefcase and took out a stack of files. Alone on a private jet, Liz spread her work on the seat between them. The pilot and copilot sat behind the closed cockpit door.

"I have orders here for you from General Campbell. You're to remove these people from the raid. We'll go to each, and you'll say their full name and rank, then I remove you from my raid. They'll be told to reply; I'm leaving the Team Valor raid led by Richard Hayes. Pay close attention. We want to know if you can tell if they've left the raid."

"I doubt I'll be able to tell." Rick turned the pages, lines of concentration forming on his brow.

Liz said, "Before and after you remove them, I'll be performing simple tests. The tests should show us if it worked, but anything you can add will be helpful."

"I should try saying I remove you from the raid out of their presence. See if that works or if we need the formal naming," Rick said.

"Yes, let's try that too. We'll start with him." Liz pointed at a portrait. "After I do my tests, I'll call you. Try to remove him from a distance, and I'll rerun the tests. We're starting with him because he wants to leave. My theory is it'll be easier if both parties agree to leave."

"Yeah, that makes sense. In the game, if someone logs off, you can't remove them until they log in again, or six hours passes. Waiting on someone who disconnected was a real pain. At least that's how it worked when I played. It might've changed. I haven't raided in years."

"I've read the reports from when you formed the raid. No one noticed any difference. Everyone thought you were maybe a little crazy until Sara healed them. You're sure you don't remember anything about the process, anything at all?"

"Sorry, no, just what I reported. I didn't know what was going on either. I did it to humor my brother who, I admit, I thought was delusional. But I was willing to go along with it. He'd found us after all. And everyone wanted to leave. We would've pretended to be rabbits if he'd asked."

"Why did he pass you lead?"

"Well, at the time, I thought it was because he was upstairs guarding the door and I was closer," Rick said.

"And now, do you still think that?"

"Yes, and we'd talked only the week before about me inviting my entire squad to raid with them. I think, subconsciously, he thought that."

"That wasn't in any report."

"Well, no, is it important?"

"No idea," Liz admitted. "It might be. If Charlie already believed you and your squad would raid together, he already had a preconceived perception of them. I thought they were completely unassociated with him, this changes that perception."

"Team Valor all knew and agreed to raid with us. I should've reported that, but it happened a week before."

"If these removals work, we'll try inviting a complete stranger."

"When you're looking for this stranger, make sure he isn't in the service. The service is now their guild, or at least it might be. The feeling is similar, for me, anyway. If Charlie joins when he's eighteen, it probably would be for him too."

Liz made a note of their talk.

When they arrived at Elgin Air Force Base, Liz went right to her office and called Rick, who had checked into a nearby hotel.

"When I buzz, just say you remove him. Keep it short and simple. Then wait for my call."

Corporal Delton fidgeted outside her office, nervous fingers making furrows in his short brown hair. He was one of the men who didn't wish to work with the magic and hated to be reminded he was still in their raid. He'd signed numerous confidentiality agreements and received money for his silence, but Liz thought he'd have gladly denied the existence of magic for free.

He'd asked for a transfer and was doing his best to pretend the entire incident in Iraq had never happened. Talking of magic made him extremely uncomfortable and he always prefaced his replies with, 'I thought I saw,' as if even now with the evidence of his own eyes he didn't believe it.

Liz gestured him to a seat and handed him a wooden puzzle. "Corporal Delton, take a seat. Only a few simple tests today. Please, remove the loop." The stopwatches loud tick filled the small room. "Okay, squeeze this as hard as you can, please." She handed him the small machine that measured grip. "Okay, one more. This will sting a bit, I'm afraid."

The corporal grimaced as Liz made a one-inch scratch on his forearm and timed how long it bled. Then she buzzed Rick. After five minutes, she repeated the tests.

A pleased smile lit her face as she thanked the corporal, ordering him to return at the same time tomorrow. Still smiling, she called Rick.

"That appeared to work. Tomorrow, I'll repeat the tests. Tell me exactly what you did."

"I said, I remove Corporal Dalton from my raid aloud while picturing his face and then pictured the steps I would've taken to remove him. Opening the raid tab, right clicking his name, and picking remove from raid on the list."

"Very good, try this one without picturing anything if you can help it. I realize it's like trying not to picture a pink elephant after someone says not too but give it a try. Then try with just picturing it in your head. We want to learn as much as we can about this. If we can remove someone, I'll get permission to add someone."

"You should get Oz here," Rick said. "He can tell by looking who has magic. And maybe get Hawk too and see if they change 'color' to him."

That's a great idea," Liz said and dialed immediately when she hung up.

Liz called in the next person, ran the same tests, and buzzed Rick. Again, she waited five minutes and repeated the tests. That person received orders to return tomorrow as well.

After submitting her report, Liz flew back to Baghdad on the orders of General Campbell.

"Come in, Major Harris, I read the reports. I wanted to talk in person about the results." General Campbell gestured to a chair in front of his desk. "Please, take a seat. All no-goes were successfully removed?"

"It appears so, all my tests indicate it. Oz confirmed they were magic free. Hawk saw no change in color but could tell by looking at them they were no longer in his raid. He has no idea how he knew though," Liz said as she took the seat the general waved her to.

"Richard Hayes successfully removed everyone without even speaking to them. He didn't even need to stay in the zone," she continued.

"Yes, I see here he did it by stating the

name and saying I remove you from my raid."

"All the buffs go once the removal happens. I'm now in the raid. There are experiments I want to try as a raid member. He can invite and remove me at will with or without my agreement. It's a fascinating study."

"Some people you tried to invite couldn't join, has that been resolved?"

"Yes, and no. Their perceptions are again affecting them. Only people who've raided with them in the past, people they see as friends, and Marines have been able to join their raid. In effect, allies. So far, every Marine invited could join with no problem. My theory is that when Rick asked his brother to invite his entire platoon to raid with them, Charlie thought the Marines. He didn't know individual names or at least not many. They all agree they thought of it as playing with the Marines."

"Army personnel could be invited before, they can't now?"

"No. They saw men in uniform, and to them, it was a Marine, a friend of Rick's, already invited. Everyone said they considered those hostages Rick's platoon. The hostages considered themselves a group. The magic can't be fooled. If they know someone isn't a

Marine, they can't invite them."

"Have you tried putting a civilian in a Marine uniform?"

"Yes, it didn't work. What's interesting is we tried with a group of fresh cadets both before and after they took their oaths. Once they gave their oath, they could join."

General Campbell rubbed his chin thoughtfully. "Yes, perception plays a big part with their magic, the zones, and now personal perception. I took an oath and am now a Marine. What about friends? I'm assuming they can't just say you're my friend."

Liz shook her head. "No, they tried that, and believe me, Sara really wanted it to work. We took her to a children's hospital and even though she liked them, and wanted to heal them, she couldn't. Rick said he liked the children, but none could accept the invite. Just liking someone isn't enough, you have to be their friend, and again, they can't fake it. There has to be real ties, simply stating it doesn't work."

General Campbell tapped the list of current raid members. "So, six raid spots remain?"

"Yes, Rick invited Major Nelson, three of his men, and me. No one new was informed."

"The report you sent me about Sara and

Rick going to the naval hospital and healing the Marines is worrying us. While I agree it's a good thing, it's also dangerous; we can't reveal this secret."

"In one weekend, she healed two hundred and forty-four men. The plan is to visit all of the hospitals as time permits. If we could consolidate them somehow to cut down on travel time that would be helpful. Even post-traumatic stress can be helped with Soothe."

General Campbell nodded. "We're trying to work out a way for her to heal all of them. The problem is it's so unbalanced. We can't claim a new miracle drug because it only works on Marines. Sooner or later someone is bound to notice there are no sick Marines."

Liz nodded in agreement as she said, "Right now, Sara and Rick are visiting the hospitals using the cover of video gaming. They talk to their target about the game. Sara signs autographs, and sometimes Stasia goes too. They get the person to say they'll join the raid. As discreetly as she can, she heals them, and Rick removes them from the raid and they move on. The process can take over an hour. It'll be a long time before she puts a dent in them. I recommend letting her continue. If she isn't allowed to heal them, it will seriously upset her, and when we go public, we can honestly say we were trying to help them."

"That was our thought too. Perhaps we could issue the Marine oath to retired Army personnel." The general sat back in his chair, rubbing his temples before speaking, "There's so much we don't know. Let her visit injured Marines, but tell her it must remain discrete and limit the time she spends doing it to, say, twenty hours a month for now. A new cover story would be better."

Liz shrugged. "That was the best we could come up with to get the raid invite accepted. Sara and Stasia are famous raiders. You'd be amazed at how many of the Marines recognize them. Even without healing them, it cheers them up."

"All it will take is one of those Marines with a little imagination to put the visit of Seraphim the healer together with a miraculous cure. Especially, if she cures everyone she visits."

"Few of her cures are dramatic, being a disease of some sort. Most don't realize they're cured for a while. Broken bones or minor wounds she leaves alone. It'll be a long time before anyone notices."

"Okay, keep her away from anything noticeable. And keep the heals toned down when you can. Have her use heal-over-times, not full heals. Let her cure the disease, but time heals them, that sort of thing."

"We tested Sara's healing abilities on a wide range of people. She can only heal her raid. Outside of the raid, she could heal Mrs. Morales, Agent Lewis, and me. We were the only ones she considers friends. Oz's bandages work the same way. It's a much weaker heal, and after three applications you hit a timer, first ten minutes, then twenty. After twenty minutes, the timer resets effectively limiting you to ten bandages an hour. For a severe injury, it might be enough to sustain life, but it would take days to heal. Hawk's healing aura works better, but he needs to sit near plants or Oz in tree disguise.

"Again, I don't think he could cure a serious injury that way, but it would probably sustain life. It also calms people even if he isn't touching them, although it works both better and faster if he is touching them. His calming aura is always active. He doesn't need to be by plants for it to work but it works better if he is. Hawk sitting in a forest gives off a peaceful vibe; you should try it sometime. It's very relaxing, better than any massage." Liz finished with a small laugh.

"Oh," Liz said suddenly, "before I forget,

Agent Lewis put together a list of everyone they could find who raided with them in the past. It should give you more options on raid composition. They've raided with a wide assortment of people."

"That's a good idea, but it'll be a while before we do that." General Campbell leaned back in his chair, swiveling slightly from side-to-side. "More study needs to be done first, we've barely scratched the surface."

Liz paused and tapped the graphs she'd prepared. "Our knowledge is growing. Every day we learn something new. Magic existed such a short time and look how much we've already learned. Not just about the magic either. Dr. Elliot has made some big advances with Sara's help. The use of harmful mapping methods or watching under microscopes as a healing takes place has moved our medical knowledge decades ahead. Every day I say a prayer of thanks it happened to those children and not someone who'd abuse that power. I shudder to think what they could do if they weren't the honorable people they are."

General Campbell nodded in agreement. "Well, we don't know for a fact they're the only ones, but it seems likely. We're scouring news archives looking for any evidence of the lightning or any event explainable by another magic user and haven't found even a hint. Passengers on flight four-fourteen appear to have disappeared without a trace. We're being as careful as we can with the magic users we have. Reputation gains almost ruined our chance to work with them. More and more I realize their existence will change the world as we know it. A good working relationship is our number one priority now."

The reports Liz had written under his left arm, General Campbell cradled the newest reports in his right as he knocked on the door.

The president and Pierce Taylor greeted him. General Campbell slid the report across the desk. "One hundred and twelve bodies have been recovered and positively identified. That leaves forty-six potential magic users at large, and if they did the same thing as our magic users and formed raids with the rest of the survivors, maybe as many as two hundred and thirty super humans."

Pierce tapped the report. "The chances of their survival aren't good. Team Valor had medical care, and during the beginning of the transformation were trying to be the game characters. What are the chances the plane wreck survivors were?

"The survivors had nothing, not even food or shelter. Divers recovered bodies left still buckled into plane seats, dead on impact or by the lightning strike itself. No attempt had been made to free them. From experience, we know the lightning stricken would've been unconscious for forty minutes, and that's not adding in injuries from a crash. Other passengers would've had to tow them to safety. I think we can safely assume most would've drowned."

"True, but who knows how the magic works?" The president said as he flipped through the report. "And you're sure of these specs?"

General Campbell leaned back in his seat and crossed one leg over his knee. "Yes, this is the current specs for all missing game players, including the friends and spouses that were traveling with them and played the game too." The general turned to Pierce. "The fact that they aren't there means they're somewhere. Someone survived. Many someones. Luggage was missing from the plane, and a few suitcases were found intact on that small atoll. Either someone picked them up or... they used a mage portal and left."

Pierce shrugged and smiled slightly.

"Where to? We had agents at their homes. No way could they miss a hundred people popping up. If it were just the magic users missing, I could believe it. The druids, mages, and rogues could sneak away and with the wizards help the others could too but not that many. None of their families have been contacted. I'm sorry, but you can't convince me that in over a hundred people not one of them would contact their loved ones if they returned to civilization."

"That's a good point, but something happened to them," General Campbell said.

"Yes, I believe they all drowned when the storm reached them. By all accounts, the island they were on was dangerously flooding. The storm was extreme. And if they did have magic maybe they decided to risk a portal and ended up falling through the earth or outer space or just dropped for miles until they hit the sea."

The president said, "Still— the magic users could've survived a long drop. Maybe even saved some none magic users."

"Yes, but say they dropped over the ocean. The druids would live, but how long could they keep the others afloat?"

"They had a ranger for an air bubble," General Campbell said.

"Who would've to sleep sometime. They had mages so had food and water, but no way to move. They would've needed the druids to pull them through the water. We know the magic runs out. Eventually, they wouldn't have had enough."

"Our group could do it," The president said as he flipped his copy of the report closed.

Pierce Taylor withdrew a sealed report marked top secret from the file. Warnings covered the file stating the direness of reading without permission.

"Team Valor could save themselves but not their raid if they were dropped too far out to sea. I wrote out a report on the likely abilities used to survive either trying to swim away or being ported somewhere hostile to humans like the sea or a desert. It's all in this folder. They would've been weak and barely recovered. We're talking swimming and if they landed near the mages home in the North Atlantic Ocean the water would've been cold. If the druids or anyone else lived, there's been no sign of them. They haven't contacted their families, collected winnings, or touched bank accounts. We'll keep looking, but I think we can assume they're either captured or dead. There is no scenario I can imagine where a rogue could be held against its will never mind four of them. I really believe they're dead."

President Carmichael rose and paced to his windows. "I never thought I'd say this, but I certainly hope so."

- 15 -

SARA RETURNS

Sara returned home the first week of March. Her father and stepmother were on the way to South America, and Charlie was relieved they'd left Sara behind. Team Valor showed up five minutes after she arrived home.

"I'm so glad you're back!" Charlie gave her a quick hug before moving away to give everyone a chance to greet her.

"God, me too. I hate New York. It's so cold and dark. I missed you guys so much." Sara gave everyone another quick hug. "What did I miss in training?"

"Meh, don't worry about it." Stasia shrugged. "You'll catch up. Besides, you were doing most of what we were anyway on the laptop."

"I brought us hamburgers and stuff for a picnic." Oz held up the bag. "Let's hang out by the pool and soak up some rays."

Sara grinned at him. "Is Marcy coming?"

"No, she's at her grandmother's for the weekend, but I'm sure you'll see her this week." Oz headed to the pool.

"She'll be at my birthday party Friday night." Charlie ran his hand over the soft blond hair growing back on Sara's head. "You can go, right? You're not locked in here like in New York?"

"Yes, I can go. I just have to be home by ten." Sara grinned at Stasia who'd ordered Charlie's present, custom-made miniatures of their characters Chief and Seraphim, for her.

"I can go to the classes too. Guthrie set up fake language classes. My dad will be amazed at how fluent I am. The housekeeper is new. As long as I don't cause her any trouble, she won't care where I am. So far all she's said to me is, 'Very good, Miss.'"

"Sara looks better already," Hawk whispered to Stasia as they fixed plates of food.

Sara sat on the edge of the pool, kicking water at Oz and laughing.

"She does look better, stronger, less fragile. Maybe a few more days of sun and those circles ringing her eyes will disappear too," Stasia whispered back.

At nine thirty, they left.

"I'll bring junk food tomorrow and we can stay here and get more sun," Charlie said as he kissed her good night.

Sara gave him one of her special just for him smiles. "That sounds perfect."

Four hours later he found himself with Stasia, Oz, and Hawk, in his underwear, by her bedside. Confusion changed to worry. Everyone wore nightclothes. Sara shook, clutching her covers to her tear-streaked face.

"Oh jeez, I'm so sorry. I didn't mean to summon you. I had a bad dream."

"Yes, we see that." Stasia grabbed Sara's robe, putting it on over the purple lace teddy she wore. She went to Sara's bathroom, wet a washcloth and grabbed towels. When she returned, she threw the towels to the boys.

Charlie sat on Sara's bed, hugging her while Stasia wiped Sara's tear-streaked face with the wet cloth.

"I'll call Liz for a ride home." Oz gestured for Hawk to follow him.

"Don't let anyone see you, please," Sara called after him.

"Want to tell us about it?" Charlie stroked her back. Her distress made him angry, surprising him with the intensity of his reaction.

"No! I don't want to think about it. I'm so

sorry I dragged you all out here." Sara sat up straighter, avoiding their eyes.

"That's okay, we don't mind." Stasia exchanged a quick glance with Charlie and stood. "I'll go check on our ride, and no one will see me," she assured Sara with a laugh.

Charlie kissed Sara's temple, snuggling against her. "You can tell—"

"No," she interrupted, "I'm fine; it's okay." The shaking had stopped, and she was calm now, which calmed him. Charlie stayed with her until Liz arrived. "Go back to sleep. I'll be back in the morning." He gave her another quick kiss before leaving.

"So, what's all this?" Liz asked as she picked up the kids, stifling a laugh at the lack of clothing.

Hawk gripped the towel tighter around his waist. "Sara had a bad dream and summoned us; she didn't mean to."

"I see," Liz said. "I'll speak with her. If your parent's question where you were, have them call Captain Sanders."

After dropping them off, she returned to her warm bed. When her phone rang at five thirty, she groaned.

"Sorry, we need another ride," Oz said.

"Sara?" Liz asked.

"Yeah, this is starting to worry me," Oz

admitted.

"We'll handle it. Stay hidden until I arrive in an hour or so." Liz hung up and called Guthrie. "I'm on my way to pick up the kids. They're fine," she added hurriedly. "Sara had a nightmare and summoned them. This is the second time tonight, and she isn't doing it on purpose. A specialist might be needed if this is post-traumatic stress from the fight in Iraq."

"Okay, I'll pass this up the chain. Let me know what you find out."

Liz headed to Sara's house again. Sunrise had turned the sky a beautiful pink by the time she arrived. Deciding to talk to her right then, she called Sara's cell phone, which Oz answered.

"Have Sara come downstairs. I want to talk with her. She can tell Mrs. Shaw I'm stopping to say hello on my way through town."

"I will, but it's a new housekeeper. Tara fired Mrs. Shaw. We'll hang out in her room until you're done."

Five minutes later Sara came downstairs wearing sweat pants and a heavy sweatshirt. Dark circles ringed her eyes and a scared, almost desperate look, covered her face. She let Liz in and led her to a small den where she closed the door behind them. "I'm so sorry. I didn't mean to do it!" she burst out when the door closed.

"Take a minute here, Sara. Have a seat, and tell me what's going on," Liz said as calmly as she could.

"It's nothing, well, not nothing, just nightmares. Before I'm awake, I summon them."

"Could you tell me about your nightmare?"

"I'd rather not," Sara said in a small voice and looked away, nervously pleating her fingers.

"Have you had them long?"

"They started about a week after I left."

"The same dream?"

Sara nodded unhappily.

"Every night?"

Sara didn't respond, staring down at her hands twisting together in her lap. Finally, she said, "It's just a dream. I'm not crazy or anything."

Liz laughed. "No one thinks you're crazy. Everyone has bad dreams once in a while."

Sara nodded but said nothing.

"Sara, tell me what you dream. If I don't know, I can't help you."

Sara swallowed heavily. "I'm in a dark room, and I'm stuck in there. And I feel myself dying like my life is being sucked out, and it hurts, and I scream for help, but no one comes. The dark gets darker somehow, and I don't know where I am. I'm stuck there alone, and I'll always be there, alone in the dark, and I try to find a wall or a door, but I can't. Everything's dark, and no one comes...."

Tears trailed down her cheeks, and she dashed them away.

Liz put an arm around her. "And you dream this every night?"

Sara nodded. "Usually two or three times. I know it sounds stupid, but it's terrifying. Tara says I'm crazy and only babies are afraid of the dark, but, Liz, it isn't the dark, it's the being stuck there alone. I can't reach anyone. People talk in the distance, but no matter what I do, they don't hear me."

"Well, first— never listen to Tara again. I take it you told your father you were having bad dreams?"

Sara sighed. "He heard me yelling. That's why the electronics ban. Tara thinks electronics cause nightmares and depression."

Liz nodded. "Were the dreams last night just as bad?"

Sara's brow wrinkled. "No, they ended sooner, but that's because Stasia woke me."

"Sara, I think you're having that dream

because you *were* stuck all alone. I'm prescribing you lots of sunshine and fresh air. Lack of sunlight could be affecting you. Let's see if this helps. Also, I want you to summon everyone every time the cooldown is up. Let's tell your subconscious you can get help anytime you need too."

"I don't want them to get mad at me. I just returned and already I'm causing problems." Sara swallowed hard and turned away.

"They won't be mad. I'll call this a drill, part of your training. Give this a few days and see if it helps. When you're home from school tomorrow, summon them and come to the warehouse together. Class will be held outside in the sun for a few days. We'll stay in a nearby hotel tonight. Start your summons at zero-nine-hundred hours and summon them every time your cooldown is up."

Sara nodded, appearing relieved.

"Stay in the sun today, Sara. Send them out, and I'll take them home. I'll be half a mile up the street." Liz hugged her before driving up the street to wait, and call Guthrie.

"I don't think we need to worry too much, it has nothing to do with Iraq."

Liz told him about Sara's dream. " I think, if she'd been closer and had the dream she would've been okay, but because the summon wouldn't work out of the zone, it got worse instead."

"Yeah, I can see how that could happen, and I understand the nightmare, she *was* trapped there in the dark."

"I'll get rooms as close as I can to her and tell the kids were doing a practice on this."

Guthrie laughed. "Tell them whatever you like, but they aren't stupid, they'll figure it out."

"Sara's embarrassed. I told her we wouldn't say anything."

"Okay, I'll tell the parents were going on a small field trip."

Liz hung up and waited. Stasia, Hawk, and Oz, showed up five minutes later.

"Charlie is staying here. He planned on coming over today anyway," Oz said.

Liz nodded and drove them home again. She told them they'd be doing small field exercises and to pack sweats to sleep in, but they wouldn't miss school and dropped them off at their homes. "Be somewhere you won't be seen at zero-nine-hundred-hours today," she warned as she drove away.

Charlie and Sara made breakfast. Both already wore bathing suits, his borrowed.

"So," Charlie said, trying to sound matter-of-fact. "Want to tell me about the dream?"

"No. Let's eat outside, okay?"

Not willing to upset her more, Charlie dropped it. They brought their food outside and sat in the weak morning sunlight by the pool. The way Sara tipped her face to the sun, the need on her face, worried him.

"I'm supposed to summon everyone at nine. Liz wants me to practice." Sara picked at her breakfast.

"Sure, that's cool," Charlie agreed.

"I know this was supposed to be our day, but Liz thinks —"

Charlie interrupted her, "Sara, it's fine, I don't mind at all. We do need to practice your summons; she isn't wrong. I wonder if we can resist it if we're awake."

"We'll find out. I'm supposed to do it every three hours when my cooldown is up."

Charlie grinned. "Let's summon them into the pool."

Sara laughed. "Stasia would kill me if I ruined her new sneakers. How about the roof?"

"Has to be the pool house roof or your neighbors could see us."

They talked about other places they could summon to and were soon laughing. At ten of nine, Charlie lifted Sara to the roof. She climbed on, and he intercepted her.

"It's nice up here," Sara said happily, resting on the warm slate roof tiles.

Charlie nodded agreement. Afraid of breaking the roof tiles, he moved closer carefully. The early morning sun warmed the tiles pleasantly as they waited. At nine o'clock, she summoned everyone.

Stasia laughed when she realized where she was. She wore shorts and a halter-top with bare feet and carried a small bag tied tightly in plastic. "I expected to be summoned into the pool."

"Aww, you knew?" Sara pouted, then laughed.

"Well, it didn't take a genius to figure out when Liz told us to be alone at zero-nine-hundred," Stasia said with a small laugh.

"Summons tests every three hours," Charlie said, keeping his voice light.

Sara appeared unhappy to him with drawn cheeks and a nervous smile as if she expected them to begin yelling at her at any moment.

"Sounds fun." Hawk grinned.

"Yeah, I want to see if we can resist it if we're awake." Charlie smiled gratefully back. Sara could use Hawk's company. His aura would make her feel better.

"Not today though," Sara said quickly.

"Sure, we can try that later," Charlie agreed. "Last one to the kitchen cooks!" he yelled and jumped from the roof.

Charlie was last. Sara pulled herself past him at the last second and reached the kitchen before him. They made potato salad and cut up fruit and vegetables. Sara took steaks out of the freezer to defrost, and they made a cake.

"Let's bring the fruit to the pool. I'm hungry already," Hawk said as he swiped some frosting.

The rest of the day they spent hanging out by the pool. Sara summoned them underwater at noon and fell asleep right after, in the sun, lying next to Charlie.

"So, anyone else not buying the, 'we need to practice this?'" Oz asked softly.

"Duh!" Stasia spread suntan lotion on her legs and threw the bottle to Oz. "Do my back, please."

Oz laughed. "I would've done it without the Sweet-Talk."

The smell of coconuts filled the air as he rubbed the lotion on Stasia's back.

Stasia giggled softly. "I'll do yours too if you want."

They lazed around quietly in the sun. At

five of three, Charlie glanced at his watch. "Should I wake her?"

"Yes." Stasia nodded. "Liz wants her to summon on purpose, not in her sleep."

"I'll wake her." Hawk grinned and did a cannonball into the pool, splashing everyone on that side.

Sara gave a small shriek, sat up abruptly, and lay back down with a happy sigh. "This is so nice," she whispered to Charlie as she snuggled into his side.

"*Mmm*," he agreed as he kissed her bare shoulder. Her warm presence by his side eased him. He hadn't even realized he was so tense.

"Hey, Sara," Stasia called, "summon on my mark. I want to see if it's faster than a jump!"

Invisible, Stasia stood on the fourth-floor roof of the house. "Ready when you are!" Sara hollered back as she moved to an empty spot.

"Mark." Stasia jumped and appeared by Sara right as she fell past the first floor.

"It worked, but I wouldn't want to do that over a pit of alligators."

"Let's start dinner now; I'm hungry." Hawk patted his lean stomach.

"God, you're always hungry!" Stasia rubbed his short hair.

"I'll light the grill," Charlie offered.

"No, I'll light the grill," Oz said, laughing.

Liz arrived at nine thirty to pick them up.

"I'll be back in a few hours," Charlie said as he kissed her good night.

"You don't mind?" Sara ran a hand along the buttons of his shirt, avoiding his eyes.

"Looking forward to it actually. Wear that nightshirt again; I liked it." He grinned and kissed her again.

The summons at twelve and three were uneventful. Liz picked them up and brought them back to the nearby hotel. Sara was dressed in a school uniform when she summoned them at six. They arrived dressed for school.

"Sleep okay?" Charlie murmured as he hugged her in greeting.

A real smile crossed her face. "I did. I haven't slept this good in weeks. I'm sorry your sleep is being disrupted though."

Charlie kissed her before replying. "We don't mind." He lowered his voice. "I like seeing you at night. I hope Liz makes you do this for a while. A few more hours and we'll be together," Charlie said and kissed her quickly.

At three, she summoned them again, and they took the bus to the warehouse. Liz drove Sara and Stasia to Sara's house afterward.

"So, how was the new school," Stasia asked, turning to look in the back seat at Sara.

"Exactly like I expected it would be. The other girls either ignored or stared at me. At least they didn't say rude things about my parents though."

Stasia winced and reached back to pat her knee. "Don't worry about it. You always have me."

Sara laughed and touched Stasia hand, which still rested on her knee. "Yeah, I'm used to it, and I'd rather have you."

Stasia grinned, squeezed her knee, and released it before turning around to face forward again.

Sara sighed and turned to stare out the window. Liz pursed her lips but said nothing.

At six, Sara summoned them, and Charlie had pizza.

"This rocks. Hot pizza delivery. I wish I had your Call-for-Help, Sara," Hawk said as he grabbed another slice of pizza.

"Yours is cool too," Sara said.

"Not as cool as this." Hawk slid the hot pizza onto a plate. "Sure, knowing in what direction I am, and being able to travel faster is fun, but an instant summon can't be beat."

Everyone left after dinner except Charlie.

"We have an hour until they're back."

He pulled her close and kissed her neck.

After three days, Liz asked her to skip the night summons. Sara agreed and reported sleeping through the night without dreaming. Over the next three days, she gradually stopped summoning. A week passed with no nightmares or unplanned summons.

"Thank you, Liz," Sara said quietly as Liz did the routine weekly blood work.

"Are you feeling better, less alone?"

Sara shrugged. "I think I'll always feel alone, but I don't feel trapped anymore."

Liz frowned. "You're not alone, Sara. We're all here for you."

"Yes, until my magic runs out or my friends move on. Everyone is alone. I think the trick is to like yourself so you don't mind being alone."

"To some extent that's true. But you isolate yourself if you don't trust in friendship. I'm not saying you won't get burned; everyone does, but try to trust in it. Even if your magic disappears, I'll still be your friend. I was your friend before you had magic. Well, before I knew you had it," she corrected herself with a smile. "It's true I wouldn't see you as much if you didn't have the magic, my work would take me away, but my feelings would be the same."

Sara nodded. "Well, whatever fixed it, the sun, or letting my magic loose, or being home with my friends, I'm better now, and I thank you."

"You're welcome." She gave Sara a hug and made a note after she left. Hypotheses: being unable to use the magic causes nightmares or depression. Possibility of other negative manifestations; more research needed. She added the note to her report and returned to work.

A man cruised by the warehouse, filming with a small, concealed camera.

His job was to work out where to make the snatch. He didn't think it would be here. The warehouse remained heavily monitored with guards patrolling outside, and they had access to weapons here. School remained a possibility, but he wanted to take them separately, without so many witnesses. With limited manpower, he would have to use other methods.

- 16 -

GEARING UP

"Hey, Sarge, what's in the boxes?" Hawk asked as he and Stasia entered the room and spied the big pile of boxes that Charlie and Oz were examining.

"Late Christmas presents from the United States Army," Guthrie answered with a grin. "Give me a hand here, would you?"

"Sure," Hawk said, and Stasia nodded.

"Give these boxes to Major Harris and put this one on the table."

The kids examined the box's contents with interest.

Charlie held up a pair of black pants. "Armor?"

"Yep, we got new stuff custom-made for you," Guthrie agreed. "Pants, vests, and helmets; you guys go try on this stuff." He handed out the clothes to the gathered kids. "Where's Sara?"

"With Liz," Charlie said absently as he held a pair of pants against his legs.

Guthrie headed to the back room where he found Major Harris and Sara reading the manual that came in the smaller box.

Sara held up a small circular device. "These go under our clothes and monitor our vital signs and send them to this." A device resembling a cell phone, except longer and not as wide, lay on the table in front of her. "The gloves read our finger movements and connect to those devices and will supposedly trigger a cool-down automatically."

The gloves fit snuggly. A moment later, she'd linked the gloves to the bar and booted it up. Small pictures appeared on the screen.

Sara uttered a short laugh. "These are exact duplicates of our spells icons from the game."

A small timer overlaid the spell icon and began a countdown when she cast Soothe on Liz and a Minor Shield on the staff sergeant.

"Sweet!" Sara exclaimed, grinning at Liz. "And look, these lines here will show me my party's health and my hots. This is awesome. It's just like the game interface."

Liz attached the small monitoring devices

to Sara. A green line filled on the device on Liz's arm. "I wouldn't count on these though, Sara. Severe damage can happen quickly."

Sara nodded and continued to examine the readouts. "You know what this needs? a distance indicator. In the game, if you're out of my range, your bar is a different color. There were even addons to show the exact distance."

"Try a holder they sent to clip the spell-bar to your arm." Guthrie held out one of the bulky plastic clips.

Sara put the spell-bar device in the holder and strapped it on her wrist. It covered most of her forearm. Then she flexed her fingers and swung her arm.

Charlie entered, wearing his new pants and carrying hers.

"What's all this?" he asked, examining the spell-bar on her arm.

Liz explained and hooked the monitors to him while he activated a bar and entered his name.

"Are the gloves waterproof?" Charlie asked as he flexed his fingers inside the tight gloves. Wiring made lumps on his palms and knuckles and he hoped the bulky gloves wouldn't hamper his grip on his sword or break if he hit something.

"Water resistant," Liz read the manual. "Not recommended for prolonged immersion. Washing them quick with a damp towel is suggested."

"So, we shouldn't use them in the rain?" Sara opened her manual, searching for the answer.

"The manual doesn't say. I'll find out." Liz made a note. "I'll see if they can add a range indicator too. Let me know if you think of anything else."

Sara left to try on her pants and Hawk, Stasia, and Oz put on the spell-bars.

"Let's learn to use these but keep your watches too." Charlie tapped the Suunto Core watch still on his arm. "Practice both ways. Let's try the rest of this gear." Charlie sorted through the bulletproof vests until he found one that would fit him. "The black face masks go under the helmets, but do we put the headsets on under or over them?"

"Over," Guthrie said after examining the item in question.

"Liz, you know what this outfit needs?" Stasia fussed with the belt at her waist. "A retractable clip so we can clip ourselves together for a levitate run. That way we could still use our hands."

Liz made a note.

"Okay, try on the sheaths. Charlie, this one's for you." Guthrie handed Charlie a complicated looking assortment of matte-black belts and buckles. "Tighten these good now, and that box over there has a shield in it. The shield hooks onto this clip here, it's a quick release, just pull, but you might need help getting it back on again."

Guthrie handed him a classically shaped shield with the Scout's emblem painted in matte colors on the back.

"I can summon my weapon, so I can drop one of my swords to grab my shield." Charlie practiced grabbing and replacing his shield. "Hmm, getting it on my back again is taking too long."

"Perhaps we could use a magnet instead?" Liz suggested. "Charlie is strong enough to grab it and break the connection; he could just let it go."

"Maybe." Guthrie examined the clip arrangement. "Yeah, make a note of that, Major, and we'll give that a try. Stasia, those throwing stars go in the front, in those small pockets there." Guthrie showed her how to arrange them. "This belt goes over your chest armor, and these daggers are for you. This sheath is for Oz. Your summoned dagger should fit perfectly and the flap snaps down if your trying to hide the glow on the hilt."

He rummaged in a big box on the counter and brought out a smaller box, which he opened. "Hawk, this is for you. This is a specially designed Night Force scope with custom features, but if they interfere with your magic, let me know."

Next, he handed Hawk a brand-new M110 SASS. "This is also yours, and this holster is designed to fit it. I know you prefer a bow, but we thought the rifle wouldn't cause as much comment. This gun will hold a larger clip. The fact that you don't actually need bullets shouldn't be obvious if you use this one. Long range and semi-automatic features should help camouflage the magic. We want you to practice with this and use it, time permitting, instead of your sidearm."

Reminded, Charlie threaded his black leather belt through the beltloops and adjusted the holster for his old forty-five. Everyone carried a gun, more as camouflage then because they used them. Every day they practiced at their indoor range and were growing proficient.

Guthrie took a stack of MK 3 knives encased in black sheaths from the box, handing one to each of them, then three Ka-Bar knives. Stasia received two, Charlie one.

Charlie was given too thin boxes which, when opened, held two, matte-black gladiuses custom-made to fit his hand. Charlie's eyes lit when he swung it, and he ran a thumb lovingly along the sharp edge.

Sara snickered.

Charlie laughed and ran his thumb over her bottom lip.

Guthrie cleared his throat and Charlie hastily dropped his hand.

"They sent everyone a pair of these binoculars and night-vision goggles that fit over your helmets, but let's try them later. For Sara, they sent a new cloak. This one is washable and lightweight, considering it's composed of Dyneema, the same stuff they use in bulletproof vests. They also sent these backpacks designed to fit over one Oz conjures but they haven't been tested yet. This will be your standard gear, guys."

Guthrie fussed with the strap holding the dagger to Stasia's thigh and frowned. "I'll get this fixed so it lays flat, Stasia. Get fully suited. Let's make sure the gear fits."

In ten minutes, the kids lined up in their standard formation. The facemasks and gear made it difficult to tell them apart. The weapons they carried and their heights were the giveaways. "Okay guys, let's go to the basement and cast on the target dummies. The major and I will be monitoring on these tablets that tell us what your spell-bars show. Take this nice and slow. We're checking for precision timing here."

Guthrie led the way downstairs to the target dummies. Long, low, cement walls enclosed the two-thousand-square-foot area, making an ideal spot to cast without fear of being seen. Scorch marks and holes pockmarked the walls, marking where spells had impacted. Everything that happened in the basement was monitored and recorded with the results sent to the scientists who were still trying to figure out how they did what they did. A scientist was there now, hooking something up to one of the target dummies.

Charlie nodded a greeting and got a brisk nod in return. The scientists seemed uncomfortable around them and as far as he was concerned the feeling was mutual. He much preferred how Liz and Guthrie treated him.

The scientist's nervous glances and worried frowns grew wearing. Part of him agreed they had reason to be wary, but it wasn't like he'd gone looking for a fight.

The men they'd killed in Iraq had attacked

him, not the other way around. He tried to remember the scientist saw what he was capable of and were afraid and not hold it against them. Mostly, he ignored them.

"Okay, Sarge, we'll test it nice and easy," Charlie agreed. They each had their own dummy, and they cast on them checking the response time on the spell-bars.

"Mine isn't working." Stasia tapped the bar with a gloved finger and frowned. "The health bars show, but none of the timers are registering, Sarge."

Guthrie flipped through the manual. "Try a reboot. Reenter the connection ID into the spell-bar. It's the number on the inside tag on your glove. Put that number in the login field and then your name, now try that."

Stasia cast a timed move and glanced at her spell-bar, which now showed a timer counting down on her spell icon. "Nice, it's working now." She continued casting her spells, checking that each registered. "Sara, can you see on your screen when I use my defensive cooldowns?"

"No, they could probably program that though by putting the icon under your health bar like in the game," Sara said.

"Good idea, I'm making a note of it." Liz wrote it in her notebook.

"Have them color-code the spell-bar cases too." Stasia flexed her fingers and shook her arm, making sure the bar wouldn't move. "If we're gearing up in a hurry we can tell them apart that way. Use the same colors the game designers did. Sara should have a white case, and Hawk's green, Oz gets purple, and Charlie's should be blue, and mine red. All our gear can be color-coded that way. Put a small tag inside the pants and vests."

"Sounds good, I'll make a note of that." Liz wrote it down.

Guthrie glanced at this watch. "Take the spell-bars home, but don't let anyone see them. They have other features you should try out. Take a manual with you. Learn to switch the background lighting without looking and to turn on and off the audio signals. Leave the rest of the gear here but put it on when you arrive tomorrow. From now on, wear it for all practices."

Charlie stifled a laugh; Sara and Oz were already reading the manual and looking thrilled. Ever since they'd received the magic, they read constantly. The thicker and duller the book, the happier it made them. If you took their books away, it made them super cranky. Charlie had seen Oz read a phone book once because nothing else was available.

"Ten more minutes and go change." Liz returned to her office to call about the suggested improvements.

Team Valor continued to cast and check timers. "When I use my staff to cast it's giving me a regular shield timer." Sara tried another cast. "My right pinkie finger isn't working correctly."

"Extra gloves are in the box; we'll check it tomorrow," Guthrie said. "Go change. Leave the new gear in the lockers."

"I have an idea," Oz was saying to Sara when they left the room.

Charlie grinned and shook his head certain Oz's idea required Oz to take apart and reassemble a spell-bar.

Charlie stuck his head in Liz's office to tell her they were leaving. "I'll get Sara to her bus." Charlie took Sara's hand.

Liz frowned. "You're supposed to wait six months before driving anyone else under the age of eighteen."

"The bus stop is four blocks away. We can walk there." Charlie rolled his eyes.

"Fine," Liz agreed.

"See ya tomorrow, guys," Stasia said. "Is anyone going to be online in the study room tonight?"

"Me." Hawk sounded grumpy. "I wish we

could play our game instead."

"Me too." Oz slapped Hawk on the back. "I have too much time on my hands now. Maybe we could play a new game?"

"Not yet, Oz, sorry." Liz smiled crookedly. "There's too much chance your magic will become confused. Let's stick to the one-year plan and see where we are then."

Oz sighed and nodded.

"Come home and eat with us, Oz." Stasia put her arm around him. "You know your dad won't mind."

Oz nodded again, and everyone left. Sara and Charlie headed to the bus stop in one direction, and the other three got in Guthrie's SUV.

Charlie put his arm around Sara once they left the building. When they rounded the corner, he drew her in for a kiss.

"Mmm," Sara made a contented sound and leaned into him. "I've been dying to do that all night."

"Me too," Charlie agreed and kissed her again before taking her hand and heading to the bus stop. "Spring dance is Friday. You still want to go?"

"Yeah, I guess so." She didn't sound enthused.

"We don't have to if you don't want to."

Charlie kissed her temple.

"I want to dance with you, it's just..." She held a hand to her short hair.

Charlie pulled her close, running a hand through the soft, silky strands. "You're so beautiful, Sara. Even when you were bald, you were the most beautiful girl I've ever seen." He kissed her again.

She stood on tiptoe and held him as tight as she could, returning his kiss.

"I don't want to embarrass you in front of your friends," Sara said as she stepped back and ran a nervous hand through her hair.

Charlie put his arm around her, and they continued to her bus stop. "Don't be silly; my friends will love you. We'll have a good time, I promise— a nice, normal, date. Are you staying at Stasia's after?"

"Yeah, she invited me; we have to be back by eleven."

"The dance ends at ten thirty— plenty of time to walk you home."

"Maybe we could leave a little early?" Sara's voice lowered, and her eyes darkened as she pulled him down for another kiss. "And take time alone. We never get any time with just the two of us."

"That sounds like a plan."

No one else waited at the bus stop.

Charlie pulled her close, kissing her again. The bus's arrival surprised him, he was so caught up in her. She broke away and hurried on, waving from the window as it pulled away. He headed back to his mother's car he'd left at the warehouse and never noticed the man in the dark-blue sedan following him.

The week flew by. They went to school in the mornings and the warehouse in the afternoons where they worked out the bugs in their new gear. Friday arrived, and the girls didn't show up for practice.

"They're taking the day off. There's a big dance, and they need time to get ready," Liz said when Guthrie asked where they were.

Guthrie frowned before laughing. "Sometimes, I forget they're teenage girls." He let the boys go early.

Charlie was nervous. He hadn't been until the girls hadn't shown up for practice. Now, he wasn't sure what to wear. If they were taking an afternoon to get ready, a t-shirt probably wasn't right. After a quick hunt through his closet, he settled for a light blue, short-sleeve, button-down shirt.

After a moment's debate, he put on sneakers instead of his regular boots. He made a quick stop in the bathroom where he brushed his teeth, added a little hair gel, and was good to go.

The sun was still up, the night comfortably warm, as he walked to Stasia's house. They planned to get pizza together. Oz was bringing Marcy, and then everyone would go to the dance.

Hawk opened the door before he knocked. Camila greeted him pleasantly, and he tried to make small talk. The girls came out of Stasia's room together, and he'd stopped talking to Hawk's mother and had taken three steps toward Sara before he even realized he'd moved. A flushed burned his cheeks.

Camila smiled and told them to have fun, but not to be late.

Heat infused him as he took Sara's hand and he couldn't wait to get her alone. The girls had both had their hair done. Sara had new blond highlights, and her hair hung longer in front than the back now, almost like a boy's cut. *But no boy ever looked that sexy in short hair,* he thought.

She wore a simple, dark-blue dress with short, tight sleeves made of soft, clingy material that reached her knees. The diamond pendant he'd given her for Christmas glinted in the low, narrow V and small, sparkly, earrings peeked from her hair.

The high heels she wore made her only a few inches shorter than him. Her fingernails and toenails were freshly polished, and she smelled amazing. He was glad he hadn't worn a t-shirt.

Stasia also wore a dress, a red one, with Chinese characters and flowers climbing the left side. The dress hugged her from neck to knees with a slit up the side so she could walk. Her dark brown hair was gelled back with small spiky bangs in front. Red shiny earrings dangled from her ears and she wore red heels so high he was amazed she could walk in them.

He offered an arm to both girls, and with smiles, they accepted. When they reached the sidewalk, Stasia took her brother's arm, and they went ahead. Charlie stopped and pulled Sara in for a quick kiss.

When her hands slid under his shirt to his back, the kiss lengthened. He rested his forehead on hers. "Maybe we could skip the dance?" he asked, his voice deep and low.

Sara smiled and kissed him again, running her hands along his spine. "Nope, you and I are going to dance and have fun, but we can leave early," she promised. "Stasia and I spent too much time on dancing outfits to waste them."

Charlie smiled and pulled her into his side. The pizza parlor down the street from the school teemed with kids who'd had the same idea. Oz waved them to a table he'd staked out.

"It's nice to see you," Marcy said, giving Sara a friendly smile.

"You as well. Oz tells me you won the mathematics Olympics in eighth grade."

They ordered pizza and talked about school. "This is nice," Sara whispered to Charlie, "we need to do this more, a nice, normal night."

A group of boys stopped at the table. "Ah, you must be Sara," one said, eyeing her from head to toe. "I've seen your picture in Video Gamer's magazine. It didn't do you justice. If you get sick of Chief, I'm available."

His friend elbowed him, wincing at Charlie.

"No chance of that." Sara leaned into Charlie's side as he glared at the boy.

He wasn't really angry, a fact apparent to Sara if not the boy. If he had been angry, the boy would have fled. The thought made him smile complacently.

"What about you, Stasia, no date tonight? You could go with me," the boy asked hopefully.

"No thanks. We can dance though if you ask nicely." Stasia smiled at him.

The boy smiled back, and the group moved on. One saying loudly, "I can't believe you said that in front of Chief."

Sara giggled and glanced at Charlie, giggling again at his expression.

"You look too good for this crowd," he mock complained as they walked to the school.

"I wanted to look good for you." Sara squeezed his hand.

Charlie paused, holding Sara back as the others entered the building. Music billowed from the doorway every time someone opened it.

A shiver ran over her as he slid his hands down her sides and placed a soft kiss on her lips. "I love you," he said, running his hands down her sides again.

"I love you too." She kissed him, and they stood there, holding each other, till someone cleared their throat. Charlie took her hand and led her into the building.

This is perfect, Charlie thought as he held Sara for a slow dance.

He'd introduced her to his friends, and she'd won them over, as he'd known she would. Hannah had been rude, but that was expected. Sara ignored it.

Seeing the two girls side-by-side wasn't flattering for Hannah. Where Sara looked elegant and sexy, Hannah's dress was too tight and too short. The Harpies gathered at the table Oz had claimed when they'd entered and were waiting when they finished their dance.

So much for perfect, Charlie thought with a grimace as he led Sara to the table.

Heather Perry elbowed Haley Perez as they arrived. "So sad you lost all your hair in that accident, Sara," Heather said in a sugary tone. "I'm sure it will look good again— eventually."

"She can always buy hair implants and get plastic surgery like her mother." Hannah smirked at Sara, then took a quick step away from Charlie.

"Dork," Stasia said. "They didn't have them when her mother was alive. Sara's mom had naturally beautiful hair, just like Sara. You might want to look into that though; you're going to need them if you keep frying your hair getting that ratchet look."

Hannah rubbed her arms and sidled further from Charlie as she spun to face Stasia. Her eyes were narrowed and her fists clenched. "At least I can get a boyfriend."

Stasia snorted with laughter, and Sara grinned.

"Wow, that was truly lame, Hannah." Oz leaned back and laughed too.

"What's with you and the ugly girls?" Hannah sneered at Marcy.

"I don't date the ugly ones, like you," Oz said coldly.

Before Charlie grew angry enough to do more than make Heather take another step back, Stasia smirked and said, "Um, your boyfriend is hitting on Kelly. Maybe you better go insult her a while." Stasia pointed to the dance floor.

The Harpies spun around. Hannah's date stood in a close embrace on the dance floor, even though fast dance music played, not slow.

"Bitch!" Hannah said as she flounced away.

"Back at you!" Stasia yelled and laughed.

"Sorry about that," Charlie said when the Harpies left. "They have no manners at all."

"And they're stupid!" Stasia chuckled.

The Harpies loud yelling carried over the music as they confronted Kelly.

"I'm going to show Sara around. Can we meet you at your house at eleven?" Charlie asked Stasia hopefully.

"Sure, my brother will see me home. You all know how defenseless I am." Stasia rolled her eyes and laughed. "Just don't be too late, okay? I don't want to lie to my mother."

"We won't be, I promise." Charlie set the timer on his watch. "This beeps, and we go straight home."

He led Sara from the dance.

"Your friends are nice. That was fun," Sara said as they left the building.

"It was," he agreed. "Why don't we go see the football field?"

Sara laughed. "I've been there a hundred times to watch you play."

"Not in the dark you haven't."

"*Mmm*, no I haven't." Sara leaned into his side. "Yeah, show me the football field."

Exactly at eleven, they were at Stasia's house. Hawk let them in. Charlie kissed Sara lightly on the lips.

"See ya tomorrow at the warehouse."

The door closed behind her, and he practically danced down the street to his house. This had been the best night of his life.

The man watched as Charlie entered his house. Tonight would've been a good time to take them, but they weren't quite ready yet.

Still busy lining up buyers, the general had overruled him about snatching them before they went to their summer camp.

He wished he hadn't quit his job. If he'd stayed, he would've had better access, but that bird had flown.

Blueprints for their houses lay on the seat beside him. The general assured him the snatch would be soon. The mercenaries he'd hired would have no idea what they were up against.

He hoped the tranquilizers worked.

- 17 -

EMANCIPATION

One week before the start of Cub Scout Camp Sara entered the office, a drawn expression on her pale face.

"Sarge, we have a small problem. My father is sending me to a private girl's school in France for the summer. Tara convinced him I need polish. I tried to talk him out of it, but he won't budge. He says I need refinement more than nature."

Guthrie placed the file he was reading on the desk. "For how long?"

Tears filled Sara's eyes. "He said until September, but I think he means to keep me there. The tuition bill was for a full year."

"And you don't want to go? You don't have to attend this camp, you know."

"Of course, I don't want to go. I can't stop him though; he'll make me go."

"Go where?" Charlie asked as he entered. "What's going on?" he said sharply when he saw Sara's face. He stepped in front of her, glaring at Guthrie.

"Nothing we can't handle." Guthrie held up his empty hands.

"My father is sending me away for a year," Sara said at the same time.

Tense fingers grabbed his waist, and Sara leaned into his back. Charlie turned horrified eyes on Guthrie, pulling Sara into an embrace.

"Sara, you aren't sure it's for that long." Guthrie rose and placed a light hand on her shoulder.

"Two weeks would be too long," Sara said, her voice muffled by Charlie's shirt.

"What do we do?" Charlie rubbed his hands up and down Sara's back, trying to comfort her.

The thought of being separated from her horrified and angered him. In a year, she was bound to find someone new. She was too beautiful, her mother too famous, her father too rich. She never seemed to notice the interested glances she got when they went out, but he did. He growled low in his throat and pulled her closer.

"I'll call Captain Sanders. You two do nothing, you hear me?"

"I won't go!" Sara's voice trembled. "I'll run away first."

"No one is running anywhere. We'll handle this. Go get started on those map problems we laid out. Show your work. Write out the quickest, safest, and stealthiest route. Then work on the timing for moving your gear using invis. Assume metal detectors; plan the best way to cross in the shortest amount of time. There's a detector set up downstairs to practice on. Sara, we'll handle this. Go get started."

Charlie and Sara left the room; he pulled her into the bathroom, one of the few unmonitored rooms in the building. "If you go, I'll follow. I have enough money saved to go there too."

"Your parents won't let you spend your college fund to stay in Paris with your girlfriend."

"No, but they would let me go so you wouldn't be alone. I know they would, and, Sara, if they try to separate us, we'll both run away. I promise you, we'll stay together." Charlie hugged her. "I love you. We belong together."

His unreasonable anger made his palms sweat. If her father had been there, he would attack him to end the threat against her. He knew that was irrational, and an overreaction, and tried to get his anger under control.

Sara nodded and clutched him. The lashes framing her eyes sparkled with tears as she looked up at him. "I love you too, so much it makes my heart ache, but I couldn't let you upset your parents like that. I love them too."

"And they love you. You'll see, Sara, I'll talk to them tonight. They won't let you be taken away."

Charlie reluctantly released her. Her obvious reluctance to be separated from him too didn't ease him. He grew angrier by the moment, the strength of his anger shocking him. Then he had a new thought. Sara wasn't only his girlfriend; she was his sun priest. Just thinking of his sun priest defenseless where he couldn't reach her made him feel sick.

Still holding her hand, they entered the classroom and told the rest of the team what her father wanted to do. Angry looks darted over Sara's bowed head.

Stasia's expression turned thoughtful, and she exchanged a slight nod with Charlie. His shoulders tightened. Stasia felt it too. Oz and Hawk both looked furious and Sara looked scared. *Maybe her nightmares were magic related and would return if she were separated from them?* A wave of anger left Charlie trembling. Sara was probably terrified of being separated from her team, not just her friends. A sun priest needed a team, which is why not many people played them. They were weak solo players but powerful in groups. Getting a sun priest ready to raid was difficult unless, like Sara, you had friends to help you farm the gold needed to buy spell upgrades. He'd never thought about it before but Sara had never played alone.

Oz laid a hand on his sheathed knife and nodded slowly. Charlie's shoulders eased and he sat. Team Valor wouldn't let anyone take their sun-priest.

Guthrie called Captain Sanders. "We have a problem," he said when the captain answered.

"Yeah, we're already aware of it. Agent Lewis informed us last week. We were hoping we could avoid this, but we're moving forward on emancipating her."

"What's the time frame on that?"

"Well, that depends. Agent Lewis had analysts look at the situation, and they believe the threat of emancipation will be enough to keep her here, but it'll also ruin their relationship."

"Not much of relationship to ruin, but I'll tell her that. If she goes through with this, will she have enough money to live on until she's sixteen and inherits her mother's estate?"

"Yes, but she won't need to. Major Harris agreed to become her guardian. Sara will receive the same pay as always with her housing allotment going to Liz."

"Well, someone better tell the kids. I think they'll run away together before being separated."

"Yeah, we're aware of that too. The entire team would likely go. I shudder to think what they would get up to with no adult guidance. Security's been doubled. Guards will patrol at the warehouse and their homes until you leave for camp. Not that guards can stop them." Captain Sanders sighed. "Mr. Martin will be in touch with Sara later today. Keep them with you until he arrives. If they're determined to elude us, we won't be able to find them."

"I'll speak with her and see if she's willing to be legally emancipated. I'm a bit worried about Charlie's reaction to all this. It took an effort of will to approach them. He was so upset his protective aura activated against me. And we all know what he's capable of if angered."

"True, but Hawk reports he sees you as green, friendly, so you should be safe… well, from magic at least, but I suppose he could still rip your head off." Captain Sanders snorted back a laugh.

"Ha, ha, very funny. Let's see how amusing you think it is when he glares at you like that." Guthrie sighed. "Not that I think he would harm me, at least not over this, but feeling his protective aura is chilling."

"Other than that, how's everything going there? Are they ready for boot camp?"

"More than ready. Wait until you see them, everyone has grown. The classes here taught them a lot, they're extremely focused. Everything they do, they do to the best of their ability. Taking orders is another story. Don't get me wrong, they listen well, but because they choose too."

"Yeah, we're aware of that. They're too smart to blindly follow orders. It's both an asset and a liability. As long as they trust the person giving the orders, it should remain an asset. This camp should show us all some things."

"Everyone on your end is ready?"

Captain Sanders laughed. "You have no idea. Eight Marines fresh from CSO training and three newly minted Army Rangers are gung-ho to work with them. We're getting everybody set up now in the same gear the kids are using. The Scouts watched the videos you sent and have ideas of their own. I'm excited to see what they can do together."

"Me too," Guthrie agreed. "See you soon. I better go check on them. They're being too quiet."

The small room used as a classroom was silent. Everyone appeared to be concentrating on the maps.

Charlie narrowed his eyes at him when he asked Sara to accompany him. With a fake smile, swallowing heavily, he escorted Sara from the room, keeping both empty hands in sight.

"Captain Sanders was already aware of the situation and has a plan in place." Guthrie rested his hand on her shoulder. "Sara, this is just an idea, you can say no, and we'll work something else out." He led her to a chair and sat across from her. "Do you know what emancipation is?"

"Yes, and I thought of that, but didn't think I could do it."

"We can do it. It might take time to become official, but it can be done. Mr. Martin will be here tonight to show you the legal papers, but, Sara, you need to understand something. Emancipation is permanent. Our profilers and analysts say if you do this, your father will likely write you off forever. He isn't a forgiving man."

"Yes, I understand that. When you say a while, how long do you think?"

"Mr. Martin would have a better idea than me. Sara, this is a big decision, and it's unfair of us to pressure you into it. The magic could disappear; you and Charlie could break up. We're talking about your father never being able to forgive you."

Sara shrugged. "I'm supposed to love my father, but really, I feel nothing. He's a stranger to me. I wish we were closer, but that will never happen." She paused a moment. "Well, maybe not ever. If magic can exist, maybe he could change. But if he can't forgive this, then I don't want his forgiveness. Maybe he should worry about getting my forgiveness for ignoring me for fifteen years. Materially, he took good care of me. I never missed a meal, had nice clothes, and went to good schools, but my mother paid for those things. Not once, in fifteen years, has he ever said I love you, or even how are you."

"Sara, I want you to think about this, and talk to Charlie and his parents. If you still want to proceed after you've spoken with them and talked with Mr. Martin, we will. Right now, your father's in Brazil. We can fax the paperwork to him. Let us handle that, okay?"

Sara nodded. "Thanks, Sarge."

"Okay, get back to work, and, Sara," he said as she headed to the door. "Don't do anything drastic, even if this doesn't work, or you decide not to file. Let us handle this, okay?"

"Sure, Sarge."

The door closed softly behind her.

He checked the monitor, assuring she entered the small classroom. After watching a few minutes, he called for more security.

Sara spoke with both Charlie and his parents. Everyone was at Charlie's house when Mr. Martin arrived with the papers for her to examine.

"Major Harris agreed to be your guardian," Mr. Martin said as he handed the file to Sara. "As an emancipated minor, you technically don't need one, but if we can show a judge a plan in place for a stable, safe home life, it should help tremendously. The judge will be told you'll be using your own money and your inheritance from your mother to support yourself. In reality, Major Harris will receive money for your food and board using the same arrangement as the other parents. You'll continue to collect the same allowance as usual from the government with the remainder of your pay going into a bank account you can access at eighteen."

"How long will this take?" Sara scanned the documents he handed her.

"Well, that depends on what your father does, and there's only one way to find that out."

"Okay, let's get started," Sara said firmly. "Where do I sign?" Without hesitation, she signed the papers placed in front of her. "Now what?"

"Now you call your father and inform him. I'll fax him these papers, or I can call him if you prefer."

"No, that's fine, I want to say goodbye." Sara took out her cell phone and put it on speakerphone.

Her father answered on the third ring. "This better be important, Sara. I'm on my way to a business dinner."

"Yes, I'm sorry to bother you. I'm calling to inform you I've filed for emancipation."

"Sara, don't be ridiculous. You'll like the new school."

"This isn't about the school, Father. I want to choose where I live and stay in one place. I have enough money to support myself."

"I see," her father finally said.

"I appreciate that you've taken good care

of me, but I can take care of myself now."

"Your stepmother will be upset."

Sara remained silent.

"Fine, I'll sign the papers. Do you already have a place to live? I hope it's not with that boy."

"I do, and it's not. Would you like my new address?"

"Email it to me. Sara, I ask you to keep this quiet for your stepmother's sake."

"I won't mention it."

"Thank you. When can I expect you to be out of the house?"

Sara looked at Mr. Martin.

"Immediately," he mouthed.

"I can leave right away."

"Fine, I return in three days and expect you to be gone by then. The locks will be reset. Not that you aren't welcome there, it's an insurance consideration. If you change your mind, you may come home. I wish you well, Sara. If you ever need me, call, and I'll do what I can. A deposit will be made in your account that should provide adequately until you inherit your mother's estate. Goodbye, Sara."

"Goodbye, Father," Sara said softly as she hung-up.

"That went well." Mr. Martin rubbed his

hands together and gathered up the signed papers.

Sara nodded. "He doesn't dislike me; he's just indifferent."

"No, it's not indifference," Mary put an arm around Sara's shoulder. "It's inability. He doesn't know how to be a parent."

Charlie hugged her. "Are you okay?"

She nodded against his chest. "Yes, he was kinder than I expected."

"Me too, I think he loves you in his own way." Charlie said not because he believed it but to comfort her as he kissed the soft blond hair covering her temple.

This must be breaking her heart, he thought unhappily.

He couldn't imagine how painful it must be to be discarded so easily by your father. He glanced at his father who watched Sara worriedly. His mother looked both angry and worried. They loved her, but they weren't her parents.

"I suppose," she agreed, doubt clear in her voice.

"I'll send the paperwork off. Once he signs it, I'll file it. This should go through quickly now," Mr. Martin said.

"Call Stasia, and we'll get you packed up. Will all your stuff fit in Guthrie's SUV?"

Charlie asked.

"It should. If not, I'm sure the housekeeper will send it along. It shouldn't be a problem."

Charlie pursed his lips. She seemed calm to him, almost happy, and it worried him that she could hide herself so completely from him. "Sara, you can tell me if you're upset about this."

She laughed and hugged him. "I'm not though. Actually, I feel closer to him than I ever did. That was the most affection he's ever shown me. To him, this isn't changing our relationship, it's a business deal. Really, I'm fine, Charlie. No one can send me anywhere now. I'll get to choose. Believe me, I'm happy about this."

He nodded and hugged her tighter, wishing he could protect her feelings like he could her body, wishing there was an enemy he could kill for her.

Three hours later, Sara frowned at the large pile of boxes in the entranceway. "Man, I have way more stuff than I thought."

"Well, you can store a lot of this stuff." Stasia picked through the piles. "And some can get thrown away. Do you need all these old clothes and computers? And what about these books?" She gestured to the boxed books beside the door that towered head height.

"The baby clothes my mother picked out. I have pictures of us together, and I'm wearing them. I can't get rid of them, but I can store them, I guess. The dresses were hers too. Someday I can wear them, and they remind me of her. They can go in storage too.

"I read most of these books…" She trailed off and pursed her lips, clearly not happy to leave her mountain of books behind.

Charlie stifled a laugh. He hadn't realized her book collection had grown to these mammoth proportions. Oz was already sorting the books and making a pile.

Charlie sighed, knowing he'd be shuffling Oz's collection to make room for these. Oz's bedroom was lined floor-to-ceiling with books, mostly borrowed, and he'd taken over part of the small living room he shared with his father who never complained about the books that appeared as long as they didn't block the television.

Captain Sanders delivered new books weekly and had learned to leave the old ones in place or he was sent to retrieve them when Oz or Sara just had to reread something to make sure they understood the author's intent, which Charlie thought was silly since they both remembered everything they read perfectly. He thought they both just like to hold the books, to see the knowledge surrounding them.

Sara said, "Take whatever ones you want. There's only a few I really need, I guess. The computers can go. They were my only way to see you guys, but I guess I don't need them anymore."

"No, you don't." Stasia pulled the computers from the pile with Hawk's help. "Whenever you like, you can summon us."

Sara grabbed a box containing an old computer. "Let's make some piles here." In twenty minutes, three piles teetered in front of the door. A big mound to be gotten rid of, a small pile to keep, and another, medium-sized stack, to store. They loaded up the back of the SUV and Major Harris's car. The new housekeeper agreed to send the rest to a storage facility and discard the garbage. They let her think Sara was preparing to attend school in Paris.

Major Harris rented a small two-bedroom apartment about five minutes from the warehouse. The apartment had a kitchen with an island that sat two, and seating for four at a small table that adjoined the living room. The entire apartment was barely bigger than Sara's old bedroom. Every room was painted the same off-white.

The boys brought the boxes into the living area while the girls unpacked in Sara's room. Sara's bedroom already held a full-size bed, a desk with a comfortable desk chair, a dresser, and a matching nightstand. A door to a decent sized walk in closet, a bookcase, and another door leading to her small bathroom lined one wall.

Charlie gazed around the room. To him, this was a nice room, clean and neat. It looked nothing like Sara's old room, but she seemed okay with it even though to her it must look cheap. She was used to twenty-foot ceilings and elaborate moldings. Paintings by famous artists had graced her walls, and he knew for a fact Tara had spent more wallpapering the front drawing room than his father made in a year.

He was glad she'd agreed so easily to get rid of most of her books. They'd never have fit in this small room.

Liz entered carrying a box. "Last one, where do you want it?"

"Anywhere." Sara gestured vaguely about her without glancing up from the carton she emptied.

Oz hooked her computer up in no time while Charlie and Hawk unpacked the books she'd saved.

Liz cleared her throat. "Technically, you're an adult, but you're in my care. Let's set a few rules so we can all get along. If you make a mess, clean it up; we don't have any servants. Anyone you want can come over, but be considerate. If it's early or late, keep quiet. Let me know where you are and plan to return, and I'll do the same. Charlie can visit, but please keep the door to your room open.

"As for food, we'll figure out what we want to eat in advance and write a shopping list. We can both cook and clean up afterward. We'll enroll you in the same school they attend next year, and I'll bring you to your last two days of school this year, okay?"

"Thanks for doing this, Liz," Sara said in a soft, shy voice.

"It's no problem, Sara. I'm sure we'll get along fine. I'll help you however I can."

Sara and Stasia hugged her.

"Oh, and I hope you like cats," Liz said as a black and white one sauntered in.

Sara burst into tears, waving her hands to stop Charlie from coming to her. "I'm fine. I'm happy. I always wanted a cat, but my father never allowed pets because Tara doesn't like them and they hampered his traveling." She leaned down and crooned to the cat. "Who's a pretty kitty?" The cat obliging rubbed against her.

"Prince approves of you," Liz said in satisfaction. "Don't let him outside."

The cat stopped rubbing on Sara and jumped in Hawk's lap where he settled in purring.

"What do you guys say to pizza tonight?"

The man paced and kicked at the cheap furniture as he waited for the general in a shabby motel room in Massachusetts.

When the general arrived, the man vented his anger by kicking the door closed. "This is taking too long. Something is happening. The guards have been doubled. If we keep waiting, we'll miss our chance. Someone else will grab them. Hell, maybe somebody already tried, and that's why they doubled the guard. The more training they complete, the harder it will be to take them. While they're at camp, we have no shot. Strangers will immediately be noticed in the area."

"I'm in charge of this operation— not you." The general flicked imaginary lint from his immaculate uniform. "You're being paid well to get this intel. I've located two buyers, and both want the girls. Make sure to grab them. The boys aren't worth as much, and the rest of their raid is worth even less, but we can sell them all. Have you gotten access to any of the reports?"

"No." The man spun and kicked a faded, blue chair across the room. "It has Fort Knox security. Once you have them, do your own research."

"My clients want more proof. I'll need more video."

"And we'll get it. When we grab them, we can force them to perform."

"Don't contact me again. I'll contact you. Assure each group goes to their assigned place, and it's imperative you get the healer, rogue, and mage. Make all efforts to preserve the healer, the mage is expendable, but know when he dies so does your money for him." The general handed the man a briefcase. "This is where to take them. Arrange for a boat. Keep them there, do the tests, and make the videos. Plan on being there a week after you get me the video while I settle with the buyer. I'll contact you again in October when the last teams will be in place."

The general stalked out. The man flipped

through the briefcase. Now he had time on his hands. Time he could use finding his own buyers. What would it hurt to have a backup plan, cutting the general out? He owed him no loyalty.

The general paid him for the intel but didn't make use of it. He didn't understand how dangerous and hard to control these kids would be. The more he found out, the more he regretted taking this job, but it had appeared so simple at first. Sure, they could fight like demons, but a little tranquilizer, some restraints, a hostage or two, to keep them cooperative, it seemed so easy. But he'd seen more now. He didn't think it would be possible to capture Anastasia. No way would he be anywhere near that attempt.

Charlie and Sebastian would be manageable, especially if they got the parents. He was afraid of Oliver, what he did was purely magical, and he was sure they didn't know all his abilities.

Sara was the real money. Not only were her abilities worth more, but she would also be the easiest to take and control. He would make sure to be there when they took her.

Her abilities were magical as well, but benign. Without her team, she was helpless. He looked forward to putting her in her place.

Jumping from that helicopter had caused him a lot of trouble. If she thought waving a gun was a threat; he had some gun waving to show her.

- 18 -

CUB SCOUT CAMP

Four days later, Team Valor arrived at their private boot camp.

"I hope they don't separate us." Sara rested both hands on the window as she stared at the rough wooden buildings coming into sight.

"We're here to learn to work together, so if they separate us, it won't be for long," Oz reassured her.

Charlie gave her a quick kiss on the temple and leaned over her shoulder to peer out the window. The rough dirt road they drove down looked deserted. No other vehicles had passed them in forty-five minutes. They'd passed through a gate in a chain-link fence and another stretch of dirt road and then through another gate; this one locked with both a padlock and a mechanical keypad. A narrower dirt lane led into a small valley.

"Home-sweet-home guys," Guthrie said as they pulled up to a small wooden building. "This is Camp UBM Practice, or as it's affectionately called Cub Scout Camp."

"That sounds promising." Stasia rolled her eyes.

A row of squat metal buildings lined the road that circled around a grassy square with a few trees and three picnic tables. It reminded Charlie of a college quad. An obstacle course and track where visible in the distance. Metal rooftops peeked over a copse of pine trees. Low hills covered with junipers and pines formed a dense green background.

Guthrie exited the car and gestured expansively. "Okay, this building where we are now is HQ; the phones are inside here. The main office is here. Right next door is our cafeteria slash dispensary. Next, we have the women's barracks. You'll be staying there, girls, and the following two buildings are men's barracks.

Across the compound, in the smaller wooden buildings is officer quarters. Major Nelson will be in charge here, and Captain Sanders will be here now and then. I'll be around too sometimes, but you'll take your orders from the major.

"Major Harris won't be here until the last week. Go get settled in and changed. Wear full armor unless told otherwise. When you're off duty, you can wear the fatigues. At night, you can sleep in sweats or skivvies, it's up to you. This will be similar to boot camp like you've been reading up on. Be on time for meals and lights-out. Good luck, guys. Make me proud."

After exiting the car, they grabbed their bags and separated. The girls going in one barracks the boys another.

The first week at Cub Scout Camp, they did basic physical drills followed by obstacle courses and hikes, both with the Scouts and alone. As time went on, they started simple scenarios with gradually increasing complexity. Captain Sanders flew everyone to practice drops without parachutes, using Sara's Levitate.

Sara held Todd Jones in a tight embrace. Even with a chute, the jumps scared him.

"Don't worry, I won't drop you," she whispered. "One drop like this, and then you can wear a chute."

Wind whipped by them as they stood in

the open door of the plane waiting for Brenda to tell them to jump.

Todd nodded jerkily, keeping a tight grip on Sara.

Brenda said, "Go."

He closed his eyes and jumped, holding Sara hard. When the levitate took hold, his grip relaxed.

"Sorry," he mumbled as his hold slackened.

Sara laughed. "This is hard for everyone. Tony threw up on me. You're doing great. You can have a chute for the rest of our jumps, but I swear I won't let you fall."

"With a chute, and you, this could even be fun," he agreed. Todd's grip relaxed even more the closer they drifted to the ground.

Sara punched him on the shoulder.

"Tomorrow's jump will be in a bigger group. I promise you'll be one of my first levitates."

Todd grinned at her.

She waved as she headed back to do another chute-less drop with Sam.

Todd ran off to meet Hawk. They were practicing using his air bubble underwater and working on learning their own version of sign language along with standard combat signs.

Captain Sanders and Major Nelson

observed from a distance as Team Valor and a team of Scouts worked a fake extraction of another group of Scouts.

"Chief always ends up being in charge," Major Nelson said with a short laugh as they watched Charlie send Hawk to a new position using hand signs.

"His decisions are almost always correct, and he's always fastest making them." Captain Sanders gave a small shrug. "I don't know if that's because they wait for him to do it or if he's naturally faster."

"I think it's part of his magic," Major Nelson said. "He was their leader. I think he always will be. They lead groups he's not in fine but put him in the group, and everybody listens to him. Look at my men, they outrank everyone there, and have more combat experience and training, and they listen just like the rest do. Hell, even I do it," the major admitted, sounding embarrassed.

Captain Sanders nodded and held the binoculars to his eyes. "The UBM raids we studied showed he's always had a good grasp on the tactical situation. He's also a natural at using people to the best of their ability. Sara helps him with that. Watch them set up a scenario sometime, she'll shake her head a tiny bit if he picks someone for a spot or job she doesn't agree with. He asks for options and, very tactfully, she'll point out something better. I've talked with people in their old guild, discreetly of course, and they always did that."

"When they get the chance they still fight the same way," Major Nelson agreed. "Chief sets the strategy. Sara does the positioning. Hawk calls out targeting. Oz and Stasia kill things with Stasia checking the area, calling for special circumstances, and reminding everyone of timers. Oz calls for all of their crowd control while Chief oversees the entire thing." He paused thoughtfully. "Even without magic he would've been formidable, he's a natural warrior."

"Do you think the magic is aging them prematurely?" Captain Sanders followed Oz's movements through his binoculars as he climbed the side of the building. "Physically, Team Valor is indistinguishable from the more mature Scouts."

"No, Liz assures me they're right where they should be, it just seems like it because they're so physically fit. I admit, Charlie doesn't look like a typical sixteen-year-old boy. If I just met him, I would guess eighteen or nineteen. Stasia looks the same as ever. Hawk is taller now, we expect him to reach a bit over six feet before he's done growing. Charlie will be bigger, his brother's size at least. Pictures of Rick at sixteen show they look a lot alike. Charlie is more muscled now, but he works out more than Rick ever did. Oz hasn't changed much, he was always slim and fit, he's more muscular now, but the exercise here explains that. Sara has changed the most. Every day she looks more like her mother. Liz assures me that's normal as well. Regardless of the magic, she would've resembled her. The fact they're so intelligent also makes them appear older than they are. They don't fidget or act like young teenagers."

"We need to remember they are, even though they don't look it," Captain Sanders said. "I recall being that age and thinking I knew everything. We can run into real problems if they decide they don't need adult supervision."

Major Nelson grimaced. "It's hard to balance, giving them free time and privacy, while assuring they aren't doing anything they shouldn't."

Captain Sanders chuckled. "If Charlie figures out the Scouts are keeping him from meeting Sara alone on purpose, there'll be hell to pay."

Major Nelson laughed too and winced. "I

can't blame him for wanting time alone with his girlfriend, but I can't let them have that time. Not while I'm in charge. We really don't need a teen pregnancy here. This would have been so much better if there were no girls on Team Valor to begin with."

Captain Sanders laughed again. "They'd still be teenage boys. You think this a problem wait until the other start dating girls who don't know a thing about all this. Keep them busy and tired. In a few weeks, they go home, and it's Charlie's parent's problem. Major Harris will talk to Sara about safe sex. She'll be talking to all of them about it."

"The sooner, the better," Major Nelson agreed as he watched them carry the straw dummy's they used as hostages from the house.

Chief held one under each arm and walked easily. An easy hop took him to the top of an eight-foot cinderblock wall. The mannequins tumbled to the grass as he leaned down, pulling Oz and then Sara up. He drew Sara into his side for a moment but didn't kiss her. After lowering both Sara and Oz off the wall, he gave a hand to the remaining Scouts. Stasia and Hawk stood beside him on the wall, both jumping there effortlessly and lifting their teammates over. Everyone jumped down, and Chief picked up the dummies and jogged after his team.

"The dummies are weighted," Captain Sanders said. "Two hundred pounds each and he's carrying them as if they really are straw. This scenario needs to be redone using less showy tactics. No normal man could carry them like that."

"I want to redo this scenario with just Team Valor and an all-out effort not trying to hide their abilities."

Captain Sanders gave a small snort of laughter. "Do that last. They're likely to destroy the house."

"It would be so damn cool to do what they do," Major Nelson said wistfully. "I wish I could throw fireballs or heals."

"You play a mage now?" Captain Sanders glanced at him in surprise.

"No, I'm still a warrior. But I do love to Spell-Steal the fireballs." He flicked his finger in the Spell-Steal pattern and pretended to toss a fireball. "You know, it's a good thing they were such organized players. If they used addons or even different key binds this would be much harder to learn."

"Their layouts are logical," Captain Sanders agreed. "We all use it, it's mandatory. If we ever get magic of our own, we'll be ready."

"Any word from higher up about letting them attempt to infect one of us?"

"Nothing official. Pierce is running simulations. I don't think they'll let them try though until we understand the magic better. Five people with magic who can't be stopped worries them. Besides, they have no idea how to do it."

"That concerns me too," Major Nelson admitted. "They're honest, trustworthy people though, which eases my mind." He grinned at the captain. "At their age, I don't know that I would've been as trustworthy. If I had Stasia's precog, I would've dragged Oz to the nearest casino and been driving a Lamborghini with my ill-gotten gains in days."

Captain Sanders laughed. "Yeah, at their age I would've bought my plane and had Oz disguise me as a movie star or something to score girls. I was hopelessly shy and crazy about flying."

"Stasia doesn't even shoplift, which she could do effortlessly; her moral character is very strong. Liz told me she shops a lot in her free time but doesn't buy much. Liz is keeping a careful eye on her. Some of the things Stasia wants are expensive. The temptation to take them must be overwhelming, but she hasn't yet," Major Nelson said admiringly.

"The United States was lucky when the magic came to them." Captain Sanders gestured to the Scouts gathered in the distance. "All of them are good people, not one slacker or troublemaker in the group. What do you think the odds of that are?"

"Pretty good actually," Major Nelson assured him. "The eight Marines were already headed for full time military careers. Granted, not in their current fields, but everyone had plans to make the military their careers. The Army Rangers did too. Staff Sergeant Guthrie was already a lifer; my men too. They went through training with no buffs. They're dedicated. The entire process tends to weed out the weak or weak willed. Before any of this, these guys all wanted to be part of something larger than themselves and to aid their fellow Americans. Now that they have these special abilities, well, I think, they feel it more, the need to use them to help others."

"True," Captain Sanders said thoughtfully. "We did drop the no-goes, leaving only the dedicated ones. Not that they weren't good men and woman too."

Major Nelson nodded in agreement. "We have a good bunch here, men and women I'm proud to serve with."

"Me too," Captain Sanders agreed and handed his binoculars to Major Nelson. "I'm headed to town for more supplies. I'll bring back pizzas to reheat. Everyone could use a treat; they've been working hard."

"Take one of the boys and call for a summons. Let them have fresh, hot pizza." Major Nelson suggested.

Captain Sanders laughed. "All three can come; I wish she could summon me too."

"Party only spell," Major Nelson reminded him.

The captain nodded. "I'm not even in the raid now. They were using me to see if their CC was noticeable from the victim's perspective as magic. I've been sapped, sheeped, hypnotized, trapped, and frozen. Every spell that wouldn't kill me, they've tried on me. Some of them are damn unpleasant."

Major Nelson laughed. "What's being sheeped like?"

"Odd, I wrote a full report on it, but Polymorph feels like you're dreaming and confused. My legs and arms wouldn't respond as if I'd had a stroke or something. Sara was laughing, so I wasn't too paranoid, but you can't control your movements, and the perspective changes making colors appear different. You can still see and hear, but things sound slightly off too. If it happened to someone who didn't know about the magic, I'm sure they would think a weird medical condition was happening, like I did."

"I'll have to leave the raid and try it," Major Nelson said.

"Sara's hypnotize feels like sleepwalking or something. Unless she does it a few times in a row, you aren't even conscious you're doing anything. After a few times, you're aware but can't stop it. If she's trying to maintain secrecy, she should only do it twice, any more than that and the target might notice."

"Stasia's sap?" the major asked.

"The hit doesn't hurt; it feels like you blacked-out for a minute or fell asleep. Sap can be used unnoticeably. If you weren't alert, you might not even remember the hit. If she distracts first it's hard to notice it, you almost can't. Distract is cool. You don't even realize you were distracted. You would swear you were looking where you intended to the entire time."

"After I read the report, I'll let them try that stuff on me. I'll go get the boys and spread the word about pizza tonight." With ease, Major Nelson jumped over the low wall they stood at and ran down the hill.

- 19 -

MISUNDERSTANDINGS

The pizza place was the first stop where they ordered twenty pizzas to go, to be ready in two hours. A group of girls hanging out there gave the boys the eye as they entered. Oz stopped to talk as Captain Sanders ordered.

The girls seemed disappointed they weren't staying in town. Oz was invited back and to a party that weekend. Two of the girls slipped him notes when he left.

Charlie laughed when they returned to the truck. "Can't leave you alone for a minute, can we."

Oz read his notes and handed one to Charlie. "Can I help it if they're bored and never see anyone new? This note is for you."

Charlie read it, blushed, and threw the note out the window. Oz laughed and turned to Hawk. "We're invited to a party this weekend. Charlie was invited to a private party whenever he wanted."

When Captain Sanders looked worried, Oz rolled his eyes. "Relax, we know we can't go." He turned to Hawk, who looked disappointed, and punched him on the shoulder. "We'll be home soon. There'll be more parties. They were nice though. It's a shame we can't get away."

They did the shopping, loaded the truck, and headed back for the pizza. Captain Sanders groaned when they arrived at the pizza place.

Every girl in town under twenty-five had decided to get pizza tonight, Charlie thought and snickered.

"Jesus, they must be bored out of their minds," Hawk said when he saw the turnout.

Oz stifled a laugh. "Population six hundred, it would be shooting fish in a barrel. Any new face is probably welcome." Oz exited the truck, said hello to the girls he'd met before, and introduced Hawk as Charlie and the captain paid.

Hawk excused himself to help carry the pizza.

Oz told lies about where they were from and where they were going, laughing as they drove away. He handed out more notes to everyone, including Captain Sanders.

Charlie tossed his away unread. Hawk read his, reddened, then laughed and threw his away too. They split up the pizza boxes and called for a summons.

Fresh hot pizza thrilled everyone.

"O-M-G this pizza is so good!" Stasia said as she took her fifth slice. "I miss junk food so much; you should go every week for pizza." She looked surprised when Oz and Hawk laughed, and Charlie blushed. "What?" she asked with narrowed eyes.

The boys laughed harder.

"I'll go," Oz said cheerfully.

Charlie took another slice, keeping his head lowered. The heat of Sara's stare on him made his blush deepen.

Stasia narrowed her eyes at her brother. "What?" she repeated. "Ah, a girl," she said as Hawk flushed. "More than one girl," she added as her brother looked away.

"A lot more than one," Oz agreed with a smug grin, helping himself to more pizza. "We were very popular there; it's a really friendly town."

"I'm sure it was." Stasia laughed and continued to eat the pizza with an occasional smile at her brother.

The pizza sat on Sara's plate uneaten as

Charlie blushed and evaded her gaze.

Stasia's eyes widen, and she glanced at Charlie. He avoided eye contact with everyone, paying complete attention to his food and her smile changed to a frown. Another quick glance showed Sara still upset, she shrugged and turned to Oz.

"So, these girls… made some new friends then?" The red blush climbing up Charlie's neck into his cheeks made her wince.

Sara looked stricken, her face whitened, and her voice shook when she excused herself.

When Sara entered the barracks, Stasia turned angrily on Charlie. "Jesus, that was a shitty way to break up with her!"

Charlie peered up in surprise. "What?"

"Could you look guiltier?" Stasia asked in disgust. "She isn't retarded! Everyone here noticed. If you don't want to date her, that's fine, but you don't need to be an ass."

"What?" Charlie repeated in an angrier voice. "I never said anything like that."

Stasia sighed in exasperation. "Your guilt said it all."

Oz and Hawk watched wide-eyed as Stasia half rose to lean into Charlie's face.

"I get it, you met some pretty, local girls, and they liked you. Good for you, he just should've broken up with her first kindly, not let her find out like that."

"There was nothing to find out." Charlie glared at Stasia.

Oz laughed. "Nothing happened at all. You're totally overreacting."

Stasia shrugged. "If nothing happened, why was he blushing so bad? If he didn't do anything, why couldn't he meet her eyes?"

Brenda chimed in. "I have to agree with Stasia here, it was a shitty thing to do." She glared at Charlie. "In the future, you tell the old girlfriend, *privately*, before moving on."

"I haven't moved on!" Charlie yelled.

Brenda regarded him doubtfully. "If you were my boyfriend, I wouldn't believe that. You looked guilty as hell. I'm not saying you did a thing, but your blush made it clear you wanted to."

She left the table. Stasia grabbed a box of pizza and followed.

"What the hell?" Charlie yelled after them and then turned a furious glower on Oz who held up his hands and laughed. Hawk snickered, turning it into a cough when Charlie glared at him. Tony grinned at him, and Rick frowned.

"I didn't do a thing!" Charlie repeated indignantly.

Tony snickered. "I believe that, but you did sort of give yourself away there."

"I didn't want to do a thing either!" he yelled hotly.

Tony rose an eyebrow as Oz laughed again.

"That was embarrassment, not interested. Jesus!" Charlie snapped and stood.

Tony laid a hand on his arm. "It's okay to be interested in other girls. It's normal to have a lot of different girlfriends. We all feel bad when we break up with people, but it's worse to wait and let them think things that aren't true. You can want to date her and other people." Tony laughed and punched his arm lightly. "I don't think she'll agree to that, but be honest. Sara's a good kid and deserves honesty."

"Jesus Christ!" Charlie bellowed. "I didn't do a thing! I love Sara. Can I help it if girls flirt? I wasn't interested!"

Tony shrugged and continued eating. Charlie headed to the women's barrack, and his brother grabbed his arm.

"Be sure," Rick said. "If you go in there and tell her you love her and then break up with her when you get back to civilization, she'll have a hard time trusting anyone again."

"Not you too," he said to his brother in

disbelief.

"You did appear interested." Rick gave an apologetic shrug. "I believe you. Make sure you know what you want before speaking with her."

Charlie jerked out of his brother's grasp and went to find Sara. He found her crying in her bunk.

"Everyone's informed me I've been an ass. That was embarrassment, not interest. Yes, girls were there, so what! There'll be girls everywhere. I'm sorry if I gave you the wrong impression, but you should trust me. I've never done a thing to betray your trust. You know I'm not a liar. There has never been, or ever will be, anyone else for me. I love you; you should know that by now. I'll love you forever. That you don't trust me hurts." The sound of her soft crying followed him out.

The target dummies rocked under his blows as he tried to burn off his anger. Sara arrived and sat watching, but he didn't stop. He attacked the target dummy until his rage was spent and then faced her with his hands on his hips. Brow beaded with sweat and eyes narrowed, he took several deep breaths to calm himself.

She started to cast on him, and he frowned. "Stop. Don't Soothe me, don't ever do that. Let me feel what I feel. Right now, I'm angry."

"Yeah, I see that. I'm sorry," she said uncertainly.

Captain Sanders and Major Nelson watched from a distance as Charlie and Sara faced each other.

"This doesn't look good," the captain said. "Broken hearts are sure to complicate this."

The major snorted. "Damn girls," he muttered under his breath.

Charlie glared. Sara's eyes were red and puffy from crying, and his glare deepened. She said nothing, merely watched him. Minutes went by with him glaring and her pleating the folds of her t-shirt.

Sara finally spoke without looking up from her nervous fingers still twining together in her lap, "I'm sorry I doubted you, but —"

"But nothing, there's no reason to doubt me, ever! If you found me naked in bed with a supermodel, you should assume aliens abducted me and placed me there, not that I wanted to be. I would never hurt you like that. Would you do that to me?"

She shook her head no so hard blonde hair covered her face. With a trembling hand, she pushed her hair behind her ears.

"How could you think for one second I would change my mind?"

"You wouldn't meet my eyes." Sara stared down at her fingers now clenched together. "Until then, I didn't think anything bad." Fresh tears came to her eyes.

"You're a fool," he snapped and then sighed and hugged her.

She clutched him, making fists in his t-shirt.

Charlie sighed again. "This is partly my fault; I should've trusted you too. I was embarrassed and didn't want you to get mad. I'll never lie to you. You can trust me."

"I won't lie to you either," she whispered into his shoulder.

"I can't promise I won't find other girls attractive, but I can promise, you'll always have my heart."

She punched him in the arm. "I can promise, if I catch you looking, there'll be hell to pay!"

He grinned. "Fair enough." He kissed her lips. "No one compares to you," he whispered as he traced her brow with a finger.

Sara hugged him, resting her face on his shoulder. They stood quietly a few minutes.

"This is hard," she admitted in a soft voice. "I believe you mean what you say, but

I'm afraid you'll change your mind. You're so beautiful other girls will want you. How can I not be jealous?"

"Doesn't matter who wants me," Charlie said. "I only want you."

Sara shivered and hugged him tighter. "I love you."

"Forever?" he asked, his voice deep and husky.

She nodded. "Yes."

"I'll love you forever too. Please don't doubt that. I don't doubt you." Charlie pushed her gently away and kissed her lips and brow. "We both have places we should've been thirty minutes ago. Trust in my love for you, Sara. We'll be together forever, I promise." She nodded and turned to go.

"Well?" Major Nelson asked the captain as they watched her walk away, wiping tears from her eyes.

"I don't know," Captain Sanders said as Charlie patted the target dummy and jogged off.

Sara returned to the barracks, showered, changed into sweatpants, and headed to bed, exhausted. Normally, she studied an hour or so before bedtime, but her books remained unopened. Stasia sat by her, still wearing fatigues, and placed a comforting hand on her shoulder.

Sara sat up, started crying, and hugged Stasia hard. "Everything's okay, it was a misunderstanding. I should've trusted him. I almost ruined everything. Being in love is so hard. I'm so worried I'll screw it up."

Stasia patted her back and laughed in relief. "I'm glad you two are good. The way he reacted, well…I thought for sure you guys were splitting up."

Sara cried harder. "God, me too. That was the worst sensation, worse than anything, even the fire in my bones when the magic hit. It scares me how much I need him. I think it would kill me if he left me."

Brenda and Joy entered, and Stasia smiled and waved them away when they approached. "We're fine!"

Sara pulled away from Stasia, wiping her eyes.

"I don't know why I'm still crying. I'm just so relieved. God, Stasia, I'm so pathetic." Sara sobbed, hiccupped, and wiped her eyes hard, trying to stop the tears.

Stasia rose and rubbed Sara's head briskly. "Get some sleep; you'll feel better. He loves you, and you love him, nothing is wrong."

Stasia hugged her again before heading to the showers.

Sara cried herself to sleep.

Brenda and Joy waited in the locker room of the women's shower to speak with Stasia.

"They're fine; she's a bit overwrought is all. It's relief more than anything. I feel kind of bad I helped cause that, but he did look guilty as hell."

Brenda laughed. "Hey, I thought so too. I couldn't imagine what he could've gotten up to in that small amount of time, but I was sure it was something."

"Unless he lied," Joy said cynically.

"No," Brenda and Stasia said simultaneously.

"He wouldn't lie, I'm certain of that," Stasia said. "Those Hayes boys are solid. Their middle names should be integrity. I thought he was tired of dating her. Boys do that, they move on to the first pretty girl who crosses their path."

Joy shrugged. "The trick is to enjoy them while you have them." She grinned, flicked her towel at Brenda, and jumped in the shower.

MAGICAL ILLNESS

That night, Sara rose from bed, tripping on the sheet tangled around her. "Charlie?" she mumbled, her gait uneven and hesitant. At the doorway, she called for Charlie again.

Joy sat up as she left.

"Sara?" she called. When she received no reply, she followed.

Sara headed straight to the men's barracks, walked in, and called louder. Her voice sounded uncertain as if she wasn't sure he was there or would answer. "Charlie?"

"Sara?" Oz sat up, rubbing his eyes. "Is everything okay?"

Hawk got up and hit the lights. "Are you awake?" he asked with a slight laugh.

Sara stood unmoving right inside the doorway. Two small red patches high on her cheekbones showed starkly against her pale face. Dark smudges made crescents beneath her half-closed eyes.

"Charlie?" she called again in a thin, wavering voice without acknowledging Hawk or Oz.

Oz glanced at Charlie's bed next to his, but he hadn't awoken. Everyone else in the room had sat up.

Joy stepped to Sara's side and said, "What's going on?"

Oz reached over to wake Charlie. "Jesus, he's burning up!" he exclaimed.

Sara lay next to Charlie, cast a heal on him, rested her face on his bare shoulder, sighed deeply, and closed her eyes. Oz reached over and touched her forehead.

"Her too."

"Everyone out of here!" Joy ordered. "Oz, and Hawk, go shower. Rick, get Major Nelson, Captain Sanders, and Guthrie. Tony, wake Stasia. If she's sick bring her here, if not tell her to take a shower."

Joy felt Sara and Charlie's brows.

Charlie opened his eyes, surprised to find himself in bed with Joy leaning over him and Sara in his arms.

"Sara, heal yourself!" Joy said in a commanding voice.

Sara made an incoherent sound and

snuggled closer to Charlie.

Joy grabbed her shoulder and shook her as Charlie sat up, his confusion changing to worry.

"She's sick?" he asked in disbelief. "What happened? Jeez, she's burning up." He placed his palm on her forehead then her cheek, then shifted her until she lay across his lap. Both he and Joy tried to shake her awake.

An incoherent murmur was the only response they got.

Joy slapped Sara's cheeks lightly. "Wake up. You need to heal yourself! Charlie is fine now."

Sara opened her eyes and cast another heal on Charlie and herself. "He needs me," she mumbled and closed her eyes again.

Joy touched Charlie's forehead, then Sara's. She glanced up, her expression grim, as Major Nelson ran into the room in his boxer shorts.

"Sara is sick. Charlie was sick, but she healed him. Keep the rest of them away from her."

"Why didn't she heal herself?" Major Nelson felt Sara's brow.

"She did." Joy's eyes narrowed, and she felt Sara's forehead again. "Get a thermometer, and we should give her saline and aspirin."

Major Nelson ran back out the door and began shouting orders.

"How're you feeling Charlie?" Joy asked.

"Tired, a bit achy. Will she be okay?" He laid his palm against Sara's brow again.

"We need her to heal herself again. Let's get her awake." Joy said as she shook Sara and slapped her cheeks again.

Major Nelson ran back in with the dusty first-aid kit. He pulled out a thermometer, and everyone gasped in dismay at the reading. "One hundred and eight-point-three. Jesus, check Charlie." Major Nelson leaned over trying to read the thermometer.

Joy checked and rechecked it. "This isn't good, his is climbing."

"I'm okay. I think I'm taking her damage. Get me bandages from Oz." Charlie stole Sara's biggest heal and cast it on her. The major ran out the door, returning in less than a minute with a stack of bandages. "Oz made them already. Rick was bringing them."

The bandages absorbed instantly on every application. Major Nelson applied bandages to both Charlie and Sara until hitting the cooldown.

Sara sighed and opened her eyes. "Why is it so cold in here?" she murmured, pushing upright, trying to get closer to Charlie. He wrapped the light blanket around them both, pressing her to his chest.

Charlie lay back in bed holding Sara against him. Her forehead resting on his cheek seemed cooler than it had been. He glanced at his watch and closed his eyes.

Joy rechecked her temperature. "The fever's going down," she said in relief.

Charlie nodded acknowledgment but didn't move or open his eyes, busy counting out the Spell-Steal timer in his head.

Joy and the major left to grab the IV set up from Rick. No one noticed the blue mist of magic as it went from Charlie to Sara.

Where their bare skin touched a light blue mist formed and reabsorbed.

Joy and Major Nelson put an IV in both Charlie and Sara. Joy took blood samples from them both and retook their temperatures. Charlie's was normal. Sara's still dropped. Sara fell back asleep after casting her biggest heals on both of them.

"When my cooldown is up, I'll heal her again." Charlie laid the back of his hand on her hot brow. "What's wrong with her?"

Joy shrugged. "No idea," she admitted. "Caught a bug I guess. She's getting better now. Let her rest and keep healing her. Are you still achy?"

"No, I'm fine. Can you get us another blanket? She's still shivering." Charlie stroked Sara's forehead again in concern. "She still seems feverish."

Joy retook her temperature. "The temperature is dropping. I'll get you a blanket." Rick followed her, leaving Charlie and Sara alone.

"Are the others okay?" Joy asked Rick.

"They seem fine. Are my brother, and Sara?"

"Charlie is better. Sara is getting better. Call Doctor Elliot and have him come here. Give the blood samples to Captain Sanders; he can fly them to the closest lab. We need to know what that was."

Rick nodded and ran off, carrying the samples.

Within an hour, Sara was fine, just tired. She fell asleep in Charlie's arms as they stood by his bed talking.

"Let her stay here and rest," Charlie said as Joy went to move her. He'd gone from relaxed to furious so fast it actually hurt. Every muscle in his body felt tensed to spring. The strength of his overreaction shocked him, but Joy was taking Sara over his dead body. He needed her right beside him.

It must have shown on his face because both Major Nelson and Joy took a step back.

Neither said anything and Charlie lay back down, taking Sara with him, but kept a watchful eye on them in case the major decided to push the issue and take her while he slept.

The thought angered him all over again, and he half sat, leaning over Sara on one elbow.

"Relax, she can stay with you till your certain she's recovered," Major Nelson said.

Charlie sat up further, laying Sara across his lap. "Did our fight cause this?" He asked as he stroked Sara's hair, letting the fine golden strands sift through his fingers. She didn't stir, sleeping so heavily it worried him.

Major Nelson shook his head. "How could it have? She must have picked up a bug somewhere."

"Why didn't her heal work?" Charlie stole her heal and used it on her again. The yellow glow filled her and dissipated. She didn't wake.

"Maybe they did, and it took a few minutes because she was so sick." Joy checked both of their temperatures again. "Rest, I'll check on you soon."

She touched the major's arm and gestured

to the door, leaving them together on the small bed. Charlie was already dozing off.

"He might be right." Joy whispered as they left. Once they were alone outside, she continued. "Sara was upset about the fight and cried herself to sleep. Maybe she made herself sick with worry."

Major Nelson frowned.

"That would explain why her own heal didn't work, she caused it. Not on purpose," she went on hurriedly. "I think she was just so upset. When Charlie healed her, she got better."

Major Nelson's frown deepened. "If that's true and Charlie was taking half her damage, she could've killed herself."

"Let's hope they don't fight again." Joy packed up the first-aid kit, fingering the thermometer a moment before putting it back.

"If you see her that upset again, call right away. Keep an eye on her, a close eye. Check her temperature frequently over the next few days; we can't let it get so high. If she hadn't been able to heal Charlie and he, her— well, Oz's bandages wouldn't be enough."

"I'll check everyone," Joy assured him. "We need to run tests when she wakes and make sure she didn't damage herself or her magic. That high of a fever can cause brain damage."

"Doctor Elliot will be here tomorrow. Sara needs a thorough examination. Hell, we should give everyone an exam and have Sara heal everyone. If we have a bug, let's squash it flat." Major Nelson stood with his hands on his hips, and his eyes narrowed, glaring at the girl's barracks.

Joy nodded and went to check everyone.

Two weeks later, Captain Sanders observed through binoculars as Team Valor finished a ten-mile run. "They're doing well, are you sure they aren't cheating?" He asked Guthrie who stood next to him using binoculars.

"No, they're running it straight. They have more fortitude than normal."

"Major Nelson wants to take them out fifty miles and see how long they take to find their way back without a locate spell."

"Them or the entire team?"

"Just them."

"I'm betting three hours."

"For fifty miles? I think you overestimate them." Captain Sanders grinned at Guthrie. "More like six to eight hours."

"We'll see." Guthrie smiled and rose the

binoculars again.

They were both wrong. Team Valor took two hours and twenty-five minutes to find their way back. The next evening, they watched through night-vision goggles as the entire team infiltrated the top floor of a building. The mission was to rescue five people in the basement without being noticed.

Flash powder rigged to explode lined the doors and windows. Ten minutes later, the five hostages stood outside, mission successful.

"They're leaving the raid behind a lot to clear." Captain Sanders noted as he viewed the recordings.

"Yeah, the raid slows them down, but they're working well with them. The new hand signals they've worked out are really helping."

Captain Sanders stopped the video and pointed at the screen. "Stasia is out of position whenever Rick is in any danger. That could become a serious liability. See, he exits the building, and she waits and checks him before going on. It's subtle, he might not even notice, but every time she hesitates before moving to her next position, and the danger now is slight."

"I'll speak with her. Keep an eye on it to see if she stops. Sara and Charlie don't seem to have a problem. I admit, I was worried about them." Guthrie leaned forward to watch the video.

"No, no problem *per-sey*, but they're freakishly in tune even when they can't see each other, more so than any other team members. Next week, I'm splitting them up doing three-day rotations. Each group will have to track and rescue and fight a small battle. We'll be giving them subordinate positions to see how they do with others in charge."

Four weeks later, Captain Sanders spoke on a video call with the president.

"The reports and videos you sent were impressive. Are they ready for assignments?" President Carmichael asked.

"The Scouts are ready and willing to go to work. The cubs… well, training wise, they're top notch, but they're still young. Major Nelson and I think we could use them domestically. Let them find lost hikers or something and see how that goes before putting them in the field."

"Yes, I read that recommendation in your report. We have a lot of money invested in them; let's get some use from it. I'll authorize

Agent Lewis to use them locally. I agree we can start them off slow and see how they do."

"Keep in mind they're still in high school. We can't pull them out for jobs without arousing suspicion."

"Yes, we're considering our options there. The boys will be juniors, the girl's sophomores and Sebastian a freshman this school term, correct?"

"Yes. Honestly, they could all pass the SAT's or ACT and get a GED. They've been doing college classes here. Keeping Oz and Sara supplied with reading matter is a full-time job. I'm more concerned with the parent's reaction if we pull them from school."

"Reputation is still a priority. Get Sara and Oz any books or supplies they ask for. The changes they made in the spell-bars are brilliant and not just the programming but the components. Dr. Elliot was thrilled with the new bone density scanner they made him and they made that from plumbing fittings and a laptop."

The two men exchanged rueful grimaces. Sara and Oz had begun requesting expensive machine parts to use in their experiments.

"I'm worried if we take them from school and it upsets the parents, our rep could lower." The president paused a moment. "Get them tutors able to keep up with them academically, but keep them in school. Before doing anything, let me talk to Pierce about the parent's probable reaction if we remove them from school. How much longer will they be at Cub Scout Camp?"

"One more week, which gets them home three days before school starts."

"Pierce and Agent Lewis will keep their eyes open for suitable missions, but I want them kept under control, no running off on their own. Don't let them be seen using magic. By some miracle, we've managed to keep this secret. Let's keep it that way."

"Yes, sir, Mr. President."

"Keep me informed," the president said and hung up.

- 21 -

GRADUATION

Major Nelson handed a slip of paper with coordinates to each team. "Okay, people, this is the last test. This will be a high-altitude jump. We're coming in from different directions and meeting at those coordinates.

"The mission is a hostage situation with six hours before the first one is killed. Hawk, and, Sara, you're with team Alpha. Stasia, Oz, and Chief, you're with Beta. The squad leaders are in command. If anyone is spotted, our operation is blown."

Major Nelson gave instructions for a few more minutes before the teams headed out.

The jumps went well; they had been practicing all summer. The groups met up as planned. Major Nelson led them to a large warehouse complex. "Alpha, are you in position?" he whispered into his mic.

"Roger that," came Brenda's soft reply. "Four tangos are on the second floor, twelve on the top floor; none on ground level."

With a wave of his hand, Major Nelson indicated that Beta was to precede him. A glance at his spell-bar showed all bars green.

"Okay, Beta, full infiltrate."

The spell icon displayed Oz cast Wink and Invisible Duo. Another glance at his spell-bar showed Stasia was now invisible.

"Hold. Explosives on the doors and windows," Oz whispered. "Bottom left window is now clear."

"We're in," Glen, Beta's team leader, said.

"Multiple booby traps line the stairs," Stasia reported a minute later. Two more minutes passed before she said, "Well, I found five people tied to chairs with explosives on their chests, but I don't think they're our guys."

"Explain." Major Nelson kept an eye on his spell-bars.

"Well, first of all, they don't match the picture we were given. Their bonds are loose enough to slip out of, there are weapons in the room, they don't seem scared, they appear eager, and they're dressed alike with combat boots on."

"Bad acting maybe? This is a scenario

after all. They aren't really hostages."

"Give me five minutes to check the rest of the building, sir," Stasia asked.

"Go."

Three minutes later, she reported. "Oz, I think you need to port through the door into the cellar."

"If I land on a trap it could blow the mission."

"If we rescue the enemy, it's blown as well."

"On my way." Oz broke the silence with a whispered, "Door's clear now. A booby trap was wired to blow if you opened the door."

Two minutes later, Stasia said, "I think I found the real ones."

"Squad leaders, move them out to Alpha's position." Major Nelson took out his night-vision goggles and watched his teams work.

"Incoming," Hawk warned. "Two trucks pulling in."

"Move those packages, Beta," Major Nelson said.

"Package's secure," squad leader Alpha replied, "moving back now."

"All squads, fallback to the rendezvous point."

"Our trail is clear," Hawk reported.

Major Nelson called for pickup. "That

was a good catch, Stasia. I should've known they would get tricky. Advance reports say no one noticed anything suspicious and the men involved are wondering how we managed so quickly. Good work team. You all did a great job keeping the magic under wraps. Keep it up."

Back at camp, General Campbell waited to address them. "Training is complete, and you've all done well. The president sends his congratulations and thanks. Scouts, you'll be sent on missions with other branches of service, and we expect you to blend in as much possible. Keep up with your training. At any time, you could be called out to work with Team Valor on a mission using all of your abilities. I don't need to remind you how important it is that Team Valor remain a secret. Everything about them and what you've learned here is classified top-secret. When you're not on missions, you'll be stationed near them to give you a chance to practice together to stay sharp. I'm proud of each and every one of you. Together we'll make America a safer place. Dismissed."

Captain Sanders stood. "The Scouts get two weeks leave starting tomorrow. Sorry, Cubs, you get three days, and it's back to school for you."

The Scouts teased them good-naturedly as the groups split up.

General Campbell met with Major Nelson and Captain Sanders in the captain's office. "No sign of the bugs return?" General Campbell watched out the window as the Scouts and Cubs parted with laughing and jokes.

"None. All the tests came back good, and Charlie and Sara were fully recovered by morning with no ill effects or symptoms since," Major Nelson assured him.

"Everyone did well here at the camp," General Campbell said as he turned to the major.

"Yes, they take orders well, and it didn't seem to bother them to accept a minor role either." Major Nelson joined the general at the window.

General Campbell turned back to the window saying, "I wish they were a bit older, but time will fix that soon enough. Let them return to school, and we'll see about sending them on small, local missions."

"We'll be walking a fine line here. We don't want them to get bored with this project, but we don't want them to have too much free time either," Captain Sanders said as he joined them at the window.

"Believe me" – a small smile crossed the general's face— "I know what kind of trouble teenagers can get into. I had two of them. Let's give them more free time, and we'll find them something they can do to put their training to use. This group as a whole is very impressive. Let's preserve the forward momentum. Keep our interactions with them positive and our rep going up."

Since Sara and Oz had pulled out the plumbing to use in one of their experiments, two of the showers were out of order, leaving three working showers in the women's bathroom. Stasia and Sara waited their turn.

"When we get home, I'm going shopping." Stasia shook out the wrinkled t-shirt she took from her footlocker. "I miss stores and mall food."

"Yeah, me too. Since we've been here, I've gotten an entire inch taller. I need to get my hair trimmed before school starts, and you'll need to help me pick out clothes. In the past, I wore a uniform." Sara rummaged in her small cosmetic bag for soap.

"Sure, we can go together," Stasia agreed.

"You think Liz will take me for my driver permit?" Sara asked as she handed Stasia the soap.

Brenda laughed. "You two crack me up. Sometimes I forget how old you are. If she won't take you, I will. Any of the Scouts would."

Joy exited the shower.

"Dibs!" Brenda yelled and darted in.

"She's right," Joy said as she toweled off her short black hair. "It's hard to remember how old you two are. She's also right that any of us will teach you if Liz won't. Take time to be a kid; you'll grow up fast enough."

"Can we wear our regular clothes now?" Stasia examined her brown fatigues and curled her lip. "I'm so tired of these fatigues."

"Yeah, go ahead," Joy agreed. "You're officially off duty and I'm no longer your squad leader." Joy rose her voice. "Gina and Lee, your off duty too. Our leaves have officially started."

The women in the showers cheered and emerged moments later smiling.

Stasia and Sara entered the vacant showers and dressed in the clothes they'd arrived in when they emerged.

Stasia snorted with laughter when she saw Sara. "Um, give it up. It doesn't fit. Wear your sweatpants."

"I think they shrunk. There's no way I'm

fatter after all this running around," Sara complained as she tried to button her jeans.

Joy and Brenda burst out laughing too. "That shirt is two sizes too small for you now. You'll never get it buttoned." Brenda threw a clean, white t-shirt to her.

"How the hell did I get fat? Why didn't I notice it?"

"You're not fat." Stasia made an hourglass shape with her hands and smiled. "Just curvier. No more girl clothes for you. We have a lot of shopping to do."

"Hmm," Sara said. "I need a mirror. How come your clothes still fit you?"

"I already was curvy," Stasia said smugly. "Like my mom. She was the same size since fourteen too. Let's go find the boys. I want to say goodbye to Rick before he leaves." The two girls left together.

"Watch out boys," Joy said softly.

Brenda giggled. "Those two in high school… I don't remember looking like that."

"I'm sure you never spent a summer training like this either. Liz will have her hands full."

"Never mind Liz, poor Charlie."

Charlie laughed when Sara showed up in her sweats. "Your clothes wouldn't fit either?" He still wore sweatpants and a white t-shirt too.

"No"– she poked him— "Stop laughing; it isn't funny."

But she cracked a smile too.

"We're officially off duty now. Let's say we take a walk?" Charlie asked.

Sara smiled and took his hand. "I want to say goodbye to Rick first, okay?"

"Sure, he's inside. One minute, I'll get him."

Charlie ran off to get his brother. Rick came outside pulling on a t-shirt over his wet head. Stasia's eyes widen at the sight of his bare chest.

Sara hugged him and kissed his cheek. He promised to keep in touch if he could. Stasia stayed to make her own goodbye.

"You know Stasia has a huge crush on him," Sara said as she and Charlie walked down a dirt path holding hands.

"Everyone knows." Charlie laughed, but a frown crossed his face. "I kind of feel bad for them. If she'd been a bit older, I think my brother would've pursued her, but there's no way he will now."

"I know. She knows too. Don't worry, it'll work out. It's not like she won't have her pick of guys."

Charlie pulled her close and kissed her.

"What about you, will you have your pick?"

"I already picked," Sara said as she slid her hands under his t-shirt.

- 22 -

RETURN TO SCHOOL

Sara and Stasia spent the next three days shopping. They fit in a trip to the nail and hair salon.

Charlie picked her up in his mother's car the night before school started and his eyes lit at the sight of her. The two days without seeing her had felt like ten, and he couldn't wait to get her alone.

"Where do you want to go?" He held the door and waited till she tucked her skirt out of the way before closing it.

"How about the football field?"

Charlie groaned. "Can't. I'm sure people will be practicing there."

"I don't care where we are as long as I'm alone with you." Sara leaned over and kissed him.

"Right, me too. So, um, the beach?"

"Sure."

Charlie drove to the nearest beach. "Hmm, it's pretty crowded; everyone in Florida might be here."

Sara giggled. "What about a park then?"

Charlie checked the GPS. "Jeez, this feels like a conspiracy. The parks close at sunset."

"I don't know about you, but I'm willing to chance sneaking into one." Sara leaned over and lightly bit his neck then kissed the spot.

Heat built in his chest, making sweat spring up on his brow. "Yeah, I think we can manage that."

After checking the GPS for the nearest park, he parked in a small shopping center, and they walked to the park holding hands.

Three minutes after they arrived, someone else came with a flashlight. The light followed them around the park till Charlie leapt into a tree and Sara pulled herself up next to him. They sat together, not speaking until the person with the light left.

Charlie leaned his forehead on Sara's. "This isn't what I had in mind." Frustration made his voice harsh.

"Me either," Sara sighed. "Let's go to my house. As long as the door stays open, we can hang out in my room."

Charlie checked the time. "Your house it is. My parents will still be downstairs at mine." He jumped down, catching her when she jumped and kissing her before setting her on her feet. When they arrived at Sara's house, no one was home.

Sara pulled him down beside her on the bed.

He was kissing her neck with one hand on her bare thigh and the other on the button of her shirt when Liz came home.

"Sara, you home?" Liz called from the kitchen.

"Yes, Charlie and I are in my room," Sara said and hurriedly straightened.

Charlie groaned softly, sat up, and put his head in his hands. "This is ridiculous. I think we're cursed. I spent all summer with you and got no time alone. Everyone knows you get the girl when you go to camp. How come all I got was a quick kiss once in a while? Then we come home and can't find anywhere not crawling with people."

Sara giggled and leaned over to kiss his neck. Her mirth fled, her breath a warm caress, and her voice was low and serious when she said. "I want to be with you too. What do other kids do?"

"No one is as chaperoned as us. This is

ridiculous."

"Nobody can do what we can either. Maybe Oz will help. One little disguise and you're a forty-year-old man able to rent a room somewhere, or Stasia can pick a lock for us and let us into a room."

"Sara, you're a genius. I'll ask him tomorrow."

"Charlie, I love you and want to be with you forever. I can't imagine my life without you."

Charlie stared into her eyes as he pulled her close and leaned back onto her bed. She fit against him as if made for him. The kiss she gave him made him moan. His voice sounded rough and low when he spoke.

"I love you too. We belong together." His hand was sliding up her leg when Liz called from the kitchen.

"You guys want pizza? I have some left."

Charlie sighed and sat, pulling Sara up until she sat on his lap. "Sure," he called. "We would love some, thanks." He set Sara on her feet and with a determined smile left the room.

- 23 -

A NORMAL LIFE

Charlie picked Sara up for the first day of school. "Don't worry, my friends all like you, and you'll make your own friends before you know it." He ran a finger over her light frown.

Hawk, Stasia, and Oz, had walked to school together as usual and were already surrounded by friends they hadn't seen all summer.

Charlie grabbed Sara's hand and tugged her into the group.

"Jesus, Chief, I thought you were on a sports ban, but it looks like you've been on the roids," One of his old teammates said after giving him a quick hug.

"What can I say, I'm naturally buff." Charlie grinned at Sara and winked.

She laughed and rolled her eyes.

"Hey, Sara, you go to school here now?"

one of Charlie's friends asked her.

"Yes." She tightened her grip on Charlie's hand in both of hers.

Charlie gave her a reassuring smile and she lightened her grasp. When Marcy arrived, she hugged Oz, said hello to Stasia, and introduced Sara to her friends. The girls wandered off together. The boys followed behind bantering and joking.

Between every bell, Charlie met her and walked her to class. Some of Marcy's friends walked with them talking and laughing with Sara. Charlie grinned at them, happy Sara had already made friends.

The football coach cornered Charlie at lunch. By the time he got away, Sara sat with Oz, Marcy, and some of his old teammates.

"He wants me to play this year too, but my doctor won't let me," Charlie explained when his friends asked what was going on.

"Our bone density is low or something," Sara said and gave him a rueful grimace.

"Yeah, we have to wear medical alert bracelets and everything. If the beeper goes off, we have to get to the doctors right away. My football days are over," Charlie said sadly. The sadness wasn't fake, he'd loved playing football.

Sara squeezed his hand. When the bell rang, he pulled her into an embrace as the kids scrambled to leave.

"Maybe we can think of something else to do instead of football?" she whispered in his ear and kissed his neck.

His eyes lit with anticipation, and he smiled. "Yeah, that would be good."

A teacher shooed them to class. He ran to catch up with Oz. If he didn't get time alone with her soon, he was going to die of frustration.

On the third day of school, Charlie's new beeper went off in second period. With an apologetic shrug to the teacher, he left. He was excited. This was their first call.

Oz and Sara were together in a math class when the beepers went off.

Sara said, "Excuse me," and left.

Oz followed, leaving the gaping teacher staring after them.

Stasia was in the bathroom; she walked out unseen by anyone.

Hawk was in English class. His teacher told him to wait.

"I can't. I'm sorry it's a medical emergency," he said over his shoulder as he ran from the room.

Everyone piled into Charlie's car, and he

drove to the warehouse where Guthrie waited. "We have a mission. Get suited up, side arms and knives only, and be in my SUV in five minutes."

Within five minutes, they were driving down the road. "We're headed to the airport where we'll catch a helicopter. An amber alert broadcasted, and we thought this would make a good first mission. Our objective is to find this girl." Guthrie handed Stasia a picture. "When we locate her, we'll intercept. No deadly force – stuns only – no razzle-dazzle visible. At no time will you show yourselves. Am I clear?"

"Yes, sir!" they said in unison.

Stasia handed the picture to Oz.

"She's that way." He pointed north.

"This isn't a parental abduction so the child could be at risk. Don't let the kidnapper see you coming," Guthrie said.

A pilot waited for them, his helicopter already running. Oz sat in back, casting locate.

"Got her!" he said as his locate indicated they'd passed over her. "This is our stop, Sarge."

The helicopter hovered, letting them jump to a rooftop, and the copter peeled off.

"She's in front of us. Valor, let's go."

They roof hopped until Oz said, "Stop.

She's under us."

"Four in the building. I can't distinguish friend from foe," Hawk said.

"Swing me down to the window, Chief," Stasia said and turned herself invisible.

"I'm in," she reported a moment later.

"I see you. One to your left, two under you, one on the first floor," Hawk informed her where the people stood in the house.

"Checking left," Stasia said a few seconds later. "Not her, going down a floor." A minute later she said, "Not her, going down a floor, but get us some backup. These are some crazy, sick bastards."

"Copy that. Backup on its way," Guthrie said. "Are you in danger?"

"Not at all, but they're completely perverted. Not her on the first floor either. Looking for a basement." A minute later, "Holy mother of god!" Stasia sounded sick. "Six children are locked in here, Sarge."

"Are any in immediate danger?"

"Negative."

"Stay with them, Stasia. Hawk, no-see-um Chief, and Sara, then go into the neighbor's house and call in a complaint about screaming next door."

"Chief, Sara, stay ready to help Stasia if they attempt to harm the children."

Three minutes later, Hawk said, "I placed the call, and the police are sending a car."

"When the officer knocks, I want you to scream your head off, Stasia, and disappear."

"Roger that." Stasia's voice vibrated with anger.

Five minutes later, a patrol car appeared. When the officer approached the door, Charlie whispered, "Now, Stasia,"

Sara stifled a laugh; they heard Stasia from where they were.

"Good thing she wasn't a paladin and able to magnify her voice," Charlie whispered, making Sara laugh harder.

The officer called for backup.

" Stasia, they're moving," Hawk said. "Chief, the one upstairs is going to the roof. Is there a door there?"

"On it." Oz headed to the trapdoor in the roof his locate revealed. "He won't get out this way."

"Stasia, two are moving to the first floor, one to the doorway."

"I can hold the door closed, should I?" Stasia asked.

"Do it." Half a mile away the helicopter circled. Guthrie bit his thumbnail more nervous than they were.

"A man is talking to the officer at the

door. Okay, the officer has him in custody."
Chief watched from the roof next door. "The
officer's entering the house now."

Two gunshots sounded in quick
succession.

"They're shooting at the door handle."
Stasia's voice rose in agitation.

Another police car pulled up.

"They're going back upstairs," Hawk
reported. "All three are on the second floor
now."

"I'll put down frost area to slow them.
Hawk, use your slow trap when they come
out," Oz said.

Hawk leaped from his building; Sara
caught him in mid-air with Protective
Companion and pulled him to her on the
roof. He ran across the building to where Oz
placed his slow. Charlie leapt back over to
their roof. Two more gunshots sounded, and
Hawk reported that six people were now in
the room.

Stasia ran up the stairs and then out the
front door. "They're in custody," she reported
breathlessly.

"Go one house over; we'll be right there,
and I'll heal you," Sara said.

Charlie belatedly glanced at his spell-bar
and noticed her health bar down. "You've

been shot?" Instantly rage tightened his muscles, and he wanted to kill the men in the house.

"Just a nick. I'm fine. I don't think I even left any blood behind." Stasia sounded angry now.

Charlie grabbed Stasia in a hard hug while Sara healed her. Stasia patted his cheek before running back to check on the kids. His rage had receded when he touched her, but he was careful when he lifted Sara to the rooftop, knowing rage would make him stronger. He was relieved he felt no need to kill the men in police custody.

"The police have this, we can go," Stasia reported.

Guthrie issued coordinates. "Be there in ten."

When the helicopter arrived, they were waiting. In thirty minutes, they were back at school.

The beepers went off again as they were getting into Charlie's car after school. Oz gave Marcy a quick kiss on the cheek before he scrambled into the back seat.

"Are you guys okay?" Marcy asked in concern. "That's the second medical alert today."

"Yeah, we're fine. It's just a new medicine,

and they need to get the kinks out. We have to go; see ya later." Oz waved as Charlie drove off.

"That was lame." Stasia rolled her eyes at him. "She's going to think we're drug dealers."

"School is lame." Hawk stuffed his bookbag by his feet. "I would rather do this."

"Well, me too, but I don't want people thinking we're dealers either."

Charlie glanced at them in his rear-view mirror. "I'm pretty sure drug dealers would be more subtle, not to mention more solo."

- 24 -

LOCATE

"This one's a missing boater." Guthrie handed Oz the picture. "We think it's serious. He was in wit-sec."

"No direction, sorry, Sarge," Oz said after a moment.

Guthrie frowned. "Is water a different zone?"

"No idea, but we can check. Get me a photo and name of someone you know is on the water."

Guthrie made a few calls and a few minutes later received a fax on his portable printer.

"The first guy is that way. Oz pointed south. "The second I can't locate."

"Okay, so international waters is its own zone. Try looking for that guy's dead body first, Oz," Guthrie said after a moment.

"It's that way," Oz said, pointing with a grimace of distaste.

The body floated face down in a weed-covered canal beside a dead-end street. Hawk tracked the footprints near it to where a vehicle had parked. Car tracks, no one except Hawk could see, led to town and Hawk pointed out a man sitting in a coffee shop.

"That's it for us." Guthrie took the license plate number and a picture. "This is Special Agent in Charge Lewis's territory now."

He and the agent spoke briefly on the phone.

"How would you guys feel about checking out more missing person cases for us? Before you say yes, there's a few thousand of them."

"Bring it on, Sarge," Oz said.

"Let's prioritize these. Do the dead ones last and youngest first," Stasia said.

"This'll take a few days to set up." Guthrie took out his phone again, and this time spoke at length. "Okay, tomorrow after school we'll get started."

The next day, a helicopter waited at the local hospital for them after school. They boarded wearing armor and facemasks, but with only knives, no other weapons.

Guthrie handed Oz a tablet. "Okay, Oz, if

they're dead, place them in this file. If you can't find them, put them in the one marked, not in Florida. If they're alive, we go after them."

Oz looked at the first picture of a smiling three-year-old girl. "Dead." He ran a gentle finger along the girl's smile and filed her before flipping through the remaining pictures. "Not here, not here, not here, bingo— this one is south of us."

They tracked missing persons till dark and found three. Four more were dead and six more not in Florida. By the end of October, they were looking for the dead bodies. Special Agent Lewis worked with them full time now.

"This is good work, kids. A lot of people will rest easier knowing where their loved ones are."

"This will take years to do." Hawk complained as he flipped through the stack of files still waiting.

Agent Lewis slapped his back and smiled. "Yeah, but they'll be years well spent. You could do it faster if you spent a full day on it instead of after school too."

"Couldn't you rearrange our school schedule or something and give us a day off from school to look? Then we could have our afternoons free again," Hawk asked.

"I'll see what we can do. We all know school is a cover. You're way past those classes now."

"Yeah, we need more time to get this stuff done," Charlie agreed. "And time to hang out with our friends." Between homework and this he hadn't had a second alone with Sara in a month.

"We'll set something up. It might take a while though. Now that we're working the dead file, you should have more free time. Keep the beepers on in case we receive any new calls."

"When do we start doing more hostage rescue stuff?" Stasia pulled out one of her knives, using it to clean her nails. "Not that watching Oz cast Magical Locate a million times isn't thrilling."

"There hasn't been any in Florida."

"I think we're ready to leave Florida if we're needed elsewhere," Sara said as she examined her own nails and frowned.

"I agree, and I'm sure Guthrie will agree. We'll do the dead files one day a week until we can free up more time for you."

"Let's get back to work." Oz pointed. "He's to the north of us."

The man answered his phone, his voice cracking in anger. "I told you we should've taken them last April. They're always together now doing those searches. We need to snatch them during the day while they're separated. The homes are too well protected at night. Without the element of surprise, grabbing them will be hopeless."

"Don't be so dramatic; we have time. Eventually, they'll run out of steam and want time off. We wait for it."

"Did you not hear me? They search and find missing people! If even a hint of our presence is made known, they can find us. Oliver is the lead on searching, but we don't know how he does it. I've seen Sebastien follow people who should be impossible to detect. The longer we wait, the more likely it is they notice something, and if they look, they *will* find us."

"If you can't capture them, kill them – it's that simple. I'm sure they have weaknesses we can exploit. Obviously, they have to look hard; it can't be too easy if they need so much time to do it. Figure out what, where, and how they search. Do something besides complain. You can be replaced, you know."

- 25 -

BROKEN DATES

"Thanks, man, I owe ya one." Charlie slapped Oz on the shoulder as Oz cast disguise, making Charlie appear to be a thirty-year-old woman.

"Are you sure about this, Chief? This is a big step, for both of you." Oz stepped back and couldn't help but laugh at Charlie's new appearance.

"Absolutely sure. Thanks again, buddy." Charlie drove to the Hilton and strolled to the front desk. "I would like a room for one night, please," he asked the clerk in as feminine a voice as he could manage.

"Name and ID," the clerk asked without looking up from his screen

"Sara Mitchel, but I won't be leaving a car here. And, um, is there any way this doesn't show up on my credit card bill?"

The clerk's smile was almost a leer. "The card is in case there's damage to the room. You can pay cash for all expenses." Charlie paid in cash and gave him Sara's real credit card and his fake license saying he was Sara Mitchel age thirty-seven. The photo looked exactly like him and nothing like Sara. He was sure the clerk assumed he was here having an affair, but Charlie didn't care what he thought. Somewhere to be alone with Sara was his goal.

The clerk handed him a key. "Checkout is at eleven. Put the key in this envelope and leave it in the receptacle by the elevator if you've made no charges to the room. You're in room two hundred twelve, that's the second floor to the left as you leave the elevator. Have a nice stay."

Charlie took the key and left. Once in his mother's car, he cast a quick spell to break the disguise and drove home.

He tried not to flush when he bought the condoms. He picked Sara up at five wearing khaki pants, brown loafers, a button-down shirt, sports coat, and tie. By the time he arrived at her house, his palms were sweaty and his shirt stuck to his back.

Sara came to the door wearing a long pink dress with thin spaghetti straps and her hair knotted in a fancy twist. A light pink sweater draped over one arm and a small bag dangled over the other. The necklace he gave her sparkled above her breasts. Thankful that Liz wasn't home to question them, he led her directly to the car. Once in the car, he kissed her, not pulling back till they were both breathing harder.

"I made us dinner reservations," he said as he started the car.

Sara placed a hand on his knee, leaning closer to kiss him again. "I'm not hungry; are you?" When he kissed her neck, the scent of roses teased him. He inhaled and closed his eyes, wanting to remember every detail of this night.

"Not at all," he admitted.

"Let's skip dinner and go straight to the room. We can always eat later."

Charlie drove right to the hotel, parked on the street, and opened her door. "Sara, you don't have to do this."

She stood on tiptoe, pulled him closer, and kissed him a long slow kiss that heated his entire body.

"I want to do this," she assured him with a smile. Then the smile fled, and she stepped back, searching his face. "Are you having second thoughts?"

"God, no, but we have time. I'm not

going anywhere."

Sara rested her face on his jacket. "I love you so much, Charlie. I wish you could feel how much I love you."

"I love you too."

The light in her eyes when she smiled made him smile too. The receptionist didn't look up when they walked to the elevator.

He wanted this night to be special, to be perfect, a night they would remember forever. He turned the radio by the bed on low to a classical music station as Sara wandered the room.

Excitement made his fingers fumble on the small dial. Sara stopped before the mirror over the dresser across from the bed and removed her hairpins, letting her hair curl around her shoulders. His breath caught she was so beautiful. He rose to kiss her neck, and she smiled at him in the mirror before turning to kiss his lips.

Each small sound she made excited him more. When she broke from their kiss, her eyes shone, and her voice trembled.

"I love you," she said as she removed her sweater and dropped it on the chair with her bag.

"I love you too." He let his coat fall to the floor.

He wanted to take this slow, to take the time to savor everything. She came to him eagerly, taking his outstretched hand and letting him pull her close to trail kisses across her cheek to her bare shoulder.

After a minute, she drew back, and one slow button at a time removed his shirt.

Every place she touched heated beneath her hands.

When she reached down and undid the top button on his pants, his breath caught, and he needed to clear his throat before speaking.

"I stopped and bought us protection; it's in my coat pocket." He ran his hand over her breasts; his pulse leaped knowing that soon the dress would be gone.

"Don't need them. I got a birth control implant. We should be safe," she murmured, moving closer, kissing his neck and down his now bare chest.

"Liz knows?" Surprised, he stepped back to see her face.

"Yes, she wasn't thrilled, but she knows. I wanted to be ready." Her hands trailed over his bare back and came to rest on his waist again. "When you touch me, I feel it everywhere, as if my entire being wants to touch you. I've never wanted anything as much as I want to be with you. Never being alone with you, just us two with no distractions, is killing me."

"I love you so much, Sara. It's exactly the same for me. I think about you all the time." Charlie's voice deepened, and his hands rose to frame her face. "When I see you at school or the warehouse, I want to hold you, to feel your skin on mine."

Charlie slipped the straps of her dress down her arms. The dress pooled on the floor at her feet. She moaned softly when their bare skin touched and continued to remove his pants.

When his pants hit the floor, he picked her up and carried her to the bed where he trailed kisses across her collarbone. The warmth and softness of her skin excited him. His breath came harder as he drew along the curve of her breast above the lace of her pink bra with one finger.

Someone knocked on the door.

They both froze. "Jesus Christ, this is a conspiracy." Charlie rose and peeked through the peephole. Foggy looking, and carrying their duffle bags, Stasia knocked again and came more firmly into view.

"It's Stasia. You told her where we were?"

"Yes. I didn't think she would come

here." Embarrassment and dismay replace excitement and desire on Sara's face. She sat, pulling a pillow in front of her.

"Go away, Stasia!" Charlie leaned his forehead on the door and closed his eyes.

"Please, open the door, Chief. I'm sorry to interrupt, but our pagers went off. You're not supposed to go anywhere without one. Guthrie is flipping out. We have to leave now."

Charlie jerked the door open. "This better not be a joke." His blue eyes blazed with fury.

Stasia handed him the bag with his gear and held out Sara's bag. "You have two minutes to dress. Please don't be late. I'm really sorry. Guthrie is parked next to your car."

Charlie grabbed the bags and slammed the door.

Sara reached for hers and dressed. The dress she wore to the hotel she crumpled into a ball and stuffed in the bag with her high heels and sweater. The lacy pink underwear she left on, leaving the sports bra and briefs in the bag.

Charlie growled and pulled his armored pants on and stamped his feet into his boots. The latches on his chest armor got slapped shut, and he snatched both their bags, noticing Sara's hands shook as she tied her boots. He grabbed her hand.

"I'm sorry. Are you okay?"

"No, are you?"

"Not at all. Let's go. Second floor, we can jump," he said, not caring who saw them.

Sara took his hand, and they jumped from the balcony in their room.

"Find them?" Guthrie glanced up from his laptop when Stasia returned.

"Yes, they're coming," Stasia said and bit her lip.

A moment later, Charlie and Sara got in the car.

Guthrie headed to the airport. "We've been called in on a hostage situation in Mexico. We'll be jumping in. Our ambassador, his wife, and five of his staff have been taken hostage.

"The target is an armed compound on the east coast, north of Aldama. Alpha and Beta teams are meeting us there. A Marine team is now missing; captured or killed we don't know. Only one escaped to give the location. Stasia, hand Chief the laptop. Examine the pictures of the bad guys, the buildings they're in, and photos of the people we'll be getting out. Floor plans should arrive soon. More captives or innocent bystanders could be inside. Our orders are to retrieve our personnel without revealing any special abilities. Major Harris will meet us on the plane with Hawk and Oz."

Twenty minutes later, they arrived at the airport and boarded a jet where they found Liz, Hawk, and Oz waiting.

"This isn't a date kids— we're working now!" Guthrie barked at Charlie who held Sara's hand.

Charlie's bit back his snarl, but he said nothing, just released Sara's hand. He put his sunglasses on and leaned back in his seat, trying to control his anger.

Sara's angry, blue gaze met Stasia's worried brown eyes.

- 26 -

LOSING CONTROL

The plane climbed into the sky, and a tense silence prevailed.

Stasia leaned away from Sara and rubbed her arms.

Guthrie repeated his briefing and handed out printouts as the small printer attached to his laptop spit them out. "Chief, head in the game here; we need you to look at these."

Charlie straightened in his seat and snatched the pages. "I see them."

Despite his sunglasses the pages seemed preternaturally bright to him as if they were drawn in 3D. Every line engraved themselves in his memory with the barest glance. He flipped the pages, slapping each on his knee after glancing at it. Sara pulled at his attention. Every noise and motion in the cabin grabbed his attention and he knew without looking where she was and what she was doing.

Guthrie scowled, and Stasia glanced between Sara and Charlie, a frown growing on her face.

"Sara?" she asked.

Sara placed the papers in her lap and squinted at Stasia. When Stasia said nothing else, she returned her attention to the papers.

Stasia swallowed hard. 'Something is wrong,' she mouthed to Oz who leaned forward, his eye's widening as he stared at Charlie.

In her haste, she fumbled unbuckling her seatbelt and pulled on Guthrie's sleeve.

"Sarge," she whispered, and when he peered at her, she mouthed, 'right now,' and jerked her head to the back of the plane. Guthrie rose and followed, a quizzical expression on his face.

"We have a serious problem," she whispered.

"Meh, we interrupted their date, and they're pissy. They'll get over it." He turned to go.

"I should have noticed when he opened the door. I saw something was off but it just hit me. Charlie has brown eyes, Sarge, and Sara's eyes never glowed before."

"What?"

"Charlie and Sara, something is wrong with them," Stasia whispered. "Something is magically wrong. The magic has them," she clarified. "We need to land right now."

"What's wrong with them?"

"I don't know, but I sense it too. It's making my skin crawl, and look at Oz and Hawk, they feel it too. The last time Charlie's eyes blazed blue, he'd just killed a thousand men…"

Guthrie regarded his small group. Sara held the printout with trembling hands. Charlie sat still with his head leaning on the seat back. Not statue still, but predatory still – a lion about to pounce– his body coiled in readiness. The sunglasses hid his eyes, but his hands gripped the arms of the chair so hard his knuckles were white. Hawk rubbed his arms as if he was cold and Oz hunched as far from Charlie as he could get.

Guthrie strode back up the aisle. "Sara, Charlie, you guys good to go?"

"Good to go." They replied in perfect unison; neither moved or looked up.

"Sara?" Guthrie reached towards her. "Your eyes," he said and took a step back. A sharp crack made him spin around.

Charlie had squeezed a chair arm so tight it cracked. Now he sat forward in his seat, his face turned towards Guthrie, his entire body tense. Guthrie took another step back and lowered the hand reaching for Sara.

Charlie took a deep breath and settled back in his chair.

Guthrie hurried to the cockpit. "We have a small problem and need to land, at once, at the closest airport."

"I can land in six minutes," the pilot said after radioing the tower.

"Do it! Stay on your toes up here," he said in vague warning as he left the cockpit.

Charlie felt like a fool. It took all his willpower to not go to Sara and finish what they'd started. He tried to distract himself, closing his eyes and going over the mission parameters, but all he could think about was her soft skin and that he wanted to touch it again. The chair arm creaked again. *This was a mission for god's sake, and we weren't alone.* He needed to get a grip. When Guthrie returned, he tried to appear less tense.

"Chief, um, Charlie, can you remove the sunglasses, please?" Guthrie asked.

Charlie removed them and glared.

"Mother of God," Guthrie took an involuntary step backward. "Okay, what's going on here kids? Where were you?"

"None of your business," Charlie

growled.

Sara made a small sound of dismay.

Guthrie reached a hand towards her.

"Don't touch her!" Charlie said with such menace in his voice that Guthrie jumped away.

"No, I won't. No one will touch her. What's wrong with her? What happened to you two?"

"We're fine," Sara and Charlie said in unison.

"Stop it. You're creeping me out." Stasia crouched in front of Sara. "Sara isn't fine, Chief. What's wrong, Sara?"

Red crept up Sara's neck, staining her cheeks. "We're here, doing our job!"

"Yes," Stasia agreed in a puzzled voice. "I get it, you want to be on your date, but you've had broken dates in the past. You're upset, I can see that, but why?"

Sara leaned forward and whispered to Stasia, "I need to touch him."

"No—absolutely not— no touching on the plane!" Stasia scrambled to her feet. "The last time we barely lived through it!"

The blue in Sara's eyes lit her face as she looked at Charlie. His brightened in response and he made as if to stand.

Stasia cast Sweet-Talk. "Please sit, Chief.

Sarge, we better land. I really, really, think they shouldn't touch up here."

"What the hell is going on?" Guthrie crossed his arms and narrowed his eyes at her.

"I'm not sure, but I think it's the magic. That blue glow is the same that hit us on the plane last year, and I think it would be bad if it got loose in here."

"Sara," Liz said. "Why do you need to touch him?"

Sara shrugged and reached for Charlie. Stasia put herself between them and took her hand.

"I really need to touch him." Tears came to her eyes, glowing, white crystal droplets that trailed down her cheeks.

"Okay, when we land, but not right this second," Stasia agreed, releasing Sara's hand and moving away.

"Please, stop talking!" Charlie said in a strangled voice. Misty blue light showed on his fingernails, and blue light leaked out from behind his closed eyes. "I won't be able to stop myself from going to her."

The effort to remain seated made him sweat. He could feel the magic inside him increasing. It pushed at him until he felt bloated and worried the energy within him would explode outward.

Stasia pushed Sara back into her seat as she rose.

"Right!" Liz said, "No more talking. Everyone sits quietly till we land." Liz glanced at her monitor, which showed their blood pressure and heart rates dangerously high.

Stasia cast worried looks at Guthrie as the blue glow crept into Sara fingertips. Every inch of skin showing on both Charlie and Sara soon shone with a soft blue glow, magic coating their skin.

The plane rolled down the runway when Liz cracked the door.

Charlie strained to hold it back and leaped from the still rolling plane. Sara pulled herself to him.

Stasia and the others crowded around the open hatch. "I expected an explosion or something," Stasia said as their hands touched. "Ah, there it is."

A bright blue light flashed above them. What looked like lightning flickered almost too fast to see, and a wave of warm air buffeted the watchers on the plane.

Charlie leaned down and kissed Sara on the lips. The blue glow turned bright white and swirled around them until Sara held out their clasped hands. The glow disappeared. They hugged, and spoke, but were too far to hear. A few minutes later, they returned to the plane.

"Better?" Liz asked.

Her monitor showed their respiration and heart rates returning to normal.

"Yes," Charlie said, "much better."

"Back to normal, I think." Sara smiled at Charlie, and he grinned back. "I still want to touch him, but the normal amount."

Charlie laughed and kissed her temple.

"So, what the hell was that?" Guthrie asked.

"My magic really likes Sara too." Charlie slid his hand to the back of her neck. Skin almost hot to the touch, heated from the weight of her hair combined with the natural heat of her skin, warmed his soul in a way only she could.

"What the hell does that mean? And why the hell does it like her so much right now?"

"I have no idea. It's not as if we planned it," Charlie pulled Sara to his side, and his hand dropped to his empty scabbard.

Liz stood and made sitting motions. "Okay, everyone, calm down. This is a big, unexpected change. Can we expect this to happen again?"

Sara turned bright red.

Charlie grinned and relaxed. "I hope so,"

he murmured, lust rising at the expression on Sara's face. He moved away from her, not trusting his willpower. "But I think we're safe for now. We can go."

"This plane isn't budging until I get a better answer." Guthrie glowered at Charlie.

Charlie sighed and closed his eyes; turning to Sara, he gave her a light kiss. "I'm sorry, Sara, we're destined to have no privacy at all. This isn't anyone's business but ours." Facing Guthrie, he continued, "We didn't know this would happen, but I think us being, um, intimate caused it."

Guthrie leaned back in his seat. "Are you saying...?" He paused a moment and cleared his throat. "Okay, are you saying having sex caused that?"

"No, not having sex caused that. We were interrupted. I think our magic wanted to mingle. I've never been in love before. Sara is the only girl I've ever wanted. I didn't realize my need to touch her wasn't me."

Sara gasped and covered her face with her hands, hunching as if from a blow.

"No, that isn't what I meant at all, Sara," Charlie said hurriedly. "I wanted you before we had magic; you know that. What I meant was, I couldn't tell my obsession for you from its. Now I can, but it's pretty similar actually."

To Charlie's relief, Sara straightened and offered him a wan smile before she resumed staring at the floor. Her dismay over their lack of privacy angered him, and it took him a second to realize Liz spoke.

"Sara, what did you do with the magic?"

"The majority we reabsorbed, but I put some into my staff." When she glanced at Charlie, tears filled her eyes. "I still love you, Charlie."

"I'll always love you. We'll figure this out." Her distress hurt, and he hated that he couldn't comfort her as he wished. More than anything he wished they could have a private moment and not need to share this part of their life with anyone.

Guthrie went to speak to the pilot. A moment later, he returned. "Buckle up, the mission waits." With an apologetic grimace at Charlie, he continued, "Okay, I realize I have no right to ask this, but for the good of our missions, please refrain from any sexual activity until we get this straightened out. That means all of you. And, Chief, if you two suddenly have an overwhelming urge to touch, inform me immediately. If I'd let you hold hands earlier, would that have helped?"

Sara nodded, and Charlie said, "Yes."

"Okay, I'll try to be more sensitive to your

feelings, but I need to know of any changes."

"Yeah, okay, Sarge, but we didn't know what was happening either. I thought my need to touch her was because we were, um, interrupted. I didn't realize my need was a magical thing," Charlie said in a small, embarrassed voice.

Guthrie cleared his throat. "Let's get back to work." He handed the laptop to Charlie. "We've received more intel, house plans, and a list of the staff there. You guys look through this stuff. I need to call in and make sure our ride is ready."

"We aren't stupid, Sarge. We know you have to report this," Charlie said bitterly.

"Yes, I do, son. I'm sorry, but I do."

"Has this happened before?" Liz asked.

"No, we've never…." Sara trailed off, turning away and blushing.

"We're never able to find time or space to be alone together. This is embarrassing for both of us. This was supposed to be private and special, not public and reported," Charlie said.

Anger flushed his skin. That they would think him embarrassed angered him more. His love life was nobody's business except his.

"I know, and again, I'm sorry. Liz and I'll make our reports. You guys study this information." Guthrie grabbed his phone and motioned for Liz to follow him to the rear of the small jet. "I'll pass this up the chain of command. You call their doctor. I think we were lucky we interrupted before they, um...."

Liz nodded. "Yeah, that much energy from just some kissing... we'll have to make sure they have a safe spot. We can't have them blowing up hotels or something."

"This wasn't in my job description," Guthrie grumbled as he called Captain Sanders.

- 27 -

SAVING RECON

Team Valor arrived in Mexico at one in the morning. Team Alpha waited there already, but Beta hadn't arrived yet. Major Nelson decided to go ahead; Beta could catch up. The drop went smoothly. Everyone wore parachutes but didn't use them.

Using a maneuver they'd practiced all summer, they formed a circle as they dropped by joining hands with Sara casting Ascension. Oz cast Magical Locate, and Hawk sensed people while Stasia towed everyone as she sprinted to the compound.

"What do we have, Hawk." Major Nelson unrolled a map of the complex. Hawk pointed out on the map where the people stood.

"I can't tell the good guys from the bad, everyone is neutral except four friendlies here." Hawk indicated the spot on the map where he 'saw' people in shades of green.

"That's probably our fellow Marines," Major Nelson said. "Standard wall cross. Sara, help Drew to the top of building two. Hawk, go with them and No-See-Um Drew, and then go to building one. Stasia, find us an open door or window, and we'll have Chief steal Sara's pull and get everyone inside. While everyone is getting in, Stasia is looking for traps and cameras, then hostages. Get them out and return for the Marines. Everyone, look sharp, silent kills only, and don't leave a mess lying around."

A simple Disarm Sensors cast from Oz disabled the camera's pointing at the wall. In ten seconds, they were across the eight-foot wall. Sara cast Ascension on Hawk and Drew, making it easy for them to pull each other to the top of the main building.

Stasia found the rest of the team an entrance, a second-floor window in an unguarded room. One easily avoided man patrolled outside in a circle around the main building.

Charlie cast Waylay on Stasia and Sara pulled herself to him. A flick of his fingers gave an ally a spell and let Brenda intercept him. He Spell-Stole Sara's pull and yanked Manny to the window. Sara cast pull right after on Major Nelson.

Oz cast Invisible Duo on himself and their last teammate waiting to come up as the patrol passed them. Charlie gave Tony Waylay, and Sara pulled Oz up. Within six minutes everyone crouched inside a bedroom while Hawk kept them informed on enemy positioning.

"They're using night-vision on exterior views," Hawk reported.

Stasia ran down hallways checking for hostages. "I've located the hostages. I need Oz to disable the motion sensors in the hall. Two guards are in the room. I can handle both."

"Two people are in front of you, Major, a hallway, I assume," Hawk said. "And eight are spread out above you. Twenty-four people are underneath you, also spread out."

"Stasia, can we remove the hostages before the bad guys notice us?" Major Nelson asked.

"If we eliminate these two guards, and the guards aren't missed, for say, five minutes, then yes," Stasia agreed.

"Alpha team, clear the building. Sara, you're with Alpha. Chief, you're with me for extraction. Oz, how are those alarms?"

"One more and good to go. I've

whammyied the alarms in the hallway in front of you. If you're going upstairs, I didn't clear there."

"Okay, Oz, get the last one down there, then come upstairs, and clear for Alpha team. Stasia will move on your mark. Stasia, when Oz say's it's clear, take out both guards and bring the hostages to Chief and me. Keep the razzle-dazzle to a minimum. We want no witnesses."

"Roger that. I'll distract before I attack."

The eager sound of Stasia's voice made Charlie tense. He wanted to be with her attacking too. It was hard to hold himself back. Much harder than it had been in practices. A grimace crossed his face, he dreaded having to report this. Thinking of the other report Guthrie had just given made his anger surge and he had to fight the urge to jump down and pull his swords. He had to close his eyes and breathe deeply while picturing Sara's sweet smile to regain control.

"Hawk, let us know if people move around," Major Nelson was saying when he opened his eyes.

"Oz, there's a patrol in the hallway you're approaching," Hawk reported.

He lay on the roof of the house, scanning with binoculars and his senses.

Two minutes later Oz said, "It's clear—go."

Thirty-five seconds later, Stasia said, "Tangos down. I'm releasing the hostages."

Brenda reported, "The top floor is cleared. "We're moving to the bottom floor now."

"I see you, Alpha; you'll hit that patrol in the hall," Hawk warned.

"We'll get them." Sara said, "I have right, Oz."

Oz cast invisible, and he and Sara got behind the guards. She cast Hypnotize, and he cast Polymorph. Brenda tied them with zip-ties before blindfolding, gagging, and dragging them into another room.

"We have movement by the gate." Drew scanned slowly with his binoculars, being careful not to break the No-See-Um he lay under. "Four trucks."

"I'm counting twenty-four new people," Hawk said.

"Sixteen appear to be hostages," Drew added.

"Get ours first. Alpha, proceed to the first floor. Stasia, what's your ETA?" Major Nelson asked.

"Two minutes," Stasia said, busy herding her charges to the window she'd entered.

"Hawk, can you clear a lane for us?" Major Nelson asked.

"Roger that."

"Okay, Chief, we're up. Go back out the window. You catch the hostages."

"Chief, patrol coming to you, I'll use my Silence Shot, you finish him," Hawk said, "To your right."

"All clear, Major," Charlie said twelve seconds later as he wiped his bloody sword on the corpse at his feet.

The violent action soothed him, and he was much calmer when he straightened. *The doctors were going to freak when I report this*, he thought angrily, then snickered. There was nothing they could do about it.

"Stasia, head to the first floor. Chief, first hostage," Major Nelson said as he lowered an elderly woman from the window.

Charlie caught her and placed her on the ground. She put her back against the wall and stood trembling with her hand pressed against her mouth. In less than a minute, all seven hostages crowded around Charlie. "Hawk, am I clear?"

"Yes, go now."

"Follow me quietly, please. And if I say get down, lay flat and cover your eyes. We might use our flash bangs," Charlie said to the hostages, feeling calm and in charge now.

His senses felt sharper than normal and his strength greater as if he could fight for a year with no rest. Each small sound the hostages made, every smell and flicker of light became a part of him, like it had on the airplane and he wondered if his eyes were glowing again. He knew without looking where his charges stood and their condition. His reflexes were on a hair trigger, and he had to smother a laugh it felt so good. He almost wished one of the men patrolling would attack them. He imagined it would feel even better to release the energy inside him.

"Stop, two men around the corner from you, Chief," Hawk said.

Chief told his group to wait and eagerly rounded the corner.

"I have left." Hawk cast his Silent-Shot as Charlie cast Waylay on the man on the right and killed him. Charlie grabbed the man Hawk shot and killed him too with one quick thrust of his sword, wiped the blade on the dead man's clothes, and placed the dead body against the wall. He was right, it felt amazing, freeing, and he wanted to do it again.

He beckoned the hostages forward while he pondered this new bloodthirstiness.

"Major, this is team leader Beta; we're

outside the wall now," Glen said.

"This crew is not climbing that wall," Charlie said, eyeing the elderly couple in the group.

"Chief, take your group to the back gate. Team Beta, meet him there. Hawk, how many?" Major Nelson asked.

"Twelve between Chief and the gate. I can take them all, but not silently."

"Hold on that, Hawk. Stay silent as long as you can."

"Hawk, anyone in the building in front of me?" Charlie asked.

"It's empty, Chief," Hawk replied.

"I'll stash the hostages while we clear."

"Agreed," Major Nelson said. "Beta, can you get over the wall?"

"Roger that," Glen replied.

"It's clear where you are, Beta," Hawk said. "Stasia, your group has eight tangos in the next room."

Charlie removed a box from his pocket and used a small blade to cut a hole in the window before him. "Watch my back, Hawk." He slid the window open, climbed in, and opened the door. Crouching, he peered around the door into the hallway leading to the front of the building. "Motion sensors line the hall. Can you get down here, Hawk?"

"On my way. Team Beta, we're in the third building to your left. Two men are patrolling between us," Hawk said.

"The bottom floor is clear except for the room with eight in it," Stasia reported.

"Return to my position," Major Nelson ordered.

"Hawk, boost the hostages to me," Charlie said and turned to the hostages. "You'll be safe here while we make a path out. Stay quiet in this room. Don't go in the hallway, it's alarmed."

"Team Beta is inside the compound, Chief," Hawk said.

"Beta, leave one man guarding the hostages in the house. Hawk, get back on the roof. Beta, and, Chief, clean up the outside. Drew, where are our new friends?" Major Nelson asked.

"Still standing by the trucks, arguing over where to put the new hostages." Drew kept his gun sights on a man holding a bound woman's arms and gesticulating with a pistol as he yelled at the other men. None of the other men had their weapons out. The machine guns they carried dangled by straps from their shoulders.

"Team Alpha, go for the four Marines in the small house, take Oz and Sara. Stasia, meet me. Let's see if we can take the new guys."

Hawk knelt on the edge of the roof and nudged the mic on his shoulder with his chin. "I'm in position on the roof. Bad angle here for the gate. Stasia, two men left that group of eight."

"Stasia, take them out. Hawk, get a better vantage for the gate," Major Nelson ordered.

"Hawk, where's our closest target?" Glen asked.

"Five are standing together behind the building where you are," Hawk replied.

"I'm clear," Stasia said, "ETA, forty seconds."

"Joy, the building before you has three men, but spread out, one on each corner, except south." Hawk did another quick survey of the area. "Alpha team, you have one tango guarding the front door."

"We have the packages," Brenda said less than a minute later.

"Oz, bandage them if needed and take them to the first group. Brenda, take Alpha and escort both groups to building one. Hawk, how's it looking?" Major Nelson asked.

"Eight appear to be new hostages, leaving fourteen baddies. I can get the men standing next to the hostages," Hawk said.

"I got the fat ass with the pistol," Drew said.

"Stasia, sap the guy with the paper in his hand. We want him alive. Beta, are you in position?"

"Roger that, we have left."

"Chief, give us a disarm, but no intercept or fear. Go in three."

Gladius gripped in his right hand, Charlie crouched at the edge of the building. When Major Nelson signaled, he rushed in and shouted his drop-weapon area-of-effect spell.

The armed men yelled in surprise and couldn't help dropping their weapons. Charlie laughed as he hit one with the flat of his blade, knocking him to the ground.

His protective aura was so strong the men cowered before him, not trying to retrieve their weapons.

Charlie was perfectly content to let his team tie them. Another laugh made Major Nelson peer at him curiously.

"Nothing, we can talk later," Charlie said.

The doctors would be happy he could control himself but whether they liked it or not he was a Protection Warrior. And Charlie loved what he was.

Two minutes later, they untied the new hostages.

"The six men in the room are running to the front door," Hawk warned as he changed position.

"Beta?"

"We have it."

"Okay, let's get our prisoners. I'll call for transport if we're clear," Major Nelson said.

"I see no one except us and our captives," Hawk said.

The major called for transportation and a helicopter appeared within minutes. "Beta, stay here and babysit this group until local law enforcement shows up. Alpha, go with our ambassador. Remain with them until they're back at the embassy. Cubs, get off at the first stop."

Charlie and Hawk helped the older people aboard the helicopter. Sara and Stasia already sat in the back. The Marines they'd rescued sat beside them. Team Alpha boarded and sat across from them, and the helicopter lifted off.

Brenda took off her helmet and facemask, and the rest of Alpha team followed suit. The Cubs left theirs on.

"Does anyone need medical attention?" Brenda looked them over and grinned. "Well, if it isn't Recon. Imagine meeting you here."

"Scout?" The rescued Marine said as a red

flush climbed his cheeks.

Brenda grinned at him. "Your teammate returned and reported where you were and they sent the best to get you. You should be flattered."

He frowned at her. "Women have no place on the battlefield."

Sara and Stasia laughed.

"Some women," Brenda agreed, "but the same can be said for some men. I passed the same training you did, plus twelve more weeks to become a Scout."

Recon pursed his lips and narrowed his eyes as he examined the group of Scouts and nodded slowly. "I never even heard of you until we saw your group train in Pendleton. How do you become a Scout?"

"It's classified. You're invited, you don't apply." Brenda grinned at Sara as Charlie laughed.

"This is our stop," Hawk said forty minutes later as the helicopter hovered over an empty road.

Sara and Stasia bumped fists with Brenda as they passed her. They slid down the ropes, letting go when they were out of sight.

"This way," Hawk said, and they ran after

him.

Brenda watched the man across from her staring after the Cubs as they ran down the road.

"Where are they off to?" he asked.

"Classified."

He nodded and gave her a devilish grin. "I don't suppose you'd let me buy you a drink when we get out of here?"

Brenda grinned back. "I'll let you buy me two."

Two days later, Brenda slipped onto a bar stool in a cantina right outside the base, ordered a beer, and smoothed her skirt. The television at the bar showed a news station, and she watched idly as she waited for her date. The news anchor was just finishing giving credit to Delta Force for the rescue her team accomplished. A frown crossed her face, and then she shrugged.

"Ouch, that had to hurt," her date said as he sat on the stool beside her.

She smiled ruefully and leaned back in her chair. "Meh, it's all good. We're on the same team, Recon."

"Call me Mike," Recon said and motioned to the bartender to bring him a beer. "The reports and the pictures showed your team doing impressive work. How many of you are there?" he asked.

"Classified." Brenda gave him a small, apologetic shrug. A name on the television caught her ear, and she spun to face the screen. Drew joined her at the bar, watching as well.

"Oh, hell," he mumbled. "I'm on it." He fished his cell phone from his pocket and strode away.

Brenda's date turned to the television where a reporter interviewed an actress on the front steps of a courthouse while pictures scrolled alongside in a cut scene.

"Tara, will you be filing for custody of your stepdaughter, seeing as how you two are so close?" the reporter asked.

"I'm not sure. We haven't talked about that yet." Tara gave a bright smile to the camera.

"Double hell," Brenda whispered.

Her date looked confused.

Brenda changed the subject. "How about some dinner to go with my two drinks? I'm buying."

A wide grin creased his tanned cheeks as he stood and offered his arm. "And maybe I can thank you properly?"

Brenda smiled, winked at him, and stood to take his arm when her beeper went off. Four more beepers sounded, as the rest of the team in the bar received notice. She sighed and excused herself. "Sorry, Mike. Rain check maybe? Duty calls."

"Sure, rain check," he said as she hurried away.

He sat back down and grabbed her beer. One of his buddies plopped down next to him.

"Aw, struck out, huh?" Mike's friend snickered.

"No, I was doing fine until they got recalled."

They sat at the bar and had another drink. The news announcer broke into the current show. "In breaking news, we've just received word cruise ship *Hera* was taken by Somali pirates on its way to Dubai. This is a small, privately run ship and unconfirmed reports say the president's younger sister and niece were aboard." The newscaster gave what details he knew as pictures of the yacht and the president's sister and niece flashed in the background.

"I wonder if that's where she's going," Mike said enviously.

- 28 -

THE MOVE

Major General Campbell attended a private meeting with the president. Pierce Taylor the head of the FBI, Captain Sanders, and Doctor Elliot were also in attendance.

"You've read the reports. Doctor, what are your recommendations?" the president asked.

Doctor Elliot steepled his fingers on the table. "First, let me start by saying, we expected and are happy with the response Charlie had to the fight. A normal man displaying those same symptoms, that same eagerness, it would be worrisome, but we need to remember he isn't a normal man. He was able to control himself, and I'm comfortable with the level of, ah, bloodthirstiness he reported."

"If he told the truth," the president said

sourly.

"No reason to think he didn't," General Campbell said reassuringly. "As Doctor Elliot says, we are aware Charlie is a Protection Warrior, and his magic will affect him. It isn't a one-sided event. He can't influence others with his aura without being influenced in return. I too am happy with his responses. It's our job to keep him under control until we're certain he can keep himself under control."

"And the magical display on the plane?" the president asked.

Doctor Elliot slid a graph across the table to the president. "We measured the magic, and it's the same radiation that was present a year ago on the plane. What we're now calling m-radiation. Secondly, they flatly refuse to cooperate in any tests—"

The president interrupted. "What tests specifically? They've always cooperated in the past."

The doctor leaned back in his chair and sighed while rubbing the bridge of his nose with two fingers. "This test would be highly intrusive, I can see why they refused, but it would help tremendously to observe and measure the effects as they occur."

The president cracked a small smile. "As I understand it, they're being sexually intimate causes this reaction. I appreciate the refusal, but we need to know if this is safe. We can't let them spread m-radiation around."

"We don't know," the doctor admitted. "As far as we know, a magical manifestation only happened twice. Major Harris reported the first known occurrence on the plane. The second, we, um, set them up for and took very good samples of m-radiation. They didn't realize the room was monitored.

"Sara can recall it, leaving none behind, but in both instances, they were interrupted. We aren't sure what the effect would be if they weren't. I think, when they were sick in New Mexico, the magic caused it as well. By all reports Sara was extremely upset. High emotional response calls their magic out. If her response didn't match his, it might cause an imbalance making her ill."

"You think because her magic couldn't merge with his, it hurt her?" The president asked doubtfully.

"I need to do more tests and conduct more experiments, it's just a theory. If that was the first time the magic exchanged, perhaps it did hurt her. Reports say she recovered when Charlie used his magic on her. Maybe, it wasn't the heal that fixed her, but the magical exchange. What I'm saying is, we don't know. We do know the magic is changing or maybe puberty is changing them," he finished thoughtfully.

"So, what's the recommendation?"

"Well, first we need a safe room, as discreetly monitored as possible, and a few volunteers. I think Sara might be able to utilize that magic on someone else, to give them magic, if enough was present—"

General Campbell interrupted, "Several Scouts who've been working on memorizing the same spells they use volunteered; all the Scouts play UBM. But I don't see any way of talking either of them into having intercourse with anyone else."

"No, you misunderstand. My theory is she could guide it to someone else. But I admit they would have to be close to her, right after, or as, she and Charlie raised the magic." Doctor Elliot smiled and steepled his fingers on the tabletop again.

"Charlie's brother is one of the volunteers; perhaps we could set something up without them realizing it?" Pierce Taylor wondered aloud.

"That's a side issue," Captain Sanders said. "We need to take into account the other three. What happens when they become intimate with someone and that someone isn't involved with project Cub Scout?"

"Oh, Jesus, this just gets better and better." The president leaned back and rubbed his eyes.

"Yes, it's complicated by our ignorance," Doctor Elliot agreed. "I'm not comfortable doing any of these things behind my patients back, but I see the necessity. The Scouts make ideal test subjects. They're already in the need-to-know loop, but the age difference is a factor. There are four women Scouts in their twenties, and we're talking about getting them to seduce sixteen-year-old boys." The doctor laughed. "I admit they could do it, and probably easily, but is that ethical?"

"Ask the boys to cooperate," Captain Sanders said.

"If we ask and they say no, they'll be suspicious if suddenly the female Scouts try to seduce them," Pierce said.

The president smacked the tabletop with his open hand. "Okay, like it or not, put a ban on sex for them, for all of them!"

Pierce laughed. "That won't stop them. Sex has been banned for teenagers for years and how many teenage parents are in this country?"

"I agree." General Campbell flipped his copy of the report closed. "Tell them the truth and provide a safe place. Monitor them, but nothing intrusive. Volunteers can be nearby. Sara is friendly with the female Scouts, use those. She would probably be more comfortable with another woman. Don't force them or trick them, ask them. Anastasia is an attractive young woman. She could take her pick of the available Scouts. And there's no hurry here. We can wait a few years."

"The Cubs need to be reminded of the dangers of spreading m-radiation to people not in the raid who can't be healed." The president tapped the tabletop for emphasis.

"Oz is the only one who currently has a girlfriend who doesn't know. We'll keep a close eye on him," Captain Sanders agreed.

"General, speak with the Scouts, inform them on the Cubs, err, condition. The process that gave Team Valor magic was extremely painful; make everyone aware of that. Lift the ban on fraternizing in ranks," the president said after some thought.

"Fine," Pierce shut his briefcase and placed it by his feet. "Let's see about getting them a safe place, but be subtle. Maybe we can move the warehouse and make it available after hours as a hangout. Remove the video from the common rooms, keep it in the practice rooms, and let nature take its course."

"Yes, that sounds feasible," the doctor agreed. "Ideally, the warehouse should be well away from anything, but still close enough to their school and homes that they use it frequently. I'll need an office and lab nearby, and we should keep the Scouts near. We're already discussing removing the Cubs from school for home schooling. Hiding the rate at which they're learning is getting harder and harder."

"Could we relocate the parents to a military base?" General Campbell asked.

Pierce said, "Potentially, if we offered good jobs and maybe private tutors. I'll need to research this a bit. Let's inform them on the ban except for Scouts and work on moving them when we can. We need a small base or community, or perhaps a large one would be better." Pierce leaned back in his chair obviously deep in thought.

"Let's meet in two months, and I want to see progress by then." The president stood in dismissal, and everyone filed out.

Captain Sanders went to break the news to the Scouts.

Liz attended a flurry of meetings as they worked out the details of moving the kids and their families.

The decision was made to move the kids to Camp Pendleton in California. A specially designed housing complex located on the edge of the base made to withstand heavy blasts using shatterproof glass in all windows was commandeered for their use.

Some of the buildings were brand-new, some older and reconfigured. The area was sunny enough to please Sara, and trees and gardens would be planted for Hawk. Better paying jobs were found for the parents and housing would be provided on the base. The facility was officially part of the base but constructed to resemble nearby housing to help them fit in locally.

Liz met with everyone involved, working out the details and there were many. Finally, she spoke with the kids.

"We'll move the day after Christmas. Team Valor now has an official contract, claiming you're independent contractors working on upgrading computer encryption and safety protocols. Oz is handling all of that but it makes great cover to allow you to live on base and collect your pay as well as getting Sara and Oz the equipment they've been asking for. You've already seen the rules and regulations for people living on base; while most apply to you, a few don't. You'll be living right next to the Scouts. It's their official home base too. The ban on fraternizing in the ranks is lifted for the Scouts only."

Liz cleared her throat. "Because of the release of m-radiation during intimate acts you'll need to be careful. Only the Scouts and Marines can be healed. As you grow older, I'm sure you'll have relationships, but premarital sex isn't an option for you. You could seriously injure a lover not in your raid. This might change as we learn more, but for right now, this is how it is. Your dormitory was constructed as strong as possible to make it safe for intimate liaisons. Nine open spaces remain in the raid. When you become serious about someone, if they agree to sign the confidentiality agreement and pass a background check, they could be offered a spot, but you must choose very carefully. A secret once told, can't be untold."

"Our mother is okay with this?" Stasia asked, sounding amazed.

"Your mother is realistic," Liz said with a smile. "You're free to stay in the same house as her as long as you like, but no boyfriends can go there. You'll be attending a local school with people of all different ages. The curriculum will be eclectic. I think you'll find it much more interesting than the school here, being more suited to your advanced abilities. We'll keep up with your training and include any Scouts present on base in a private gym. This should give you ample free time to pursue your own interests. One day a week, we'll do locating. You'll get weekends off, excluding if we're called out of course.

"We're debating letting you enlist a year early. Everyone needs to seriously think about what you want for your futures. You've been given extraordinary gifts. What you do with those gifts is up to you. As always, I'm available to talk with if you have any questions concerning this move. Sara, I'll always be available to you no matter where I'm stationed. I'll be stationed for a while at Camp Pendleton, but that could change. But as long as I live you'll never be alone."

"So, I'll have my own place?" Sara grinned at Charlie.

He hoped he didn't look as eager as he felt. Christmas felt like a million years away.

Liz laughed. "Yes, it won't be large or fancy, but it'll be all yours. Hopefully, it'll be finished by the deadline, but ready or not, we go after Christmas. That should give you plenty of time to say goodbye to friends here."

"I'll miss my friends," Charlie said. "But it's getting harder and harder to hang out with them with my secret life. It'll be nice to be with people we don't need to lie too."

Liz turned to Oz. "Will you be okay leaving Marcy?"

He shrugged. "I like her, but we aren't in love or anything, and I'm sure we'll remain friends. I'll miss her company, but we don't spend much time together anymore."

Liz squeezed his hand. "I said things would slow down a bit for you, and you'd get more free time, but I'll need a rain check for the next month or so. I think you're really going to like this. We have an opportunity to send you to an advanced driving course to learn how to drive like a pro. Regular classes here at the warehouse will be two days a week, the other three we'll learn defensive and aggressive driving. You'll learn to drive all different sorts of vehicles from motorcycles to trucks. Once we master wheeled vehicles, we can go on to planes and helicopters next year if you're interested."

"I don't even have a regular driver's license yet, just a learner's permit," Sara said.

"And Hawk doesn't even have that," Stasia added.

Liz laughed. "We realize that, and you

aren't obligated to try, but it's a great opportunity."

"I want to!" Hawk sat up straighter and glared at his sister.

"I'm in." Charlie grinned at Hawk.

"Me too." Stasia rolled her eyes at her brother.

"Yeah, I'll try it," Sara said.

"Sure, why not." Oz shrugged.

"Okay, tomorrow after school, go to this track." Liz handed Charlie a paper with an address. "Driving suits and helmets will be provided, so wear clothes that can fit under them, nothing too loose or too heavy and no layers. Guthrie will be taking the class as well; I might take a few lessons too."

"We can't wait anymore. We go now! In one week, they'll be on a military base. Take them tomorrow. I'll set up a meeting with Oliver, but I want a backup crew in place to take him out, just in case. Sara will be alone in the apartment in the early evening. When the apartment empties in the morning, drug the food. Anastasia and Sebastian are planning on Christmas shopping. A team will grab their mother. If we can't get them as they come in the house, we can use her to control them.

We aren't sure where Charles plans to be. After we snatch the others, we can pick him up. What about the Scouts?"

He sneered the word Scouts.

"Don't worry about them, I have a plan. I'll grab as many as I can get. You remember what to do if it goes badly?"

"Yes, but if we take Sara and Oliver now, we can come back for the rest. There's no need to kill them."

"If we can't capture them, Kill them. There's no second chance on this. Get both girls. You have over a hundred men at your disposal, so don't screw this up! Get me both girls!" The general slammed down the phone.

- 29 -

THE SNATCH

Charlie shifted the box to his other arm and knocked on Sara's front door. Tomorrow was Sara's birthday, and he hoped to surprise her. Prince would stay with Liz when they moved, so he'd gotten Sara a fluffy white kitten of her own.

This had been the longest two months of his life, and he still had five days to go before they could be alone unless Liz planned on being out late.

The doctor spying on them had freaked Sara out, and they'd decided to wait till they had their own apartments. While Charlie didn't want to sneak around either, the delay was killing him. Although it comforted him to know the postponement frustrated Sara too.

She clung to him when he left and sought opportunities to be alone with him just as eagerly as he did and it got harder and harder to stop. Only his determination that their first time be special stopped him from using the backseat of his car.

Sara planned to be home tonight. She intended to wrap Christmas presents and pack. *Maybe, if Liz would be out late, we can make love tonight in Sara's room.*

No one answered his first light knock, so he knocked again louder, grinning eagerly. No one answered that knock either. The door was open, so he let himself in.

Liz's outstretched arm lay on the kitchen floor in a pool of blood. The box containing the kitten hit the ground with a dull thud as he leapt to Liz while hitting his panic button, romantic daydreams fleeing his mind. Blood pooled around Liz's shoulder from a gunshot wound.

To his relief, a pulse beat in her neck. He put pressure on the wound with one hand and grabbed his phone, hitting the speed dial for Oz.

"Come on, pick up, damn it!"

Blood coated his hand in moments so he hit speakerphone and placed the phone on the floor to rip another towel into strips.

Oz answered as Charlie bandaged Liz's wound as best he could with the dish towels.

"What's up, bro?"

"Get to Sara's! Liz has been shot. Locate Sara for me." Not waiting for a reply, he ran to Sara's bedroom and wasn't surprised she wasn't in there. Furious now, he leapt back to Liz, landing so hard beside her, he shook the glass jars on the counter.

"Sara is north of me," Oz said in confusion. "I'm on my way to you."

"Call Hawk. Get him here. They took Sara." Charlie stabbed disconnect, then hit the speed dial for Stasia. She answered on the first ring.

"Did she love it?" Stasia asked cheerfully.

"Liz was shot. Get your mother and go to the warehouse. Sara's taken, and they might try for you too. Oz is calling Hawk. Call Agent Lewis if you can. Arrange for a helicopter and a jet. If they move Sara out of the zone quick enough, we could lose her."

Without waiting for a reply, Charlie hung-up and grabbed the house phone to call for an ambulance. He didn't give a name just reported a shooting and gave the address. A quick call to Major Nelson followed.

"What's up, Chief? Your alarm just triggered?"

"Check all teams. Someone grabbed Sara and shot Liz. I assume they took out the agents assigned here, but I haven't had a chance to look."

"Watch your back, I'm on it." Major Nelson hung-up.

Charlie called his own house. His mother answered on the first ring. He was so relieved he needed to swallow twice before speaking. "Mom, hit the house alarm and get in the car right now and go to the warehouse. Right now, Mom!" Without waiting for a reply, he hung up and called his dad.

"Dad, you need to go the warehouse right now."

"What's happening?" John asked.

"I have no time to explain, just hurry. I love you."

Oz ran in the door a few minutes later.

"Jesus Christ!" He winked to Charlie's side and began conjuring bandages.

The first bandage absorbed instantly. He wadded another, placed it directly on the gunshot wound and applied pressure.

"Where's Sara?" Charlie finished tying his makeshift dishtowel bandage around Liz's shoulder.

"Still north." Oz met Charlie's eyes a moment, his own eyes bleak.

Charlie nodded and rose.

Liz opened her eyes.

"Oh, that hurts," she moaned as she tried to sit. "They have her. She's unconscious. I walked in as they were leaving."

"Stay down," Oz commanded. "I made a stack of bandages for you. Keep using them."

"An ambulance is coming, Liz. You'll be okay. Who took her?" Charlie crouched by Liz, his senses so acute he knew his eyes were glowing. His hands clenched into fists.

"Six men, four wearing regular clothes; jeans, and t-shirts, nothing memorable. The other two were dressed like paramedics. Everyone had short hair. I got a military vibe, but I could be wrong. You two, get to the warehouse. I'll be fine."

"We're going," Charlie said as Oz rewrapped her wound. He handed her the house phone, and they ran out the door.

"Did you get a hold of Hawk?" Charlie asked as they sprinted to his car.

"Yes, he was with Stasia. They're going for their mother," Oz said.

"Call your father now, Oz."

Oz was already telling his father to go to the warehouse.

Charlie called Stasia. The phone rang ten times with no answer and he exchanged a worried glance with Oz.

Oz called Hawk, who answered on the

third ring.

"Twenty tangos have our mother in the house," Hawk whispered.

"We're on our way. Try to keep one alive if you can. They have Sara."

Charlie watched Oz cast locate and knew he'd lost her by his expression.

Oz grabbed Charlie's phone when it rang. Charlie was busy breaking every traffic law getting to Stasia's house.

"Sarge, we have twenty tangos at Stasia's, and we're on our way there now. Recall the security there if any are left alive. We'll handle this. We need a helicopter standing by," Oz said.

"Get us a jet too." Charlie's jaw clenched. "Our best hope of finding them is if you can stay in the same zone as her."

"I heard him. I'm on it. How's Liz?" Guthrie asked.

"She'll be fine," Oz said," An ambulance was on its way, and I left her bandages."

"I'm on my way—"

"No." Charlie sounded calm while inside he raged with a fury that flushed his skin. "Stay at the warehouse. Our parents are coming to you. Get them somewhere safe. The warehouse is compromised. You could be in danger there, so stay alert."

"Roger that. I'll call when I get your jet."

Charlie parked in a neighbor's driveway, and he and Oz ran to meet Hawk.

"Mom's inside," Hawk's glowing blue eyes met theirs. "Five men are in the living room by the front door. Seven are in the kitchen with my mom and the rest are in the bedrooms."

"Oz, invis and Ice Shield, and get between Camila and the bad guys. You protect her, and we'll get the rest. In twenty seconds, we come in," Chief said as he glanced at his watch.

Oz nodded and ran to the back of the house where he teleported through the wall into Stasia's bedroom using Wink. He cast Invisible Duo and sprinted down the hallway to the kitchen.

Stasia stood invisibly beside her mother.

Tapping his watch, he held up eight fingers, putting them down as the seconds ticked off.

Charlie charged through the door of the living room with a kitchen knife he'd taken from Sara's in his hand, yelling his attack cry then casting drop-weapon.

The five men in the living room dropped

their weapons and stared in shock as Charlie leapt and stabbed the man nearest the kitchen doorway in the throat. The corpse fell to the floor as he cast Waylay and appeared beside the man who stood in the hallway reaching for his gun on the floor.

The man held up his hands as Charlie grabbed him and stabbed him four times before he could blink. The dying man gurgled and slid to the floor, clutching at his chest.

A scuffle behind Charlie made him whirl. Hawk held a man against the wall with one hand, reaching for the gun at his waist. The man stared with terrified eyes at Charlie.

A feral smile on his face, Charlie jumped, landing atop the couch and grabbing the man hiding behind it, using him as a human shield as another man ran into the room firing his gun.

He threw the man he held into the wall as hard as he could, not sparing a glance at the wet splatter and grappled the gun from the man standing in the hallway. The gun flicked from the man's hand to Charlie's instantly. Charlie threw it as hard as he could at the now unarmed man. Men ran in the front door and doors banged open down the hallway.

Gunfire echoed in the room and the unarmed man fell, clutching at the wide hole in his chest. Wide eyed, he gaped at his bloody hands as he fell face first to the floor.

A gun sounded again in impossibly fast succession. Black smoky swirls streamed past Charlie's face, the afterimage of Hawk's Swift Shot. Before Charlie could turn, Hawk had killed all the men in the room. The two ran down the hallway.

Charlie kicked in the door to Stasia's room and leapt forward, yanking the man scrambling out the window back into the room so hard he broke his neck.

Behind him, Hawk fired again. Charlie threw the corpse to the floor and ran back to the hallway.

Hawk had a man frozen in place in his room. The man batted at his smoldering clothing while he swore between threats.

Charlie ripped the blanket from the bed and tied him tightly, proud of himself for not killing the man although he longed too, while Hawk dove out the window and fired again.

When Charlie yelled and entered the house, Stasia sapped the man nearest her, appeared behind the man on the other side of her mother, and killed him with one quick slice. Blood sprayed, and men screamed as she leapt to the next man and killed him too before he got a shot off.

Oz pushed Camila to the floor and cast a lightning bolt at the man standing in the doorway pointing his gun in their direction. The man fell as Oz cast an instant fire wave at the man beside him. The man screamed and batted at the flames as he raced from the room.

A loud fight erupted in the living room. A gun sounded, deafeningly loud, in the small kitchen. A bullet hit Oz's Frost Shield and tumbled to the floor. Fire bloomed around him as he cast Fire Shield and teleported forward.

Stasia cast her defensive cool-downs and killed four more men with a kitchen knife, leaving one who Oz took out with lighting. More gunfire broke out, and Stasia ran into the other room.

Oz summoned his dagger and shouted for Hawk to take it. After dispelling Fire Shield, he cast Freezing Rain, letting it channel for thirty seconds to put out the fires he'd started before grabbing Camila's hand, and pulling her out the back door.

Two minutes later, Hawk ran out the door and yelled, "It's clear, let's go!"

Camila shook in Hawk's embrace.

Ignoring her questions and protests, they ran to the car and sped off to the warehouse.

"Where's Sara?"

"Don't know, sorry, Chief." Oz shook his head. "At my last sighting, she was north."

Charlie nodded, not surprised. "Call Guthrie and see if our parents are there and if we have transport."

Oz called and spoke quietly.

Mrs. Morales cried in the back seat. "What's going on? Who were those people? Did you kill everyone?"

"Yes, we killed them. Other than bad, I don't know who they were." Stasia gritted her teeth, gripping her mother's hand tightly.

"Man, I better call Rick. We planned to meet." Oz took his cell phone out.

"I'll call him," Stasia said, "You talk to Guthrie."

Stasia tapped a speed dial. It rang ten times, and she called again.

Oz frowned in concern but was busy talking to Guthrie. He hit speakerphone.

"Head there now," Guthrie was saying.

"Okay, hold on." Oz held the phone in the air between them. "You're on speaker. Chief, go to the airport. Guthrie has our parents and will meet us there. Team Alpha is missing. Team Beta is accounted for and will join us."

"Rick isn't answering," Stasia hollered from the back seat.

"Yeah, he was transferred to Alpha; we're reforming the teams. That doesn't matter. What matters is we have seven teammates unaccounted for."

"Get us a jet now." Blue magic flickered around Charlie for a moment. The magic expanded away from him in swirling blue clouds lit with static, going outside the car before returning and reabsorbing into his skin. "They know what we can do. If they take her far enough away and keep moving, we won't be able to find her."

"An F-15 is getting ready as we speak. The president is issuing a red terror alert. All planes will be grounded. Oz, you go in the f-15. The pilot will transport you wherever you say. When you arrive at the airport, get suited up. I have your gear with me."

"Our house is a mess." Hawk gave his mother a hug and an apologetic wince. "One man is tied. The rest are dead."

"Agent Lewis will handle that. What's your ETA?"

Charlie glanced at his watch. "Twelve minutes." They'd been to the airfield so often in the last few months while hunting missing persons he could drive there blindfolded.

"We'll beat you there. A safe house is being arranged for your parents. I'm not telling you where for their protection."

"Fine," Charlie agreed. "Can I speak with my mother?"

"I can hear you." Mary sounded as if she'd been crying. "Dad and I are okay. We love you. Please be careful."

"I love you too, Mom. We'll get them back." Again, Charlie's magic burst from him and swirled around. It wanted Sara too. He felt it's need and fear separate from his.

When they arrived at the airport, they went directly to the usual hanger. Guthrie waited with their gear. They stripped down right there and dressed.

"We must have a traitor." Charlie grabbed his swords and sheathed them in one fluid move. The familiar weight soothed him. Every moment he grew angrier, rage empowering him. When they found who'd done this, his magic would be unstoppably strong.

"Yeah, I think so too. They knew exactly who they needed to grab first. It had to be Sara, or she could have summoned any of you back," Guthrie said.

"Why take Alpha though?" Stasia asked as

she tightened her knives and loosened her throwing stars.

"I think they were trying to capture all of you," Guthrie said as he loaded Oz's gun. "If Chief hadn't called, Oz would've met with the fake Rick, and you two would've walked into your house without knowing bad guys waited inside. Team Beta ingested tranquilizers in their food, but Charlie hitting his panic button let us get to them before they could be taken away. They should be fine in a few hours. That's probably how they abducted Sara and maybe how they planned to take Oz. Who called you to meet Rick?"

"Sergeant Rinto. He said he, Rick, and Drew were in town and Rick wanted to surprise his parents and Chief for Christmas. We planned to meet for pizza."

Guthrie nodded. "Hmm, he was on Major Nelson's team and took early retirement after the last mission, one of our no-go's. We better check on all of them. I need to make a call. Let's move out." He climbed into the helicopter. "Get us to Elgin Air Force base as fast as you can," he told the pilot and called Captain Sanders.

"Locate the no-goes. There's a possibility some are involved. Yes, I understand. We're headed there now." Guthrie hung up his phone. "Oz, we need reports ASAP. This helicopter and your jet will be the only ones with flight clearance. All commercial, military, and private planes are grounded. Zigzag up the coast trying every zone. Liz reported Sara was carried out unresponsive on a stretcher. If Sara regains consciousness, I'm sure she'll be casting her Call-For-Help. Be prepared to be summoned to her. Hit your panic button before doing anything else."

He handed Oz an extra clip for his pistol. "Your priority is finding her. When you do, we'll go in together. I want your priorities in this fight to be crystal-clear. Team Valor must survive. If that means letting a bad guy get away, we do. If that means leaving Alpha team behind, we do. Am I clear?"

"Yes, sir," they chorused.

Oz boarded an F-15, while Charlie stood grim-faced.

"We'll find her, son." Guthrie put a comforting hand on his shoulder. Charlie watched through narrowed, glowing eyes as the jet took off.

- 30 -

VIDEO PROOF

Sara woke in a small room tied to a chair. The room spun, and nausea roiled her stomach. It took her a moment to notice a man sat across from her holding a shotgun. Five other men held pistols trained on her. One man held a video camera. Someone pulled her hair, yanking her head back.

"Show us what you got, sweetheart," he said with a sneer and slapped her hard.

The door opened, and another man entered dragging Brenda, gagged and blindfolded, her hands and feet bound. Another man followed, toting Rick in the same condition. Their captors dropped them on the floor and left and a man she recognized entered.

"You do one thing, you even twitch your fingers, and I'll kill them. Do you understand me?"

Sara swallowed hard.

Sergeant Rinto sounded as if this was all perfectly normal.

She tried to nod.

The man holding her head back tightened his grip in her hair.

Sergeant Rinto removed her gag.

"Yes, I understand." Tears trailed down her cheeks.

"My buyer wants proof, so you're going to put on a show." Sergeant Rinto untied her, grabbing her hair cruelly tight, shot Rick in the leg, and then ripped his pants so the wound was visible. "Heal him."

Sara cast a chain heal and the injury disappeared. Rinto punched her in the face, rocking her head backward. "Just him! I know what you did."

The cold barrel of a gun rested on her temple as another man shot Brenda and then Rick in the stomach. Both screamed, muffled by the gags, and jerked as if trying to clench their wounds. Sara healed them both without waiting and put a shield on them. Rinto punched her again. This time the skin on her cheek split open, and she whimpered.

"Let's get serious here. We want to see a resurrection."

"No, I've never—"

The sound of a gunshot cut her off. She screamed as they shot Brenda in the head. Her shield stopped the first shots. Sara tried to cast a heal on her as Rinto shot Brenda four more times in the head in quick succession, but the man behind her grabbed her hands and squeezed.

She struggled, trying to force her fingers to move.

"Stand on her fingers. Crush them if she twitches." Two men forced Sara to the ground and stood on her hands, keeping her face down on the floor while Brenda died.

"Okay, let her up, she's dead."

Sara stood unsteadily, blinded by tears and sobbing. First, she healed herself and then cast resurrection on Brenda. Bright yellow light interspersed with sparkling blue static surrounded Brenda and Sara sagged in relief as Brenda stirred and her face reformed.

Sergeant Rinto laughed. "They'll pay so much for you. Do it again," he said, and shot Brenda in the face while Sara screamed.

"Stop please," Sara begged. "I can't do it! There's a timer, and you'll really kill her."

"So, what? We don't need her. Save him then." The gun in his hand barked, and Rick's head exploded into blood and gore. Sara cast her Mass Resurrection and attacked.

She twitched her fingers and tipped her head back, screaming her fear spell, making all the men in the room run from her in a panic. While they blundered into walls and each other, she cast a damage-over-time spell on each of them.

Men yelled in the hallway, rapid footsteps approaching as she began to smite. Orangish-yellow balls of light knocked men down and back, and she was certain she'd killed at least two before gunshots from the doorway interrupted her.

She cast a mirrored shield on herself and smiled a feral smile when the man shooting screamed and tumbled to the floor.

Another man fired, the bullets hitting her new shield and tumbling away but her fear ran out, and the men in the room began firing. The impacts knocked her back but not down.

The rate of fire increased, and she screamed shrilly as bullets made it through her shield. Blood sprayed, and she slipped in the gore on the floor.

Yellow streaks of light flew from her fingertips, healing herself and her tied teammates as she kept attacking. Sergeant Rinto fled the room.

"Grab her hands, idiots," he yelled. "Don't kill her. We need her alive!"

Someone grabbed her arm, and she threw him into a wall and kicked out. Silver Shields formed around Brenda and Rick, and she used her heal-over-time spells on them and herself.

Any men that entered range of her feet got kicked as she cast Smite and put up more damage-over-time spells on everyone in sight. Five men lay unmoving on the floor now, either dead or unconscious and more lay in the hallway.

Unable to fight effectively in the small room while healing both Brenda and Rick and being shot by men in the hallway she couldn't target, she forced her way through the door.

More shots were fired, and she fell to the ground screaming, then healed herself, and jumped back up. Another volley of shots knocked her over.

"We'll kill them if you don't stop right now!" Sergeant Rinto yelled from the hallway.

Sara didn't stop; they would kill them regardless. A shotgun blast hit her in the chest, and she went down again.

She healed herself with a heal-over-time and a Chain Heal, cast a new shield on herself, and pushed into the hallway. Someone fell on her and grabbed her arm. Someone else stamped on her hand. She screamed and fought to get loose as her fingers broke. Tears and blood covered her face. Moaning and crying, she struggled upright and shrieked as she forced her broken fingers to cast a heal and then used Greater Fear again.

While they ran away from her, she healed herself fully, put up more damage-over-time spells on everyone in sight, and started smiting, wishing she had a staff, but nothing in the room was long enough.

She cast her Lesser Fear and small glowing black balls of light dribbled from her fingertips. The balls rolled and bounced along the floor, walls, and ceiling, making the men they touched cower on the floor screaming.

Orange balls of light flew from her fingers, impacting the attacking men and making them shriek or fall motionless to the ground. More men ran into the hallway, stepping over and on the corpses lining the floor, and fired weapons at her while others shot at her blindly hidden behind doorways, giving her no line-of-sight.

Men yelled at her and each other, but the gunshots and her panting breaths drowned them out. Another round of shots hit her shoulder and more hit her legs, each a red-hot stab of agony.

The sound of gunfire reverberated in the hallway, competing with the sounds of screams. Someone came in with a machine gun, and she shrieked as the bullets tore a line through her stomach and over her arms. Blood gushed from her wounds, and she had to stop attacking to heal herself.

Someone tackled her and grabbed her hand while she was casting the heal and someone else stamped on it. She tried to get off another heal but couldn't pull her hand free or move her fingers.

"Stop!" Sergeant Rinto yelled. "We need her alive."

"She'll kill us all!" the man holding her down shouted back.

The bone in her arm broke with a sharp crack as he twisted it behind her back and she screamed shrilly. Booted feet stamped on her hands, breaking her fingers. Pain made the room spin, and she vomited and choked.

Sergeant Rinto leaned down, wound his fist in her hair, and screamed in her ear, "I'll kill them both permanently if you move. Cast one heal on yourself. Anything else, and I'll let you all die. Let her move her fingers once."

Still sobbing, she forced her broken fingers to move and cast a heal and tried to cast fear. A rifle butt hit her in the head, cracking her skull. She fell to the floor unconscious and didn't feel it when they broke her fingers into pieces.

"Jesus, and this isn't even one of the fighters," a man panted as he dragged her into a nearby room.

"Give her more sedative. We have enough video. Put her in the box. We're moving them." Sergeant Rinto glared at Sara's unconscious form. "Maybe we better check her first to make sure she doesn't bleed out."

They cut off her clothes, leaving her in her underwear, threw her in the shower, and rinsed the blood off.

"Yeah, she'll live. Put an IV in and bandage those wounds up; they won't kill her. Tie her hands down. Make certain she can't even twitch them. Keep her damn fingers broken!"

Sergeant Rinto left the men to finish tying her and sauntered into the other room where Rick and Brenda lay, surrounded by armed, angry men. He removed their gags and blindfolds. "You two okay? Not dead on me, are you?"

Neither answered him.

"One of you is all I need," he said conversationally. "I'll shoot her in the face again."

"I'll live," Rick mumbled.

Sergeant Rinto patted him on the head.

"Yes, until I kill you." He kicked Brenda lightly in the leg. "So, any ill effects? Still feeling chipper?"

"Go to hell," she said through clenched teeth.

"Be careful, Chicky. No one is here to resurrect you this time."

Brenda just glared at him.

Sergeant Rinto eyed the blood splattered walls and the dead men on the floor. "Lucky for you, I didn't like them much. Give me any trouble, and your cub will pay."

Two men entered a few minutes later, and dragged them out, throwing them back into the room with the rest of team Alpha.

"Take them to the van in pairs and don't let your guard down; they're tougher than they look," someone said from the hallway.

Four men grabbed Joy and Drew and dragged them out. Joy was still unconscious. Drew struggled until a rifle butt slammed him in the head.

"For every hit you take, the girl gets two, so knock off the shit!" the man who hit him said and smirked.

In thirty minutes, they were on a boat. The smell of salt air and the rocking motion made it clear.

"Nighty night," the same voice said, and a

needle poked Rick's arm. He knew nothing else.

Sara woke in the dark. Both gagged and blindfolded, she could neither see nor speak. Agony shot up her arms as she tried to move her fingers. The pain in her arm and hands caused her to whimper as she pulled and jerked, trying to free them. A high moaning shriek was all she managed behind the gag, sobbing as she rocked from side-to-side trying to get free.

Wood surrounded her, and she started to hyperventilate, imagining herself buried alive. She tried to move her fingers as she waited, sobbing over the sharp stabs of pain. If she could loosen her fingers, the pain would stop in moments. After what seemed like hours, someone finally entered. The door squeaked open, and footsteps approached.

"Awake already? You metabolize this stuff fast, nighty night." A needle pierced her arm, and the world disappeared.

Oz flew up the coast, over Georgia and the Carolinas, over Virginia, Washington, and

Maryland and then across Pennsylvania and Connecticut. They landed to refuel and flew over Massachusetts and New Hampshire. The flight went to Maine and over to Vermont and down to New York. They covered Michigan and headed back to Florida covering Ohio, West Virginia, Kentucky, Tennessee, and Alabama. He didn't get a glimmer anywhere.

"Okay, do it again," Guthrie said when Oz returned. "This time go out to international waters; try there, then make the loop again. We might have missed them before."

Oz grabbed a bathroom break and a sandwich and climbed back into the jet where a new pilot waited.

The remaining Scouts had gathered in Washington. Agent Lewis sat at a small table inside a conference room at Bolling Air Base. Papers, maps, and empty coffee cups littered the table. It had been two days, and they hadn't spotted Sara or Alpha team yet.

"Oz, we want you to fly over Canada, and then we'll go to the Middle East and try there. We won't give up. We'll find them," Guthrie said.

"New intel has come in. We've been tracking Sergeant Rinto's known associates and tracing his every move," Agent Lewis said. "We found a man in Massachusetts Rinto talked with at the harbor about hiring a fishing boat. The man remembers he carried Canadian money. Now, that might mean nothing, but it's worth checking. We have permission to fly over Canada. Oz can check each province in twenty-two hours. In six hours, we leave. Go get some sleep, Oz. We'll catch you up on the rest of this briefing when you wake."

Oz nodded and went next door, stretched out on the floor, and was asleep in seconds.

Charlie stood over his sleeping form, the scowl on his face deepening. Oz had spent the last forty-eight hours crisscrossing the United States casting Magical Locate constantly. Now his mage was exhausted and his sun-priest still missing.

"Team Beta will go with Team Valor," Major Nelson was saying when Charlie entered the room. He stopped speaking until Charlie sat at the table. "We know there is a link here to ISIS and Sergeant Rinto. What we don't know is if he's working for them or if he's the one in charge. We're proceeding as if he is. Agents are checking everywhere he's been and setting up a timeline to check his whereabouts. The men killed at the Morales house had known ISIS links. The lone survivor isn't talking yet.

"Because we think the Canada angle is a real possibility, we want Team Valor and Beta to fly to Quebec. If"— Major Nelson glanced at Charlie's furious face and straightened, saying firmly— "when, Oz finds her, we'll be close. These printouts show known associates of the men killed. We'll have Oz look for them too. One more day remains of the red alert. The president will lift the flight ban in four hours." Major Nelson rose from the table. "Our plane leaves in one hour. Dismissed."

Charlie, Stasia, and Hawk stayed seated as everyone else filed from the room. The Scouts stopped and offered words of encouragement as they passed.

"We'll find her, Chief," Stasia said, putting an arm around his shoulders.

He nodded but didn't reply. Blue magic swirled around Stasia before returning to him. His jaw tightened with the effort to control himself. That brief contact, when his magic had touched Stasia, inflamed him even more. Her fear and anger enraged him anew. He hadn't slept since Sara had been taken and felt no need for sleep. The magic and his rage sustained him.

Sweat beaded on his brow and it was all

he could do to remain seated. Only by telling himself repeatedly that rushing out wouldn't help was he able to remain in the room.

They headed to the airplane to wait. Dressed in black with sunglasses covering their glowing blue eyes everyone who saw Charlie scurried away, casting fear filled glances over their shoulders. His aura was so strong people in offices with their doors closed exclaimed. He caused a panic just leaving the building, making people run away calling for help.

His magic felt satisfied with that response, but it didn't ease him. He didn't care about these people. These people weren't his enemy. He wanted with a need beyond desperate to find his enemies. Forcing himself to sit and wait was the hardest thing he'd ever done.

Agent Lewis boarded the plane twenty minutes before it was due to leave. "Change of plans. We found a house in Massachusetts we want Hawk to see. We're going there now." He led them to a waiting helicopter.

"What did you find?" Hawk asked.

"A mess. We want you to look at it and see if you can find anything we missed. The man you captured at your house has a connection to this address, so we think it's related. We don't know for sure though."

With a small wince, he handed Hawk a stack of photos. "This could be completely unrelated. Don't get upset."

Hawk took the pictures and rifled through them, his face whitening. "I can't tell a thing from these. I need to go there."

Stasia grabbed the pile from him and stopped on one. "She was there. I recognize the clothes." Stasia's breath caught on a sob.

Charlie took the pictures from her.

Photographs of blood-saturated clothing laying on a floor nearly black with blood and gore were followed by individual pictures of the clothing spread out. A long-sleeved shirt, red from blood, with a black and white cat on the front pierced with so many bullet holes the cat was almost indistinguishable. Jeans that were so riddled with bullet holes they barely hung together. White sneakers red from blood.

He sighed in relief.

"Stasia, she didn't have a shirt like that, and her sneaks are bright blue."

Stasia sat with her eyes closed. "She went shopping with me the other day; she just bought them. She said the cat reminded her of Prince."

Charlie turned in horror to the picture of the clothes again. "Are you sure?"

Stasia nodded.

"Jesus Christ, she must have been shot fifty times!" Blue magic leaked from his skin as his anger mounted.

"Seventy-two," Agent Lewis said softly after reading his notes. "But she could easily be alive using her own heals. We'll keep looking." He cleared his throat. "Brain matter smeared the wall of the room where the fight took place. Two people were shot against a wall in this room."

The blood-smeared wall in the picture Agent Lewis handed them showed two distinct marks of extreme violence.

"Quite a lot of blood is splattered about that room, and we're running the DNA samples now. I'm hoping Hawk can track her from there."

Thunder rumbled in the distance although the day remained clear. The small hairs on Charlie's arms rose as the smell of ozone built.

"Keep it together," Stasia whispered. She hugged him tightly. "We need their help to find her."

Feeling Stasia close and unhurt helped calm him. He pulled Hawk into an embrace and hugged them both till his breathing steadied.

Agent Lewis watched, biting his lip and

rolling the report in his hands.

When Charlie stepped from the plane, the armed and armored soldiers surrounding it hunched and rose their weapons.

"Stand down!" Agent Lewis bellowed. "You're protecting them," he called in a voice laced with irony.

Charlie snorted, his glance lingering on Major Nelson who stood behind the nearest group of armed Marines. It was clear to him the major thought he would rampage and had brought these men to stop him. A smile formed beneath his face mask.

"Thirty seconds. That's all it would take me," he said to the major.

Major Nelson blanched and tightened his grip on his rifle.

"You aren't my enemy though," Charlie continued in a normal voice, proud of himself for his calm tone. "Yet," he added. The magic roiled within him then settled and the men facing them eased.

Stasia snickered quietly.

"All green to me," Hawk said loudly and slapped Charlie's shoulder. He rose his face mask and gave Charlie an exasperated glance, then rolled his eyes at his sister.

The major nodded and lowered his weapon.

"This way to the helicopter," he said and gestured them to proceed him.

The surrounding soldiers straightened looking interested and alert but not afraid. His aura wasn't affecting them now, Charlie thought in satisfaction, glad he was gaining some sort of control.

"These are my men," he whispered to himself.

Stasia heard though and squeezed his bicep. "They are and will follow where you lead."

Charlie pondered that until they arrived at the scene.

Agent Lewis escorted them past the police tape and news vans. The armor they wore made them impossible to identify, and reporters yelled questions after them.

Charlie barely heard them, his entire attention was on Hawk, willing him to be able to follow.

Hawk searched and followed a trail invisible to everyone except him. He jogged along the road for seventy miles leading them to a pier in Boston Harbor while Agent Lewis trailed in the car with Charlie and Stasia.

"Okay, they took a boat. Nice work, Hawk. Let me see what I can find out."

Agent Lewis started making phone calls.

More agents showed up while Team Valor waited in Agent Lewis's car. Charlie was practically crying with the effort to hold his magic back. He wanted to fight, to rend and tear his enemies and bath in their blood. He craved violence with a need he'd never experienced before.

"Okay, we need to get to the airport. You're going to Quebec." Agent Lewis said when he finally got back in the car.

"Have they found them?" Charlie's eyes were full of hope, and his hand caressed the sword he held unsheathed in his lap.

"The boat that docks here went to Montreal four weeks ago. We'll find them. Every second that passes, we grow closer."

Stasia nodded and sat back in her seat.

"Guys, she's most likely alive, they need her alive." Agent Lewis laid a light hand on Charlie's shoulder.

"They have team Alpha and shot two, which we know are dead. The Scouts are our family…" Hawk trailed off and cleared his throat.

Agent Lewis nodded. "We'll find the people responsible."

Charlie said nothing. Rage coursed through him. God help them when he found them, he had no mercy in him.

- 31 -

OZ FINDS SARA

Sara woke again in the pitch-black, not a sliver of light showed. Her fingers were numb. She attempted to move them but had no sensation other than pain. She'd lost count of how many times she'd awoken alone in the dark, how long she'd struggled to get free.

A metallic sound when she moved informed her she still laid on a metal table. At first, she'd been happy to not be encased in wood but the tinny metallic sound the table made terrified her now. It sounded like she imagined an autopsy table would sound.

A scream tried to claw its way from her throat, but all she managed was a soft whimper behind the gag.

Time had ceased to register. She didn't know if it had been hours or days; it felt like forever. The dull throb in her arm flared into agony as she strained again to wiggle her fingers. Only pain remained with no sense of movement. Afraid she would vomit and choke, she stopped trying, unable to feel her fingers anyway. A hoarse sob was all she could manage as she wondered if they had cut off her hands.

Am I on a dissection table? Are they cutting me up one piece at a time? The thought horrified her, and she began to cry and struggle futilely till pain made her head spin.

Voices warned someone approached to inject her again. She almost welcomed it as a relief from pain, but if she was unconscious, she couldn't cast Call-for-Help.

Again, she tried to cast her Call-for-Help. The door creaked as it opened, but not even a flicker of light lit the darkness surrounding her. The sun, she needed it; she craved it. If she didn't feel sunlight soon, she would go mad.

The agony from her broken arm made her sob as she tried with all her strength to cast her Call-for-Help.

"My passenger disappeared," the jet pilot said in confusion.

Charlie closed his eyes and took a deep

breath. Oz had found her. The magic surrounding him receded as he let himself become excited at the prospect of violence.

"Don't be alarmed. Return to base," Major Nelson ordered the pilot. "He's using a new stealth ability to jump from the jet, and we're tracking him. I don't need to say this is highly classified, do I?"

"No sir," the pilot said. "It worked very well. None of my indicators for a hatch opening sounded. If he hadn't been connected to my interior sensors, I would've assumed he was still there, but unconscious."

One moment Oz sat in the back of a jet with his eyes closed, casting locate, the next he stood in a pitch-black room. Voices warned him men approached the room. A soft click sounded loud in his ears as he unholstered his gun and got ready to cast. Two men talking at the door drowned out the small noises he made. A hand outstretched, he backed up slowly, putting space between himself and the approaching voices as he prepared to fight.

"This is stupid, let's just turn a light on," one man said.

"No, our orders are she stays in the dark, no light at all. Give her the shot, and I'll check the IV."

A narrow beam from a pen light barely pierced the darkness, making the men mere dark shapes in the pitch-black room. A muffled moan as the light flicked on made Oz tense.

"Let's have a little fun with her before she goes," the other said.

"Touch her, and I'll kill you myself. She's worth two-million dollars. You're worth shit."

"Who would know? All this trouble for one girl— those Marines aren't even being kept this secure."

The light played over a table and sheet draped form and the moan increased.

"Shut up, stupid. We aren't touching her! Give her the damn shot."

"Don't get your panties in a bunch, I gave it to her. I don't know what the big deal is, we'll kill her if we keep giving her this shit every six hours."

"Go check on the others. I'm finished here."

Oz hit his panic button and reached for his cellphone as the door closed behind the two men. "I found her."

"Where are you?" Charlie's voice was tight with emotion.

"That I don't know. We entered Quebec

airspace, and she summoned me."

"Put her on."

"This room is pitch-black, and I can't see her. I think she's unconscious now." He told Charlie everything he'd heard.

"Get her out of there."

"I'm trying."

Oz used the light on his phone to survey the area. A metal gurney in front of him held a cloth-draped figure. Sara was tied chest, waist, ankles, and hands and covered with a cold, wet sheet. The wounds and bruises covering her body made tears come to his eyes. Not reporting her condition, he made a stack of bandages and applied one while he worked on untying her.

"We're in a basement of some sort with a dirt floor, and cement walls. I need both hands for a minute." Oz put the phone down and conjured his dagger.

He holstered his gun and cut Sara loose, being careful of the blood-soaked bandages holding her smashed fingers to a small board.

The tape binding her swollen, black fingers to a plank that went under her back parted easily under his blade. He almost cried when he saw they'd nailed her fingers down and had to fight back nausea as he pulled her fingers free, glad she was unconscious and felt nothing.

He slapped her cheek trying to rouse her but received no response. Once he assured himself no bonds remained, he picked up his phone, cradling it between his shoulder and cheek as he conjured bandages to wrap about her bleeding hands.

"Oz, we've found you," Guthrie said a few minutes later. "Jesus, okay, two hours, Oz. You're in the freaking boonies."

"I can't wake her. She's untied. I'm getting us out of this room. My phone will be on in my pocket with your end muted. I don't want you giving me away."

Oz cautiously tried the door to the room and found it unlocked. Gun in one hand, cell phone in the other, he opened the door and peeked out. No one waited. With a last glance at Sara, still on the table, he went to investigate.

A set of stairs leading up stood in front of him. The basement consisted of one other large room and a small closet that held cleaning supplies. He tucked his cell phone beneath the strap that held his radio to his shoulder with the speaker above the chin plate for the mic and holstered his gun.

Careful of creaking steps, he listened at the door. Hearing nothing, he tried it. The door was locked, so he winked through it into an empty kitchen.

A quick check of the door across from him revealed a cramped pantry. Afraid to leave Sara alone, out of his sight, he returned for her.

The light sheet covering her was cold and wet. A hose on the floor, he assumed they used to clean her, dripped icy water. The crooked angle and black streaks crawling up her arm from her black fingers made him wince.

He tied her broken arm to her side with conjured bandages. It worried him wrapping her in the damp sheet, but he had nothing else. Her normally warm skin felt cold and clammy.

Trying to be gentle, he carried her up the stairs through the now unlocked basement door and headed towards the living room.

Two men talking in the other room drew closer.

He changed direction, easing into the pantry with her, and listened at the door.

"No, we go tonight," one man said. "The general is sending a ship. Once we're in international waters, he won't be able to find us. We need six more hours."

"What about them?"

"Save two, we're dumping the rest."

"Can we have the women then?"

"Jesus, whatever, who cares! Find out what two Rinto wants first though."

The refrigerator opened, and an electric can opener sounded. "Who the hell cooked this slop?"

"I'm sick of your whining. Cook it your damn self."

Oz tensed, anticipating the man coming to the pantry for food.

"Screw it, I'll eat on the ship. I'm gonna talk to the boss."

"Yeah, you do that." The other man sounded disgusted.

Oz listened to the quiet sounds from the kitchen as he took out his phone. He texted Stasia, 'the general is the traitor,' and put the phone back on his shoulder. Another man entered, followed by three more all talking over each other.

The bottles behind Oz rattled as he backed into them, getting into the farthest corner of the small pantry. The door knob twisted. Oz turned himself and Sara invisible as far from the door as he could get in the tiny area.

A man turned to speak over his shoulder as he turned on the pantry light. "There isn't much in here. Want the pasta?"

"Yeah, any canned sauce?"

"Yes, basil, meat, or marinara?"

"Meat. I guess."

Oz watched tensely as the man grabbed the items from the shelves. When he walked away, Oz slipped out the open pantry door and headed to the front room when more men walked in that way. The men laughed and joked about the pictures they'd taken of Sara being their payday.

A frown of concentration crossed his face as he memorized what they looked like. Later, he would be able to find them. No one involved with her abduction would be able to hide from him.

Slow and careful, he eased up the stairs, hoping they wouldn't creak. A long hallway ran in front of him with both open and closed doors and a lot of men. Three or more men loitered in every open room he passed. A man sat in a chair before one of the shut doorways.

Alpha team was probably behind the door.

A quick glance at his watch showed him twenty seconds left on invisible. Oz got as close to the wall as he could and teleported through, hoping the man sitting before the door wouldn't notice the flicker when they became visible as Wink took effect, or disregard it if he did.

Chained to the radiators, Alpha team sat on the floor of the empty room. Oz waited in the corner to see what the sentry did. After a few minutes, he decided the guard hadn't spotted them and bent to examine Rick.

Gagged, blindfolded, and manacled he was bloodstained and filthy. Before removing Rick's blindfold, he whispered who he was, placed Sara in his lap, and removed his gag.

Each member of Alpha team received a personal visit as he whispered help was coming and loosened their blindfolds and gags so they could remove them with a quick headshake.

A minute's effort produced conjured bandages, and he wrapped everyone. Joy lay on the floor untied and unmoving. With relief, he found a pulse, slow and weak, but there. The chains holding them were beyond his ability to loosen, his conjured dagger barely scratched them and he wished he'd rolled a wizard. He needed a key.

Drew sat in front of the door with his hands chained before him. The chain passed through the radiator to Brenda whose hands were behind her back. He unholstered his gun, racked it, and placed it in Drew's hand, dropping the extra clip in his lap.

Oz returned to Rick. "How long till they check on you again?" he whispered.

"No set schedule, but they were just in here," Rick whispered back.

Oz nodded and peeked out the window. His eyes narrowed as he lifted the phone to his lips. "This place is prepared for us. Spikes are spaced every six inches, ten feet out from the walls. Don't hop over. Dogs are chained every twenty feet. I'm guessing to alert if Stasia passes by but they must not know Hawk can control them. Or maybe they're meant to distract him. Cameras line the inside of the walls and three-man patrols, both stationary and walking, are talking on their radios constantly. I'm in an upstairs bedroom, fourth door on the left. This window faces north and has an off-white lace curtain going across the top. The window is unlocked. Alpha team is with me, and all except Joy are awake, chained down, and I can't get them loose. I'm turning mute off but speak quietly. What's your ETA?"

"One hour, forty-five minutes," Charlie whispered.

Oz squatted by Drew again. "Okay, if they come in, I'll hold Sara and invis. If it wears off, I'll attack and try to hand you the key. You get everyone else free while I hold the door. Once everybody is free, go through the window and to the right. There's a small shed there we can use as cover. I'll make everyone bandages," Oz said as he made them. "Use one on every cooldown if you're hurt."

He positioned a stack of bandages out of sight behind everyone, trying to leave them where they could grab them with their chained hands. Oz wrapped a new bandage on Joy's wrist. The first bandage had disappeared already. Sara's had absorbed, so he wound more around her hands. He used a new bandage on everyone, being careful to hide them in case the door opened suddenly.

"Brenda, when you're free, take my dagger. Rick, you carry Sara. Marcus, bring Joy. Tony, go out first. Sam, and, Todd, you go last," Oz whispered to each of them.

Nothing in the room could cover Sara. The black shirt he wore under his armor reached her thighs. The wounds, bruises, and dried blood covering her showed starkly against her white, pale skin. His eyes narrowed, and he gritted his teeth. *Someone would pay.*

With a wince, he wrapped her again in the damp sheet, handed her back to Rick, and put his vest back on. The bandages he'd applied were already absorbed. Sara's fingers looked a bit better to him, less swollen anyway, and they'd stopped bleeding. He kept making the rounds of bandages until they stopped disappearing.

Oz listened at the door ready at a moment's notice to use invisible on himself and Sara. "You hear my voice, ditch the gags and blindfolds," Oz told them. "Wait as long as we can for our backup."

After taking Sara back from Rick, he sat in a corner holding her on his lap, applying his bandages to her and Joy every time the cooldown allowed.

When the guard in front of the door spoke; he ripped the bandage off Joy, picked up Sara, and cast invisible right as the door opened.

A man entered and gazed out the window for a minute before prodding Joy with his foot and frowning at Brenda. Still scowling, he left the room and locked the door.

"ETA?" Oz whispered as he committed the man's face to memory.

"Thirty-five minutes," Charlie answered.

The longest thirty-five minutes of Oz's life passed in complete silence. Joy lay on the floor unmoving. Sara remained unconscious in his lap.

"We're here," Charlie announced. Cold anticipation filled his voice.

CHIEF

A helicopter passed over the house and men outside yelled. Oz laid Sara in Rick's lap again.

"When this starts, I'll invis you two."

More men yelled as the helicopter returned and someone came to the door. Oz cast Invisible Duo on himself and Rick as the door opened.

Two men stood at the door, one entered the room. Oz used his dagger and slammed the door. The dead body thumped to the floor, blocking the door. Oz frisked the man but didn't find the keys.

After casting Ice Shield, he opened the door and cast an instant Fire Wave on the man standing there holding a gun. The man screamed and shot him. Lightning flickered from Oz's fingertips, knocking the man back. The gunman fell to the floor dead. Flames licked over the smoldering corpse. Oz dragged him inside the room and searched him.

"Got um!" he shouted, dropped the keys in Drew's outstretched hand, and ran to the window in time to see Team Beta drop from the helicopter over the house.

Oz opened the window and shot a fireball into the group of men holding a rocket launcher aimed at the helicopter.

Stasia fought already, waylaying her targets, showing up behind them, using her daggers and disappearing as the men turned to fire on her. He winced as a bullet hit her leg. Stasia didn't seem to notice; it didn't slow her at all. He ducked back as bullets flew in his window.

"I see you," Hawk warned Oz. "You have eight men incoming."

Oz returned to the hallway. "I'm ready with a fireball, Hawk, say when."

A large orange ball of fire sailed down the hall as Hawk said now.

"Again, Oz," Hawk said.

So, he threw another one.

"They're retreating," Hawk said.

Oz ran up the hall and threw a fireball down the stairs. Chief yelling *Oorah* echoed over the sounds of gunfire and screams. The

Scouts echoed him.

"Where, Hawk?" Oz asked.

"You're clear on the second floor. Thirty or more men are on the first," Hawk reported as he shot his rifle as fast as his spells allowed and targets presented themselves.

Oz threw another three fireballs down the stairs. Flames licked up the staircase from the first floor, and smoke billowed in dense, black clouds.

"Window is good to go." Hawk held his position, covering the window.

Charlie ignored the rappelling lines and jumped from the helicopter directly to the roof of the house. With a sword in each hand, he bounded from the roof to the ground. Rage surged through him, empowering his magic. A swirling mist of blue magic lit with bright sparks of static surrounded him.

When he hit the ground, he cast Waylay and appeared in a group of five men hunkered behind a small barricade before the front door.

A thrust with his left hand killed one man instantly. He cast Fury, so he could attack two-handed doing twice the damage, and killed the other four men in moments. He tipped his head back and screamed his attack cry, a loud *Oorah.*

His attack cry not only increased his speed it halved the damage he took and increased the healing done by each attacker, reflecting more of the damage they did back at them.

Thunder rumbled overhead, and Charlie laughed as he swung his sword. All around him men screamed and fired, the gunshots impacting and ricocheting off him, kicking up dust and impacting the car behind him with load clangs.

One must have hit the gas tank because the car exploded sending chunks of metal and a wave of hot air over him. He yanked a foot-long sliver of metal from his shoulder and leapt forward into the closet group of men.

It took him less than three seconds to kill four men. They managed to do nothing except heal him completely.

He charged, whirling his swords with both hands as he rushed to the next cluster of men, blocking the shots coming at him with crossed swords. A hard swing with both swords and he left dead men lying on the ground.

Another group of men rushed from the house firing their M-15's on automatic.

Charlie hopped up and over a nearby van, wrenched the door off, and used it as a shield as he rushed forward into the men firing at him. Bullets thudded into him, which he ignored, not even feeling them.

More men exited the house, firing as they came, and split off into different directions. He dropped a sword, yanked his shield from his back, and rushed forward, using it to block the next fusillade of bullets.

Smoke poured from the doorway, and he screamed his berserk attack. Sara was in the burning building. Rage caused the blood to throb in his veins blocking sounds; he didn't hear Hawk or anyone else in his headset.

The Scouts echoed his attack cry as they received his battle buff and attacked in a wild frenzy.

Guthrie had followed Charlie out of the helicopter using the rappelling lines. By the time he reached the ground, Charlie had already killed twenty men.

Charlie yelled, and the buff hit him. The cry burst from his lips as he rushed forward and attacked. A loud *Oorah,* which echoed from every Scout.

Upstairs, Oz ran back into the bedroom yelling, "Just me!" as he came through the door.

Brenda stood against the wall with his dagger in hand. Drew crouched in the corner holding the pistol on the door.

Hawk still reported positions in his headset. "Go, the window is clear!" Gunshots sounded impossibly fast, the rat-a-tat-tat blurring into one continuous rrrfffttt. Hawk was shooting right overhead with magical speed and precision.

Tony jumped out the window. Marcus hopped down and Drew lowered Joy to him. Brenda went next, and they lowered Sara. Todd, Rick, and Sam followed. Oz fireballed the doorway a few times before jumping. He cast Wink right before he hit the ground and landed twenty feet ahead of his group.

The house was a blazing inferno now, and men ran from it. Oz cast lightning until no enemies remained in sight. Alpha team took shelter behind the shed with Oz guarding them.

Hawk still lay on the burning roof covering them.

Oz hesitated.

"Stay with Sara," Hawk ordered.

"Roger that." Oz winked to Sara's side.

Charlie screamed his attack cry again. No more live foes remained in sight, and wild fury pushed him. He needed to kill his enemies, to kill everyone who'd harmed those in his charge.

The spikes in front of the wall were no obstacle. One leap put him on top of the barricade, and he ran along it, balancing easily on the narrow top. Men ducked and scattered at the sight of him. Their weapons weren't slowing him. The shots that hit him didn't faze him. Using Waylay again, he landed in the middle of another group hiding behind the wall and with fierce joy killed everyone.

The sword in his hand dripped blood and men screamed as he swung. Bullets thudded into his armor, must falling harmlessly to the ground. The few that penetrated he ignored. Bright lightning flickered in his peripheral vision, and he headed to it.

Oz was casting lightning on men spread in the bushes at the edge of the yard firing on them. Charlie leapt over the spikes and intercepted the man Oz attacked, killing him in one swing. The dead body tumbled to the ground in two halves. The men in the trees screamed and ran; Charlie ran much faster.

The men shrieked as he slashed. Turning from the dead bodies, he surveyed the area. Oz had already killed the fourth man. Another glance showed him his brother carrying Sara's limp body, her bright blond hair a startling contrast to his brother's black clothing.

The pulse in his neck increased. Conflicting desires made him stagger forward. Giving in to his rage, he straightened and scanned for more enemies. A flicker of movement caught his eye and he'd bounded forward and killed the three running men before he'd consciously decided to move.

The fire reached the roof, which fell in with a thunderous crash. Smoke and leaping flames obscured what fighting remained on the other side of the house. Charlie cast Valorous Leap, landing on the wall again to better survey the yard.

Only corpses met his satisfied gaze. The pulse in his neck calmed. Two minutes later, when Hawk reported all clear, Charlie heard him and was again in control of his actions. He was able to sheath his sword by the time the helicopter returned.

"Oz, get Alpha team on that copter. Beta stay behind. The Cubs were never here. You know nothing about the fire. I want photos of each dead body," Major Nelson ordered. "Beta, get me every piece of intel you can from this house and those corpses."

Charlie leapt again, landing twenty-five feet away and ran to the shed Alpha hid behind.

One look at his brother's furious expression and Rick handed him Sara. Charlie's eyes glowed so brightly they cast shadows on his face.

Sara's limp form in his arms sent another wave of rage through him. It was all he could do to not put her down and go seek out more enemies to kill.

There is no more, he told himself firmly.

A bloody, bullet-ridden Stasia appeared. Gunshot wounds covered her, and a jagged cut marred one cheek. Oz handed her a bandage. Charlie spell-stole Sara's heal and used it on Stasia. The cut knitted together and wounds disappeared in seconds.

Hawk showed up when they reached the helicopter. "Sarge, I'm not going with you. Someone drove away, and I'm going to follow."

Charlie's sword appeared in his hand without his consciously willing it there. It took an act of will to sheath it and remain with Sara. To go with Hawk would be foolish. He would slow him, but worse, Charlie didn't think he could stop himself from killing anyone they ran into, guilty or not.

"Roger that; be discreet. We'll follow in the helicopter," Guthrie said.

Hawk darted off, and Charlie followed

Oz into the helicopter where Oz handed out bandages to everyone.

Brenda opened the medical kit and put an IV in Joy's arm and another in Sara. She took out the stethoscope and listened to both.

"Joy has pneumonia. Her breathing is very labored. Keep putting bandages on her when you can. If her pulse and blood pressure drop more, we'll have to use Hawk."

Brenda took each of Sara's hands in hers, washed them off with bottled water, and gently manipulated each finger. She snapped a few back into place, opened a sterile packet, and took blood samples.

"Chief, I need to see her for a minute. Hold up this blanket to give her what privacy we can."

Brenda unwound the sheet that wrapped Sara and removed the black shirt. Her frown deepened at the sight of the handprints on Sara's white skin. A soft sound of distress issued from her as she took in the unhealed bullet wounds and bruises.

Charlie leaned over Brenda's shoulder as she examined her. Oz's bandages should've healed her wounds by now. Only severe internal damage could account for this many injuries remaining. His breath caught sharply at the handprints. Someone had grabbed Sara cruelly hard on her arms and inner thighs. Her ankles and wrists were black from bruising. Tight bonds had left deep purple bruises, shading to an ugly red, across her chest and waist. Black streaks ran up both her red, swollen arms where blood poisoning had set in.

Charlie used his Spell-Steal, stole Sara's Massive Heal and used it on her. "Why aren't the bandages and heal helping her?" Charlie asked as he rechecked Sara's wounds, not seeing any noticeable improvements.

"They are, but she has a lot of internal injuries. I counted nine unhealed bullet wounds. Keep bandaging when the cooldown is up. Steal her heal spell every time you can but use it on Joy next."

Brenda checked Sara's pulse and breathing again.

"Sara isn't in danger no matter how bad this looks. She's out cold, probably for five more hours and doesn't feel a thing." Brenda wrapped Sara in a dry blanket and placed her back in Charlie's lap.

Conflicting needs again assaulted him. Sara's condition demanded action. Dried blood and gore covered Brenda's face and matted her hair. Charlie's gaze scanned his brother and his blue eyes brightening even more.

Bullet holes ringed with dried, crusted blood riddled his brother's clothing. Flaking, black blood covered the side of his head and cheek. Someone had shot him in the face. Magic burst from Charlie and swirled about the cabin in a static-lit blue cloud, coating each person for a moment before returning to him. The magic swirling through the helicopter brought the Scout's feeling to him in a confusing mix. They were horrified, angry and afraid. His brother felt guilty, the guilt and horror growing as he stared at Sara.

Brenda glanced up as she rechecked everybody.

"Calm down, Chief, before you give yourself a heart attack. We're okay now. None of our wounds are life-threatening." She ran a hand over Joy's short, black hair. "They gave Joy too much sedative. I'm more worried about Joy than Sara."

Charlie held Sara as gently as he could, adrenaline still so high he heard a slight buzzing in his ears and his hands shook.

"Why would they hurt her so badly if they wanted her? That makes no sense."

"It's my fault," Rick said, avoiding his brother's eyes but unable to avoid the magic that rushed him when he spoke. "They were murdering Brenda and forcing Sara to rez her on video. They threatened to do the same to me. She knew the rez timer would kill us and they didn't care. She went crazy trying to save us. The more they shot her, the harder she fought."

Rick's horror and fear were clear to Charlie and apparently everyone near him as the Scouts reached to him and Charlie felt their love and worry.

"Sergeant Rinto?" Guthrie asked.

Rick nodded, glanced at his brother's face, and winced, closing his eyes. "He crushed her hands when she wouldn't stop."

Oz leaned over to Stasia. "Did you tell them about—?"

"No," she interrupted. "We'll deal with him."

"You'll deal with whom?" Guthrie asked.

"Everyone involved," Chief turned his blue-eyed stare on the staff sergeant and clutched Sara tighter.

EPILOGUE

Sergeant Rinto got on the boat. The entire situation was a disaster, and now he needed to disappear. Not only did he have to worry about Oliver finding him somehow— he still had no idea how he did that— but he had nothing to give the buyers to show for the money they'd invested. This briefcase, the videos and files it contained, were his only proof, but the buyers wanted a live specimen.

His hands clenched in anger. Those kids were nothing except trouble. Anastasia would be impossible to capture. Sebastian or Charlie would be easier to subdue if they would authorize killing Sara. The problem was that's who they wanted most.

He should've killed the mage; greed caused this. He didn't care what Oliver was worth, he couldn't afford to let him live. The boat swerved as he reached for his cell phone.

He'd make one quick call to check in before he disappeared. Maybe the general had a backup plan, something to get them out of this situation— if they could just get their hands on the girl.

THE END

Books by S. M. SAVOY

Valor

A Warrior's Fury

Return of the Fae

You can reach S. M. Savoy at
authorsmsavoy@gmail.com

Or Ace Lyons Publishing for new releases
and upcoming books at:

https://www.acelyonbooks.com

Upcoming Book in this Series

SUN–PRIEST'S MAGIC

Valor Book Three

The magic evolves, connecting Team Valor in ways they couldn't foresee. They're back together, but not safe. They must track down the people responsible for planning Sara's kidnapping and eliminate the threats if they hope to lead a more normal life with their secrets intact.

Connected by magic and love, Sara and Charlie vow to stay together. A vow the magic seals with lightning, revealing it isn't a passive ability that they possess, but a living entity that possesses them.

This new connection might be more than they bargained for though. Now privy to his wife's emotions, the terror she feels is all too clear to him, enraging both he and his magic.

And to keep his new wife sane, Charlie is willing to do anything.

A protection warrior full of rage and deadly dangerous, Charlie now has more than just his secrets to lose. With or without the blessing of his handlers Chief will seek vengeance. And when Team Valor joins him on a mission to destroy their enemies, no one is safe from his wrath.